W9-CKB-718

WALKING

INTO

MURDER

Book One

Laura Morland Mystery Series

JOAN DAHR LAMBERT

Joan Dahr Lambert is the author of CIRCLES OF STONE, published by Pocket Books (a division of Simon & Schuster) in 1997 and in paperback in 1999. It is the first book in the Mother People Series. Two further books about the Mother People, STAR CIRCLES and ICE BURIAL, will be available soon.

CIRCLES OF STONE was also published in Spain, Israel, Japan, Korea, Germany, Sweden, Norway, Holland, Italy and Denmark.

Thank you to Diana Finch of Diana Finch Literary Agency, who offered valuable advice and support throughout the process of writing WALKING INTO MURDER.

My thanks also go to John Paine, of John Paine Editorial Services, for his sympathetic and skilled editing and his enthusiasm for WALKING INTO MURDER.

Additional thanks go to my husband and all the members of my family for their consistent encouragement and for patiently reading innumerable drafts of WALKING INTO MURDER without complaint.

CHAPTER ONE

Laura peered in dismay at the battered wooden stile. The Cotswold Hills of England were littered with stiles, as well as the fences they helped people to cross, but she had never come across one as dilapidated as this. The bottom step had rotted away, the top one tilted precariously and was almost chest high. She would have to be a gymnast to get her foot up there.

The first stile she had come across on this long distance walk had charmed her, she remembered grumpily. *Filled with the romance of history*, she had told herself as she imagined the generations of farmers and walkers who had trod its weathered boards. Then, however, the step had been lower, the weather perfect, and she had been full of energy. Now she was bone-tired, a dense fog with pelting rain had rolled in, and the temperature had dropped precipitously. Worse, she was lost. The walking path had disappeared into a sea of mud made by trampling cows. What had ever made her think she could walk the hundred plus miles of the Cotswold Way alone?

Raising a leg as high as she could, Laura levered one mud-encrusted knee onto the sloping step. Encouraged, she hoisted the other knee up and slowly raised herself to a standing position. She wobbled there unsteadily and then dared to fling a leg over the fence. The step collapsed under her other foot and she toppled into the mud on the other side. It was at least a foot deep, smelly and icy cold.

If it was mud. More likely it was cow manure.

Wrinkling her nose in distaste, Laura tried to stand. She failed, due to the fact that one of her boots was stuck fast in the muck. Grabbing it with both hands and a fund of pent-up frustration, she yanked. With an odious sucking noise, it came loose. Attached to it were at least five pounds of glop. How was it possible for a bunch of cows to produce so much of the stinking stuff?

She stood up hastily, startled by the sound of pounding feet. A man materialized out of the mist and ran straight at her, arms outstretched.

"Thank goodness I found you!" he exclaimed, and swept her into a close embrace. Laura's body went rigid with shock. Then indignation took hold.

"Let me go!" she hissed, shoving at his chest. The arms held her even closer, and to her horror, lips began to move passionately along her cheek.

"Play along with me," the man pleaded in an undertone. "A life could depend on it. Pretend you're my wife and we got separated when I went to look for -"

Another voice interrupted, startling Laura so badly that she clung to her unknown accoster. "By jove! Telling the truth about a missing wife after all. Still, I shall have to bring you both back. Can't go anywhere in this bloody fog anyway."

This voice was very English, brought pictures of fireplaces and dogs and country manors into Laura's mind. The idea of a fire and a manor, or any kind of house as long as it was warm and dry and had a bathroom, seemed like salvation. So did the idea of an English gentleman who might rescue her from this madman.

He hadn't sounded mad, though, only desperate. Could a life really depend on her cooperation? And what did the Englishman mean by saying he had to take them back with him? That had a menacing sound. For the first time she noticed the shotgun on his arm. It was even more menacing.

"What's your name?" her would-be husband murmured in her ear.

"Laura," she answered automatically, her voice muffled by his close embrace. She was aware of a not-unpleasant smell. Damp tweed, she thought, or was it that cologne called Tweed?

Why was she thinking about smells when she ought to be trying to escape? Laura jerked away from her unknown assailant but he grabbed her hand before she could run. Her fingers immediately felt warmer. His, she noted with satisfaction, were now well decorated with the cow muck that was smeared all over hers. She could feel the stuff oozing between their fingers. He rolled his eyes but hung on gamely.

"Come, Laura dear," he said loudly, dragging her along with him. "It seems we must do as this gentleman says and go back to his house."

Laura's instant of triumph dissolved. This was ridiculous! She was being virtually kidnapped by two large men. That didn't happen to innocent American tourists on walking trips in England, so why was it happening to her?

Because you have a positive talent for getting into trouble, Donald the Defector would have said. That was the name she had used for her ex-husband, privately at least, since the evening he had invited her to dinner and stupefied her with the news that he was leaving her.

Walking into Murder

Humiliating didn't begin to describe the experience. *She,* the Professor of Gender Studies who was supposed to know all about relationships between the sexes, hadn't had a clue that for months he'd been carrying on an affair. By the time he had finished his rapturous description of Patti, the young lady-love (his words) who had lured him away, the coq au vin and string beans Laura had ordered had congealed on her plate. Donald had speared the limp beans one by one with his fork, she remembered, and devoured them with gusto. She'd never seen him eat string beans before.

She'd never known him to do anything out of line before, which just went to show how naïve she was. She had even assumed that Donald had invited her to dinner in an effort to revive their moribund marriage.

Laura sighed. Sometimes it seemed to her that advanced degrees and academic expertise came only at the expense of common sense.

"Odd time to be out walking," the Englishman remarked, watching them suspiciously. "All this rain and fog."

"My wife has an odd preference for walking in despicable weather," the hand-holder replied, eyeing Laura warily. "She likes getting soaked. Good for the character, she says."

Laura shot him a baleful look but he only smiled charmingly and patted the hand he held with his other one. "Only teasing, darling," he said.

"If you want cooperation," Laura muttered icily under her breath, "teasing is not a good idea. Nor is calling me *darling.*"

"Sorry, darling," her companion answered blithely. A stinging barrage of freezing hail prevented Laura from

4

expressing her indignation. It was followed by lashing wind that blew her hood off and sent cold water dribbling down her back. She shivered, and then found she was unable to stop.

Paying no attention to the onslaught, the Englishman gestured them towards a maze of trees that loomed like ghostly poles in the fog. The man clinging to her hand obeyed docilely. Laura wondered why, until she noted that the shot gun was now pointed at them.

She glanced up at the man beside her covertly, trying to decide if he could be trusted to come to her assistance if that should be necessary. His curly hair was plastered to his head by rain, but even so, he was attractive. She wondered what she looked like with her hair plastered to her skull. Less attractive, she was sure.

Failing to watch her feet was a mistake. She tripped over a protruding root and fell. Her companion pulled her upright again. "Best to look where your feet are going, dearest," he advised. Laura responded with a furious frown. The man was incorrigible! And what made her think she could assess his character after five minutes when she'd failed so spectacularly to assess her husband's after twenty years?

Laura clenched her fists hard. "Quite a grip," her companion observed mildly, and squeezed her hand in return. Glaring at him, she tried again to pull it away, but he held on as if his fingers were glued to it, which possibly they were.

The path narrowed. Closely packed bushes hemmed them in on both sides and met overhead, forming a tunnel. The Englishman gestured for them to go ahead and followed with the gun. Laura hustled through. At any other time she would have enjoyed this tunnel of greenery, but now she felt only an eerie prickling along her spine.

Rain attacked them again as they emerged. Squinting, Laura made out the shape of an enormous house just ahead. Smaller buildings clustered around it. She heard the sound of horses neighing, then the clatter of hooves, and the silhouette of a large horse came into view at the top of a ridge. A small and graceful rider was perched on its back. Both vanished as quickly as they had appeared.

"Damnation!" the Englishman shouted. "Who let the senator go out?"

Laura was bewildered. Was the senator a person or the horse?

The Englishman offered no explanation. "In!" he ordered Laura and her companion in a tone that brooked no argument. Opening the heavy door of the house, he shoved them unceremoniously into a wide stone entry and loped off in the direction of the vanishing horse. Laura went inside obediently, but the other man dropped her hand and ran after the Englishman.

"Cat," he shouted. "Cat, come back!"

Laura watched him disappear into the fog again, feeling perversely abandoned. She wasn't sure she wanted to be alone in this great castle of a house. Maybe she should go out again, try to find a road or a halfway sensible person. And who or what was Cat? The missing wife perhaps? If there actually was one.

The big door closed soundlessly before she could make up her mind whether to go out again or stay put. Laura was conscious of sudden blissful silence, of dryness and warmth. Better to be warm and dry and abducted than wet and cold and abducted, she decided, feeling her shivering abate. Besides, someone in here might help her.

She looked around curiously. The entrance hall was huge, with a flagged floor and high vaulted ceiling that gave it a cavernous feeling. The stone walls were studded with lethal-looking swords and firearms. Across from her was another heavy door, a replica of the one through which she had entered.

"Please remove your muddy boots and wet jacket," a disembodied voice commanded. Laura jumped. No one was in the hall. Maybe a butler lurked behind the inner door. This seemed like the kind of house that would have a butler. An invisible one, however, was distinctly odd.

She hesitated, but her indecision lasted only a moment. Her jacket was clammy and her boots soggy, and she removed both with a sigh of pleasure.

"Thank you," the polite voice remarked. As if by magic, the door opposite her opened. Laura went through into another hall, this one more conventionally decorated with dark paintings and heavy curtains. A magnificent Persian rug stretched across the stone floor, and she wriggled her cold toes appreciatively into its warmth. Against one wall, a long, heavily carved table held a tall vase of flowers and a large number of ornate pieces of silver. A butler still hadn't appeared.

She whirled as the voice spoke again. "Please put your card on the silver salver and proceed into the drawing room," it instructed politely. A speaker system must be wired to the doors, Laura realized. How clever! Her son would love it. Mark used to play around with wiring, causing Donald to wonder if they would all be burned in their beds while they slept. Mark had looked crushed.

Since she had no card Laura went directly into the drawing room. At the threshold she stopped abruptly, her mouth open in astonishment. The scene in front of her was like a stage set. An elegant older woman rested her hands on the back of a carved Victorian sofa that was placed in the exact center of the room. She was the embodiment of a grande dame, with her aristocratic face, her aquiline nose and arched eyebrows. Just behind her stood a tall skinny youth with a supercilious look on his face. He had exactly the same eyebrows as the older woman but a distinct slouch. A pair of round wire spectacles was perched incongruously on his long nose. Neither spoke nor moved.

The tableau remained frozen for a long moment; then the woman began to slide sideways, very slowly, without changing her erect posture or her composed expression. The young man, however, looked startled. Laura heard a muffled curse and a giggle, and then the lights went out.

2.

Someone will scream now, Laura thought. *Someone always does.* She fought an urge to scream herself, or maybe to laugh hysterically.

The scream came, but not the one she expected. It was the indignant yell of a furious child. "That isn't fair, Nigel! You said I could do it."

"Well, I meant you to, but it happened so fast." The young man sounded aggrieved and surprised in equal measure.

Walking into Murder

A door opened at the other end of the room and the lights went on again. With disbelief, Laura watched the woman who had just fallen enter the room. How could she have moved that fast? Then she saw that there were two women, one on the floor behind the sofa and the new one. She took a step closer and realized that the first woman was a mannequin, a remarkably realistic one. She almost expected it to get up.

The woman at the opposite door regarded the scene thoughtfully with keen dark eyes that contrasted sharply with her snowy hair. Her gaze rested on the young man, whom Laura presumed was Nigel, and then moved to the stiff figure on the floor. She said nothing, but her dark eyebrows arched expressively, managing at once to convey veiled annoyance, resignation and a touch of humor.

"Sorry, Gram," the young man apologized. "Didn't mean to startle. We were just practicing. No one told me a guest was coming."

The white-haired woman inclined her head graciously. She must be his grand-mother, Laura decided. They looked extraordinarily alike.

Muffled giggles came from behind the sofa. The grande dame finally broke her silence. "That will do, Angelina," she said calmly.

A small girl popped up from her hiding place. All laughter disappeared when she caught sight of Laura. "Why are you here?" she demanded, stamping her foot. "You are not supposed to be here!" She sent Laura a scathing look.

Laura sent one back. "I don't know myself why I am here, and if I could I would be elsewhere," she said crisply, irritated by the child's peremptory tone – and by the fact that no one, so far, had acknowledged her presence except this obnoxious girl.

"Then you should leave," the child ordered. Her accent was as perfect as the Englishman's, and Laura wondered if she was his daughter. Like his, her manners left a great deal to be desired.

As if on cue, her thought was expressed by a younger woman who entered the room. Laura tried not to stare. She had seldom seen anyone as beautiful, or as impeccably dressed. Patti's neat little outfits and fake blond hair couldn't come close. This woman's flaxen hair hadn't come out of a bottle. It waved softly around her oval face, and her skin was so pale it was almost translucent. She had the same huge blue eyes as the child. But while the girl's eyes were frankly hostile, the woman's eyes held only mild boredom. She didn't look at Laura or even seem to notice her.

"Your manners are atrocious, Angelina," she said lazily, her tone unconvincing. Angelina paid no attention. Her small mouth was set in a discontented line that foretold more loathsome remarks.

Fed up with being ignored, Laura decided to make her presence obvious. She was tired, wet, dirty and bewildered. The least these people could do was to offer her a bathroom or a hot drink – anything but this perverse silence, as if she didn't exist.

"I would like to use a bathroom," she stated, not bothering to think of a polite euphemism. "I have been walking for hours and want to wash my hands at least."

The two women looked at her for the first time. "Of course," the white-haired one replied. "I fear we have been inconsiderate. Please take our visitor to the green room, Antonia, and see that she has everything she needs."

The youth's eyes widened in alarm. He opened his mouth to speak but closed it again and made a helpless gesture with one hand. Angelina giggled.

Laura turned away from the tableau with relief. She followed Antonia up a wide staircase and past an impressive number of doors. All were closed.

"I think you will find everything you need here," her escort said as she opened one of the doors. "There is a connecting bathroom to your left."

"Thank you," Laura replied, her mood vastly improved by the chance to clean up. She went straight into the bathroom and eyed it appreciatively. The fittings, though old, gleamed with cleaning; so did the tiles that covered both floor and walls. Thick white towels were neatly folded on an elegant drying rack, and when she picked one up it was warm to the touch. This must be one of the many grand old houses that had resorted to taking in tourists to help pay the bills, she mused. Why else the perfectly polished fixtures, the heated towels?

Reveling in the unexpected luxury, Laura treated her wind-whipped face to a soothing cream, removed every trace of cow manure from her hands and combed her rebelliously curly red hair into some semblance of order. She even found a toothbrush and a tube of toothpaste in her pack. Now she could face the impeccable grande dame and the gorgeous Antonia without feeling quite so much like a bedraggled refugee.

Her confidence restored, Laura emerged into the bedroom. She couldn't make out any details in the dim light cast by a single lamp near the door, but she could

11

see that the room was indeed green, as the white-haired woman had stated. A pale green rug covered the floor, the wallpaper had green stripes, a darker green canopy soared over the huge bed and a matching silk coverlet lay on its surface. Laura looked at the bed longingly. It would feel so good to get off her feet, just for a moment.

Tempted, she took a few steps toward it but stopped abruptly. How odd. Someone was already in the bed, under the coverlet. All that showed was part of the face and an arm. It drooped down one side of the bed, looking oddly lifeless, and the eyes were...

Laura froze, and then she screamed.

CHAPTER TWO

The scream reverberated in the room but Laura heard no answering calls. The doors, she thought helplessly. No one would hear anything through all those closed doors. They wouldn't hear from downstairs anyway.

Fascinated despite her horror, she glanced again at the woman in the big bed. Her skin had a waxy pallor that made the creamy sheets look bright by comparison, and her slanted green eyes were wide open, staring sightlessly.

Laura shivered. The hand holder had yelled for Cat to come back and this woman had a cat-like look, with her oval green eyes, round cheeks and peaked eyebrows. But if Cat was his missing wife, she seemed to be here, not on the horse.

Footsteps sounded in the hall. Laura ran to the door, aware that her legs were shaking badly. She opened it with a jerk and saw the Englishman. He was no longer carrying the gun. "I say," he began. "Sorry about all that in the woods. Acted hastily, I fear. Antonia tells me…"

"Please could you come in here?" Laura interrupted through stiff lips.

The Englishman looked surprised but followed her readily into the green room. Laura pointed at the bed.

He stared at the figure under the coverlet, bewildered. "But who is that?" he asked, as if Laura perhaps would know. "And what is she doing there?" Eyes wide with surprise, he took a step closer. "Good heavens! I think she's dead! However did she get here

13

dead?" He ran out of the room and Laura heard his footsteps pound down the hall.

She turned to follow him and saw Angelina. The child had come through the door and was inching her way toward the bed. "I think we'll go out now," Laura said firmly. Even a rude child shouldn't come face to face with a dead woman.

"I want to see her," Angelina insisted, evading Laura's outstretched arm. She ran over to the bed and peered at the dead woman. A series of expressions passed across her plump face: surprise, consternation, puzzled reflection and finally anger.

"But that's wrong!" She stamped her foot down hard on the floor. "It's supposed to be Lottie. I wanted Lottie to be the dead one! Nigel said she would be."

Her face twisted with fury and she gave the dead arm a vicious poke. Her hand shot back as if scalded. "It's cold!" she shrieked, and began to wail.

Laura lifted her up and removed her bodily from the room. Angelina kicked and screamed and pounded at her chest with clenched fists. Laura had endured her share of tantrums when her two children were young and held on doggedly until they reached the drawing room. Then, thankfully, she put the child down and rubbed her shins. Was ever a child so ineptly named? Even at birth, it must have been obvious that Angelina had not a shred of angel in her.

Angelina's screams stopped the instant her feet met the ground. Glaring at Laura, she marched to the middle of the room, as if taking center stage. The white-haired woman and Antonia, whom Laura supposed must be Angelina's mother, and the youth Nigel watched her warily.

Walking into Murder

"There's a dead woman in the green room, a truly dead one," Angelina announced in a high, shrill voice. "I know because I touched her and she's cold. And I know who killed her because I saw." With a dramatic flourish, she turned and pointed a malicious finger at Laura. "She killed her. She did it."

Laura raised her eyebrows in weary exasperation. "Oh, for goodness sake," she exclaimed. "Can no one control the silly child?"

Three pairs of eyes turned to stare at her. Laura returned their gaze with dawning horror. She saw none of the half-amused, half-resigned irritation at the child's monstrous accusation that she had expected in those eyes. Instead, she saw only suspicion.

Laura's frayed nerves snapped. "This is ridiculous! I know absolutely nothing about that poor woman and I certainly did not kill her. I am an American tourist on a walking trip, and the only reason I am here is that I was virtually kidnapped by two men and brought here."

Nigel abruptly left the room. The grande dame raised her eyebrows at the last revelation, but she didn't speak. Laura rushed on, determined to make them understand. "There really is a dead woman in the green room," she insisted. "The police should be called, and a doctor. After that, I would like to leave. I must also call the people who are supposed to be my hosts tonight so they will not send out a search party."

The white-haired woman cleared her throat. "Angelina exaggerates. And of course you must leave if you wish. You must forgive us. We did not expect a guest this evening, and we have had an unusually difficult day. We are not normally so rude." Her eyes shifted to Angelina. "Most of us are not," she amended. "Nor do we tell tales."

"But I'm not telling tales!" the child protested indignantly. "There really is a dead woman in the green room."

Antonia rolled her eyes. "There is not," she said with irritation. "You know that perfectly well, Angelina. It is only one of Nigel's games, the mystery ones he's practicing for. Though why he had to choose the green room without telling us, I cannot imagine," she added with unexpected malice.

Laura stared at her. That must be what they all thought. No wonder they hadn't reacted. Maybe they were right and the green-eyed woman was pretending to be dead. She hadn't gone close enough to the bed to be sure. She didn't think so, though. The arm had looked lifeless, and Angelina had touched it, felt its coldness.

Antonia's voice interrupted her thoughts. "Actually, we *were* expecting a guest tonight," she told Laura with a notable lack of enthusiasm. "I am afraid I forgot to tell everyone," she added, glancing nervously at the older woman. "I had forgotten myself. I was distracted…"

She turned back to Laura. "Could you give us your name?"

"Laura…"

"Laura Smith," a voice from the door interrupted before Laura could finish. The hand holder, she thought resignedly. She might have known.

For the first time she saw him clearly. He wasn't conventionally handsome as much as he was attractive. His lanky frame still had a faintly adolescent look, and a lock of hair fell boyishly over his brow. They made him look younger than he probably was, judging from the faint lines around his eyes and the gray in his brown hair. It was still damp and tousled, and she noticed traces of cow muck on his hands. That was a relief. He, at least, wasn't as perfectly groomed as everyone else in the room.

Antonia frowned. "And you are…?"

"Tom Smith," said the hand holder, smiling. "Laura's husband."

Laura scowled at him, exasperated by his insistence on the silly fabrication, and then she softened. He wasn't aware yet that his real wife might be lying dead on the bed upstairs. That would come as a terrible shock.

"But I'm not -" she began.

"Now, darling, I know you thought I couldn't come, but I've managed it anyway. Caught up with you finally, isn't that wonderful?" He grinned at her, but again she saw the pleading look in his eyes. *Don't desert me now,* he seemed to be saying.

She hesitated. Tom Smith – if that really was his name - might be her only source of help in this eccentric household. He did seem marginally saner than the rest of them. He had also warned her that a life might be at stake, and now there was a dead body.

She wouldn't expose him just yet, Laura decided, not until she knew more about what was going on – and about him.

She attempted a conciliatory smile. "Your presence is certainly unexpected," she equivocated.

"The name I was given was Dr. Morland," Antonia said, frowning at the discrepancy. "Dr. Laura Morland."

Laura's head snapped up at the sound of her name. Was she really scheduled to spend the night in this crazy ménage? Probably she was, she realized with a sense of

17

impending doom. The brochure described it as the highlight of the trip, a night in a genuine English manor house complete with turrets and titled occupants and butler – though that amenity had so far been invisible. The owners even gave tours two days a week, she remembered. Maybe wax figures were included. For all she knew, being escorted to the manor at gunpoint was part of the agenda.

"Morland is Laura's maiden name," Tom Smith replied glibly before she could speak. "She uses it professionally." He smiled appealingly at Antonia. "I hope it's all right that I've turned up, Lady Torrington. My wife and I haven't had much time together recently."

Laura lost patience. "It is long past time someone called the police and a doctor," she said firmly, "or at least went to examine the woman in the green room to see if she really is dead."

Alarm spread suddenly over Tom Smith's features. He opened his mouth to speak again but Laura forestalled him. "I recall from my notes that the place I am scheduled to stay tonight is called Torrington Manor," she told Antonia. "It would help if I knew your names," she added, aware for the first time that none of the occupants of the house had introduced themselves.

"This is Torrington Manor," Antonia conceded. "I am Lady -"

"Then you *are* supposed to be here," Angelina interrupted. "I guess you can stay then." Her tone was grudging.

"Thank you, Angelina," Laura said coldly. "Now, about the police?"

Tom Smith could contain himself no longer. "What is all this about a dead body?" he demanded. His eyes were accusing now. "You didn't tell me you found a body."

"So far, I haven't had the opportunity," Laura retorted, annoyed by his tone but gratified that someone was finally taking the situation seriously. "I thought there was a dead woman in the green room, where I went to freshen up," she explained. "It might be best if you looked at her first to see if she is someone you know," she added with a warning look.

"She's really dead!" Angelina informed him. "She's cold, and her eyes are wide open. They're green, like a cat's," she added with gory relish.

Tom Smith went very pale, and Laura was afraid he was going to faint. "But that's... that's impossible," he stammered.

"Why don't you come with me and look for yourself?" she offered, gesturing for him to precede her out the door. Instead, he grabbed her hand again and hung on tightly. This time she let him have it. His pallor was alarming.

To her dismay, the others followed as she led him upstairs. She had hoped to get him alone so she could soften the shock if the woman was his wife, but with this crowd on her heels that was impossible. Were all of them as ghoulish as Angelina?

Her dismay increased when she saw Nigel leaning nonchalantly in the doorway of the green room. He sported a Sherlock Holmes hat and a monocle, and held a pipe in one long-fingered hand. The resemblance was remarkable.

Walking into Murder

Laura was not amused. "Are you aware," she asked through clenched teeth, "that there may be a dead woman on the bed?"

"Dead woman, you say," answered Nigel thoughtfully, in a deep, cultivated voice that sounded to Laura exactly as Sherlock Holmes ought to sound. His eyebrows went up a fraction and stayed there. "Indeed! This calls for an investigation." He held the monocle to one eye and approached the bed, a faintly ironic look on his mobile face.

Laura tried to see past him, but the lights had been dimmed even more and all she could make out was a lump on the bed.

Angelina darted in front of her and pushed Nigel out of the way, eager to be the first to view the body. She stiffened and turned to Laura, perplexed. "But it *is* Lottie this time. She must have got mixed up. Lottie always gets mixed up," she added petulantly.

"Of course it's Lottie," Nigel said impatiently, forgetting his role. "I said it was going to be Lottie, didn't I?"

"But it wasn't Lottie before," Angelina protested. "It was somebody else, and she didn't look at all like Lottie."

She turned again to Laura. "It's not the same one, is it?" she demanded. "Tell Nigel it isn't! Tell him!"

"Now, Angelina," her mother reproved. "You know that can't really be true. Besides, I think it's time for us to leave. I've had enough of this game. It is horrible, macabre."

Reluctantly, Laura approached the bed, and almost screamed again. She forced the sound back into her throat. Angelina was right. A different woman lay on the bed, a woman with limp blond hair and a long bony face. She bore no resemblance at all to the green-eyed beauty who had been lying there before.

CHAPTER THREE

Laura closed her eyes and turned away, feeling nauseated. "No," she agreed faintly. "No. This is not the same woman."

Tom Smith peered over her shoulder and breathed a long sigh of relief. Slowly, his pallor receded, but he still looked grim and shaken.

"So this is a different woman," he muttered. "How very peculiar." He looked appraisingly at Nigel.

"You mean to say," Nigel asked, "that Angelina's right and someone else was here before?" His eyes widened and he began to grin. "Who would have believed it? Good old Lottie. What a glorious trick on us all. She must have put a mask on her face earlier to fool us. I wonder how she managed it."

"Who is Lottie?" Laura demanded, appalled at his cheerful tone. Did he feel no pity at all for the dead woman?

"My governess," Angelina answered promptly. "She's very stupid and I can always play tricks on her."

"Well, this time, Angelina dear, she's played a trick on you," Nigel said, still grinning in delight. Stuffing the monocle and the pipe in his pocket, he turned toward the woman on the bed.

"Well done, Lottie old thing," he crowed. "I didn't think you had it in you. But I still want to know how you managed to do the mask by yourself. That's one hell of a trick to pull off! I ought to know!"

Laura frowned. Was Nigel the mask maker? It sounded that way. Maybe he had created the grande dame mannequin, too. But who had put the cat mask on

Lottie's face? She certainly couldn't have done it. Nigel might not realize it yet, but Lottie really was dead, at least she thought so.

Nigel's voice continued, cajoling, jocular. "Did somebody help you get it on and off? Come clean, Lottie darling. Come clean for Nigel." There was no answer.

Nigel went closer. "Come on, Lottie old thing, time to get up," he went on, a tinge of worry in his voice. "The game is over. We've found you, so it's all right to get up."

The woman on the bed didn't stir. "I say, old thing, this is carrying the joke too far," Nigel objected, sounding alarmed now. "No need to lie there all day!" He reached out and shook her limp arm. His hand, as Angelina's had, shot back quickly.

"Lottie!" he said urgently, and now there was real fear in his face. "Lottie!" he repeated. "Get up!"

Nigel turned to his grandmother, his eyes filled with horror and a kind of desperate appeal. "We were just practicing," he told her weakly. His skin had turned a greenish hue, and Laura saw that he was close to tears. "We were practicing for the mystery game. It was just a game. Lottie said she would be the victim, would be in the green room. I meant to tell you…" He closed his eyes suddenly and rushed into the bathroom. They heard the sound of retching.

His grandmother went slowly to the bed and looked down at the woman lying there. Gently, she reached out and touched the cold hand. Her erect posture sagged. Even her face seemed to lose its taut structure. Laura felt very sorry for her.

Angelina's scream cut into the silence. "It's wrong," she howled. "It's wrong again, and I don't like it this way. I want the game to be right…"

Laura put an arm gently around the girl's heaving shoulders and touched Antonia's arm to rouse her. The woman looked numb with shock. She also looked terrified. "Take Angelina away," Laura told her quietly.

After a horrified glance at the bed, Antonia obeyed. For once, Angelina didn't resist. Sobbing violently, she ran out of the room.

Laura looked at the grande dame. Her back was straight again, but her face looked older, and very weary. She stood perfectly still, head bowed, as if gathering her strength.

"Thank you," she said quietly, raising her eyes to Laura's. "I fear this is not the welcome you deserve. I shall try to place you elsewhere."

"There is no need," Laura told her gently. "I'll be fine. You have enough on your hands without worrying about me. Please let me know if I can help in any way."

The old lady nodded. She turned back to the bed to look once more at the still figure, and a terrible sadness came into her face, as if something greater than a single life had been lost. Laura wondered what it was.

When the grande dame had left, she turned to face Tom Smith. He had to be involved in all this somehow, and it was past time she got answers from him. "Who are you and what are you doing here?" she demanded.

Tom Smith paid no attention. He was bending over Lottie, examining her with careful fingers. There was no sign of faintness in him now, only intense concentration and a kind of clinical detachment.

Walking into Murder

Anger suddenly suffused Laura. She welcomed it, felt it shove aside the confusion and shocks of the last few hours. "Who are you and why are you here?" she repeated. "I'm in no mood for more lies, either. I want the truth, and I want it now. Otherwise you can forget this ridiculous farce."

"I want the truth, too," Tom Smith answered grimly as he straightened up. "Believe me, I want it as badly as you."

He stared into space, thinking, but when he looked at her again, the inscrutable look had vanished. Once again, he was debonair, charming.

The man was incapable of being serious, Laura thought furiously. Didn't he care that an innocent woman was lying there dead, had probably been murdered? Why else all the subterfuge, the mask that must have been deliberately placed on the victim's face earlier to hide her identity? And then someone must have come back and removed it…

She shuddered, aware for the first time that a member of this household could be a murderer. But who? Not Nigel, surely, even if he was the mask maker. He had been genuinely upset when he realized Lottie was dead. More likely someone else was taking advantage of his talent, must have counted on using Nigel's life-like mask to conceal the real victim, perhaps to buy time as well as confuse people.

Tom Smith interrupted these morbid speculations. "Shall we find a more suitable space in which to exchange confidences?" he asked lightly. "I for one have had enough of the green room for the evening."

"I have no confidences to make," Laura retorted. "As far as I can see, all the confiding has to come from you – starting with why you told these people that I was your wife."

Tom Smith regarded her speculatively. "That isn't completely true," he countered. "For instance, you might confide what sort of a doctor you are. I really ought to know, if I'm to be your husband."

"That is *not* guaranteed," Laura shot back. "But if you must know, I am a professor. I teach and do research at a college in the United States, and I am in England to teach a seminar as well as to walk. Now let's get back to you."

"What kind of research?" His interest sounded genuine.

"On sex differences," Laura replied maliciously, "like why men prevaricate when asked questions about themselves. And why they hide their emotions behind various facades, like charm."

"Ouch!" Tom Smith looked suitably chastened. "Is that really what your research shows they do?"

"Not exactly," Laura admitted. "It's a good deal more complex than that and in my case goes back a few thousand years to the evolution of gender differences. Now – who are you? And no more prevarications, please."

The sound of water running in the bathroom reminded them that they weren't alone. When it stopped, Nigel appeared. "Sorry," he said. "So sorry." He slouched toward the door, his face twisted with tears, and hurried down the hall.

"Poor guy," Tom Smith commented when Nigel was out of hearing range. "He really didn't know. He must feel terrible. He's talented, though, isn't he, at impersonation as well as mask making."

"More talented than you," Laura replied coldly as they left the room. "Tom Smith – really! Couldn't you have thought of a more original name?"

He chuckled. "Sorry. Unfortunately, that is my name. Gets me in and out of all sorts of trouble. If you like, you can call me Thomas instead. It sounds loftier, more suitable for solving crimes, which at the moment I seem called upon to do. Or perhaps Langley. That's my other name."

"Is that really your name?" Laura asked suspiciously.

"Which one?" he countered. "Tom Smith or Langley?"

Exasperated, Laura regarded him stonily. The man changed personalities – and names as far as she knew - from one moment to the next, and she couldn't for the life of her tell what was real and what a pose - or whether to believe a word he said. Relying on him to help her was definitely out. If she hadn't been able to trust Donald, a man she had often sworn would never in his whole life do anything unexpected, how could she trust a man who never did anything predictable at all?

Laura rubbed her aching forehead. The more she knew about gender, the less she seemed to understand the kind of men who inhabited the world today.

"Both, I guess," she replied faintly, and sank down on a bench in the hall. Her legs felt too weak to support her, and a welcome numbness seemed to be setting in. She couldn't seem to think coherently anymore, either. Too much had happened, too fast.

Tom Smith sat down beside her. "I have three names: Thomas, Langley and Smith," he told her, counting them off on his fingers.

"You sound American," Laura remarked.

"Half of me is American," he replied enigmatically.

Laura raised an eyebrow wearily and didn't bother to reply.

"Sorry," he said. "Now, what are you going to call me? If we are going to get to know each other better, and I sincerely hope we are, you will need to use a name."

Laura considered. She always used full names with her students because she had found that too much informality led to endless requests for extensions on papers. Perhaps a more formal name might dampen this man's persistent insouciance as well.

"All right then, I shall use Thomas," she told him severely. "And do you really intend to solve this crime, Thomas?"

"Yes," he answered, unsmiling again. "I intend to solve this crime. And now let's go downstairs. Being near dead bodies make me nervous."

"You sound as if you have encountered a lot of them," Laura remarked.

This time Thomas was saved from answering by the Englishman. He strode toward them as they descended the stairs, looking every inch the country gentleman with his unruly hair, graying now at the edges, his ruddy cheeks and sleepy blue eyes.

"Glad to say I got Senator back," he told them proudly, rubbing his hands together with satisfaction. "Couldn't catch the girl, though." He shook his head sadly. "Too bad. Would have taught her a lesson she wouldn't forget in a hurry. Gave me a terrible start. Looked exactly like the girl on the bed! Those big green eyes, don't you know." The last three words slid into

28

each other to form a rumbling phrase that sounded like "doncherno."

Laura felt a surge of relief. The girl with the green eyes was alive and well. But could she really be the missing wife - if there was one? She had looked so very young.

Thomas made a noise somewhere between a cough and a curse and clenched his jaw hard. Laura regarded him with interest. Could he be angry because Cat was a young trophy wife who was tiring of him?

The Englishman chuckled. "Can't think why I was fooled in the first place," he went on. "Should have known better. Nigel is always making those damned masks. Jolly good, some of them. Fool almost anyone. I really thought for a minute the girl was dead!"

Laura opened her mouth to tell him that the body under the mask he'd seen really was dead, but the Englishman waved his hand. "Drinks first," he insisted. "We've treated you both abominably. Sorry about that. Had to fire the damned butler and the cook vanished yesterday. Can't think why. Paid her a whopping salary."

He frowned, puzzled. "Odd, she didn't seem the type to vanish like that. No color, if you know what I mean. Just an ordinary cook. But I suppose they don't stay long these days, do they?"

As he delivered these random thoughts, he ushered them down the hall and into a large room lined with bookshelves. A cluttered desk stood at one end of the room and a fire blazed at the other. "My study," he explained. "Only room with a good fire these days, seems to me. Now, what will you have? Drinks are on us, you know. You're our guests, Antonia tells me. Sorry I didn't know earlier. I thought…"

He stopped abruptly. "Well, it doesn't matter now, does it?" he resumed finally. "Just got things a bit mixed. Silver's been disappearing as well. That's why. Bit of a bother, actually. Makes one suspicious."

"As I said at the time, I was looking for my wife, not your silver," Thomas remarked dryly. "And I'll have a whisky."

"Yes, of course," the Englishman agreed, looking embarrassed. "Good thing you found her, what? I mean to say -"

"There is always the possibility," Thomas interrupted mildly, "that the disappearing silver and the disappearing servants are connected."

"By jove! Never thought of that!" The Englishman sounded genuinely startled. "Jolly good idea. Have to follow up on that one."

He turned to Laura. "Now, my dear, what will you have to drink?"

There was no wine in evidence, so Laura decided on whisky too. A good strong drink might help. She felt almost dizzy with fatigue, or perhaps it was hunger. She still hadn't had anything to eat since breakfast. More likely, she realized, it was shock. A strong drink was supposed to be good for shock.

"I'll have a whisky too, a small one," she told the Englishman gratefully. She took a large gulp when he handed it to her.

"Good gel," the Englishman drawled approvingly. "Like to see a woman who's not afraid of whisky.

"Occurs to me," he added in an even stronger drawl, "that I haven't introduced myself. Circumstances a bit odd, doncherno. Got off on the wrong foot, I fear." He turned to Laura and bowed low over her hand. "Barkeley Smythington–Witherspoon, Baron of Torrington, at your service. My friends call me Bark, say I talk in barks, like the dogs."

He frowned. "Where are the dogs anyway? Antonia's always locking them up. Need to have dogs about the place. Too damned stiff without them."

"How do you do, Baron Smythington-Witherspoon?" Laura replied, conscious that Thomas was laughing behind them. She wondered if one shook hands with a Baron or curtsied, a skill she lacked. She decided to raise her glass to him instead. He seemed to appreciate the gesture, since it gave him the opportunity to drain his whisky. Laura drank some of hers, too. It was really quite strengthening. Maybe she should try drinking it at faculty functions. They often engendered a need for a good stiff drink.

"No need to say the whole name," the Baron assured her as he poured himself another generous drink. "Can't get the tongue around it – trips you up, doncherno. Dropped the Witherspoon anyway. A bit too common for a Baron, I fear."

A melancholy look came into his face. "Too bad, rather liked that part of the family. More common sense than most."

He brightened. "Wonder if that's why they call them commoners?" He turned to Thomas and Laura with an inquiring gaze.

Laura knew exactly what he meant, and Thomas apparently did too. "I'd never thought about common sense and commoners, but you could be right," he said dryly.

The lord of the house nodded. "Yes. Now, where was I? Introductions - that was it."

He turned to Laura again. "If Bark is too informal," he advised her, "you can always try Lord Torrington. That's what the Brits call Barons."

"Thank you, Lord Torrington," Laura answered. She put her drink down on a table. "Now that we have been introduced," she stated in her firmest professorial tone, "I feel it is necessary to tell you that there really is a dead body in the green room. I want to make certain the police have been notified, or a doctor, or both. I feel responsible since I was the one who discovered her."

Lord Torrington spun around, spilling whisky as he turned. "A dead body?" he croaked. "But I thought it was all that bloody game of Nigel's, the one he's going to do next year. Solve the mystery, or some such nonsense.

"The tourists will love it, though," he added, brightening.

"It appears not to be a game," Thomas answered. "A woman called Lottie seems to be dead." He was watching Lord Torrington carefully, and for the first time it occurred to Laura that his persistent jocularity might be a way of covering his real thoughts. Could he be an investigator of some kind? On the other hand, he could just as easily be the killer. In either case, he must know more than he was saying about the woman's death. After all, he had told her someone might be killed.

But that was all he'd told her. Laura regarded him appraisingly. He had managed to avoid answering a single question about himself, which meant she would have to find out what she wanted to know on her own.

One good thing about an academic career was the ability to do background research. She saw no reason why those skills couldn't be applied to other kinds of investigations.

The Englishman set down the decanter carefully. He looked dumbfounded. "I can't believe it," he said. "Angelina can be a bit of a trial, but surely…" He frowned. "But who would want to harm Lottie? Are you sure she's dead?"

Laura looked at Thomas. Were they sure? She hadn't felt for a pulse or checked for a heartbeat.

She had underestimated Thomas. "I checked," he said curtly. "There was no pulse or heartbeat that I could find, and she was already cold."

So that was what he had been doing. Laura sank down on the nearest chair. "That is why I must make sure the police have been contacted," she repeated. "Enough time has already been wasted." Spotting a phone on the desk, she forced herself up again. "Is there a special number for the police?"

Lord Torrington didn't seem to hear her question. Turning away, he poured himself another drink and downed it in a gulp, then poured another. He looked dazed, uncomprehending.

"I'll look," Thomas said, and rummaged in the desk for a directory.

Laura dialed the number he gave her. "It doesn't seem to work," she reported. "Perhaps I'm doing something wrong."

Thomas took the receiver from her and listened. "That's because there is no dial tone," he informed her. His voice was neutral, his face closed.

He turned to the Englishman, who seemed lost in thought. "Lord Torrington," he said loudly, "we seem unable to get through on this line. Is there another telephone?"

Lord Torrington jumped. "Telephone? You want a telephone? Damned nuisance, those instruments. Ring at you every time you fall asleep, and then all you get is some fool at the other end."

"We need one now to call the police," Laura reminded him.

"Give it to me," he retorted, and grabbed the receiver. He listened intently. "Well, I'll be damned," he exclaimed, looking pleased. "No dial tone." His face saddened. "Old tree's finally gone," he said mournfully. "All this rain too much for it."

Laura frowned. What did a tree have to do with the telephone?

"Ah," said Thomas. "You mean a tree has fallen on the wires and that is why there's no dial tone?"

Lord Torrington nodded, still looking relieved. Was that because the hated instrument wouldn't ring and disturb him anymore, or because he didn't want anyone to call the police? Bad for business, for one thing, to have swarms of police around.

"If the telephone won't work, perhaps someone could drive to the police station, or get a doctor," she persisted.

Lord Torrington shook his head. "Road's flooded," he told her. "Always underwater when it rains hard. At the bottom of the hill, doncherno. Big dip there. Can't get a car through, even a truck."

"And that's the only way out, I suppose?" Laura queried, without much hope.

"Except on horseback," Thomas suggested flippantly.

Lord Torrington turned on him. "Can't take the horses out at this time of night," he objected in shocked tones. "Might hurt them. Valuable animals!"

Laura sighed. "So we're stuck here with a dead body and no way to get help." And, she added silently, she was stuck with two men of unknown trustworthiness, one of whom seemed suspiciously unwilling to call the police, the other about whom she knew absolutely nothing except that he was masquerading as her husband. Either of them could be a killer. It was going to be a very long night.

Nigel appeared in the door, looking even paler than before. He closed the door behind him, and Laura saw that his hands were shaking.

"We tried to call, Gram and I," he told his father. "Call the police about Lottie, I mean, but we couldn't get through."

"Old tree's finally fallen on the line," Lord Torrington assured him, sounding quite cheerful. "No use trying."

Nigel swallowed hard, as if his mouth were too dry to speak. "No," he said, "not the tree. Someone has…" He swallowed again. "Someone has cut the telephone lines."

CHAPTER FOUR

No one spoke. Without knowing she had done it, Laura took a large gulp of her drink. She choked, and Thomas patted her absently on the back. She longed, suddenly and irrationally, for a hot shower, for clean clothes. She was still in her muddy hiking socks and even muddier pants, and her untidy state made her feel helpless, unable to cope or even to think. Surely if she could just find her suitcase, have a shower and change her clothes, everything would go back to normal and she would be all right…

A gong sounded, and the door burst open.

"I made the sandwiches," Angelina shouted. "That's all we have for dinner because cook's gone and mother doesn't know how to cook, so we're to have tea instead, and I'm to help mother serve it, as there's no butler either. There's some soup, too, but it's all vegetables and it's nasty.

"It's in the dining room, in half an hour," Angelina continued, "and Gram says I'm to show you to your rooms right away, and not to be late so the dinner, I mean tea, won't get cold. Hurry up!" she chastised them when no one moved.

Numbly, Laura followed Angelina out of the room. Thomas followed.

"We were going to put you in the green room before," Angelina confided," but my mother decided the blue room would be better since there's two of you."

Laura shuddered. She really did want to know more about Thomas, but that didn't include sharing a room with him. Still, the green room was worse.

Walking into Murder

The blue room, however, turned out to be two connecting rooms with a bath between. Laura's mood lifted, and she felt even better when she saw her suitcase in one of the rooms, delivered as promised by the tour company to her next stop. She would have her own room and the longed-for shower would be hers – if a shower existed. Many English bathrooms possessed only tubs, and she had never understood how anyone could take a bath in ten minutes or less, as they always seemed to do in books.

"Do you mind if I go first?" she asked Thomas politely, indicating the bathroom. "I'm such a mess after all that hiking."

"I guess you are," Thomas agreed with unflattering honesty. He smiled, making the laugh lines at the sides of his eyes crinkle. "Mess or no, however, I find you utterly bewitching."

Astonishment rendered Laura speechless, and then, to her horror, she blushed. "Oh," she mumbled. "Thanks."

"You are quite welcome," he replied. "Let me know when you're finished."

Laura felt the blush deepening. She fled into the bathroom and shut the door hard behind her. If only she had more experience as a single woman she might know how to interpret remarks like that, or at least learn not to blush like a teenager. He must think she was terribly naïve. She was, too. She had believed him, proving all over again that she knew more about fifty-thousand-year-old men than contemporary ones. No man could find her bewitching in this disreputable state. Donald certainly wouldn't. He'd said she always looked unkempt, which had infuriated her. She wasn't really.

She just hated the tailored look and refused to wear clothes that made her look like some kind of neatly wrapped package. Like Patti.

Laura flung off her filthy clothes and stepped into the shower, which fortunately did exist. The hot water felt blissful, and she luxuriated in it for as long as she dared. Images of the dead woman came into her mind, but she pushed them away determinedly. There was nothing she could do for the poor woman now except try to find out how she had died and why.

"All yours," she called through the adjoining door when she finished, and then realized with acute embarrassment that she was clad only in a towel. She didn't want to think about the kind of remarks that might evoke.

Fortunately, Thomas didn't answer. Laura scurried into her room and rummaged in her suitcase for clothes. She always brought too much when she traveled because she could never resist stuffing in a few favorite long skirts and brightly colored jackets that might be perfect for some mythical occasion but never were. They certainly weren't right for this setting. Instead, she pulled out a new purchase, a long dark green dress of some new fabric that was supposed to be wrinkle-free. To her surprise, it was. The slinky stuff fell easily over her head and settled itself smoothly around her.

Laura glanced in the mirror. Not too bad, she decided, except for her hair. There hadn't been time to wash it and in the high humidity it exploded around her face like an untamed lion's mane. Or maybe a baboon's mane, considering the color.

Maybe a bun would work? Smoothing the unruly strands back, Laura pulled it into a rough circle and skewered it with a few gaudy pins. That would have to do. Dabbing on some eye makeup and her favorite pair of dangly earrings to give herself confidence, she knocked again on Thomas's door to let him know the bathroom was free. There was still no answer.

She found him downstairs, examining some paintings in the study. He too had changed, into a dark blue blazer. She was glad to see a few bulges in the pockets. Perfectly tailored men were too reminiscent of Donald.

"These paintings are lovely," Thomas told Lord Torrington. "Have you had them cleaned lately?"

Laura wasn't sure she would describe them as lovely, though they were the type of paintings one would expect to find in museums, and were probably quite valuable. The backgrounds were dark and the peasant homes they portrayed were little more than grimy shacks. Still, the people in them had cheerful faces, and she liked the touches of bright color that enlivened their ragged clothes.

Lord Torrington glanced up absentmindedly at the paintings. "Don't know," he answered. "Maybe Antonia did. Look the same as always to me. One of those old Dutch painters, you know. Rather good, I'm told, but I've never paid much attention to those things."

Antonia appeared. "Dinner is ready. This way, please." She sounded like a bored tour guide, Laura thought. Maybe she too was a young wife tiring of her older husband. There were far too many of that species around.

Antonia led them into an impressive dining room. More large pieces of ornate silver covered the tables, and portraits in heavily gilded frames, no doubt portraying Torrington ancestors, decorated the walls. Above the sideboard was a more recent painting of a woman with dark hair and aristocratic features that was almost certainly the grande dame when she was younger. Laura felt a stir of recognition. Hadn't she seen that face somewhere before? Not the face of the present woman, but the one in the portrait. She stared at it, but couldn't recall the context in which she'd seen it.

The grande dame, who was clearly their hostess, indicated the proper places for her guests as if this were a four-course gourmet dinner. Obviously, informality was not tolerated in the dining room, even with a dead body in the house and cut telephone wires.

"If you will sit there, Mrs. Smith," she said graciously, indicating a seat beside Lord Torrington, "and you there, Mr. Smith."

"Thank you," Laura murmured, wishing she knew how to address her hostess properly. Was she Lady Torrington? She couldn't be, though. That was Antonia, at least Thomas had addressed her as Lady Torrington.

Laura gave up and tackled her soup, trying not to slurp. The spoon, she remembered from long ago lessons, was supposed to go into the bowl from front to back, though how one got it to the mouth from that position without spilling remained a mystery, especially when the soup bowl was encased in a silver tureen that kept getting in the way. Still, the soup was delicious despite Angelina's disclaimers.

The sandwiches were another matter. They were a varied and ill-assorted lot, some with bits of green that she assumed were watercress, others with a pink paste that might be ham or fish, and a yellow one that might be eggs enhanced by a great deal of mayonnaise. Most of them, however, had a sticky brown substance inside that reminded Laura of the mud she had stared at all day. Both Angelina and Nigel were eating them voraciously, so Laura took a tentative bite. She put the sandwich down again in astonishment. Chocolate! How bizarre!

"If you don't want it, I'll have it," Angelina said, noting that Laura had taken only one bite.

"Angelina, that is not polite," her mother corrected.

"Yes, mother," Angelina answered, and coolly grabbed the sandwich from Laura's plate.

Conversation was desultory. Antonia seemed lost in her own thoughts and so did Lord Torrington. Tom Smith, who was seated beside their hostess, was talking to her about art, a subject both of them seemed to know a lot about.

Their voices suddenly ceased and Laura realized that everyone's eyes were focused on the door behind her. Antonia gave a sharp cry of fear, and Nigel looked as if he were about to faint. Lord Torrington was open-mouthed with astonishment. Thomas had a glint in his eye that looked almost dangerous. Even the grande dame had lost her steely composure, as if she had no idea how to rise to this particular occasion.

Angelina, as usual, looked mutinous. "You're dead!" she announced. "You're supposed to be dead, so you can't come in here."

Lord Torrington's astonishment morphed into triumph. "No dead body, after all," he said, beaming. "Didn't see how there could be. Not reasonable, doncherno."

Belatedly, Laura looked behind her. A duplicate of the woman she had seen on the green room bed stood in

41

the doorway, wringing her hands. Her long bony face was suffused with embarrassment.

Lottie rushed toward them. "I am so sorry, Baroness Smythington, so very much sorry that I have not attended to my duties," she said in an anguished tone, bowing until she had almost prostrated herself at the grande dame's feet. Her accent was very strong. One of the Scandinavian languages, Laura suspected.

Gratefully, she took note of the name Lottie had used. It was a strange way to find out the proper form of address for her hostess, but she was still glad to know it.

Lottie went on apologizing as if she were unable to stop. "I do not know what happens to me," she moaned, stumbling over the words. "One moment I am drinking the tea in my room, and then I am falling down, and I wake up many hours later, but I do not know where I am and what has come over me, and I..."

Abruptly, her voice broke off and she slumped into a chair.

"All right, Lottie," the Baroness said. "I am sure it was not your fault. I think all of us have been the victims of a very nasty joke."

Deliberately, one face at a time, she examined each person at the table, including Laura. "I do not know who is responsible for this outrage," she said severely, "but I intend to find out." No one met the probing dark eyes. Even Lord Torrington seemed subdued by her gaze.

The old lady rose slowly to her feet. "Shall we take coffee in the study? Antonia, I would be pleased if you would carry the tray from the kitchen." She turned to Angelina. "There are some petit fours in the sideboard. Perhaps you will bring them?"

Angelina's face lit up. "Yes, Gram," she answered meekly. Grabbing the delicacies, she ran ahead of them to the study so she could chew unobserved. The others trooped behind the Baroness, as intimidated as a group of students on their way to the principal's office.

Coffee was served and Angelina passed the petit fours, taking care to eat one every time she offered the box to someone else. No one seemed to notice except Lottie, who looked too sick and miserable to object and finally excused herself, with many repetitious apologies, to go lie down.

As if by unspoken agreement, no one in the family raised the subject that was uppermost in their minds: Lottie and her miraculous recovery. Laura suspected that the Baroness wouldn't ask for explanations until her guests had retired for the night.

She was right. "I am sure our guests must be tired," the Baroness said, rising to her feet. Laura took the hint.

"Thank you for the dinner, Baroness Smythington," she said politely, going to the door. "Good night, everyone."

"Why don't you go first, darling, and use the bath?" Thomas suggested. "I'll have a look at the weather and be right behind you."

Laura heard him saying his good nights as she headed down the hall. When he opened the front door to look outside, she heard thunder. *Great,* she told herself, *an even wilder storm as well as everything else.*

Exhaustion hit the moment she looked at her bed. It was covered with a thick duvet encased in ivory fabric with tiny blue flowers; soft pillows with the same pattern invited her to rest her weary head. Laura resisted until she had brushed her teeth and found a nightgown. Then she tumbled under the covers and closed her eyes.

Perversely, sleep wouldn't come. It often didn't. Being alone at night was the worst part of being single. She'd become accustomed to a warm body beside her in the bed, even one who had long ago lost his appeal. Why had she married Donald anyway? Sex, she supposed. That was how the species kept going. The impulse to mate was as strong today as it had been thousands of years ago. It kept going even after the job of child-bearing was over. She often wished it didn't. That empty ache never went away.

Her mind moved on to the day's events and then drifted to her children. Both were young adults now, but they still worried her. Donald's defection had come at a terrible time. She had just started a demanding new job; Melinda had just decided to get married despite multiple reservations about that patriarchal institution – now unpleasantly confirmed by her father. Mark had been in the sullen throes of adolescent rebellion and had refused to talk about anything. He had seemed most comfortable with Patti, which was hard to take, as were the sympathetic glances from other faculty members who assumed that Laura had been ignominiously dumped. In fact, she had intended to ask Donald for a divorce as soon as Mark was a little older and had calmed down, but Donald had stolen her fire. That was what rankled most of all. That and the fact that he had gone straight to Patti's after his perfidious announcement and stayed out of sight for weeks, leaving her to pay for the infamous dinner.

Laura grinned, remembering her revenge. She had come home from that dinner in a rage so fierce that she

44

had taken every article of Donald's clothing she could find and tossed each piece triumphantly out the window into the pouring rain. The sight of his soggy trousers, his shirts, socks, ties, shoes and underwear hanging limply from bushes and trees had thrilled her.

Donald had picked it all up the next day and gone back to Patti, oblivious both to her distress and to his children's. Melinda opined that he had vanished into the self-absorbed state known as male menopause, which compelled middle-aged men to prove their manhood and show off to their friends by nabbing a sexy young wife. Laura wasn't so sure. Donald had never been all that interested in sex. In her opinion, what he had wanted was an orderly life and a housewife who would uncomplainingly keep it that way. Patti seemed born for the role.

Pounding her pillow into a more comfortable position, Laura pushed Donald and her children out of her mind. Perversely, Angelina drifted in instead. Laura saw her again, looking down at the body in the dim light of the green room and then touching the arm, feeling how cold it was….

Laura's eyes opened wide. Nigel and the Baroness had touched the arm too. Both had seemed sure Lottie was dead. Only Lottie wasn't dead; she was alive, and so was Cat, and that meant…That meant the woman they had all seen lying on the bed as Lottie might not have been Lottie at all, but someone else, first with her face covered with a Cat mask, then with a Lottie mask, but it had been the same arm, an arm without a pulse…Thomas had made sure…

Laura jumped out of bed, grabbed her bathrobe and slipped quietly out of the room. She had to look at least.

Walking into Murder

The door of the green room was closed. She eased it open and peered inside. It was very dark. Probably the curtains had been drawn. Wishing she had thought to pack a flashlight, she crept cautiously across the room toward the windows. If she could open the curtains, she might be able to see a little.

She ran her hand along the heavy draperies, feeling for the opening to pull them apart. Just as her fingers found the crack, her wrist was grabbed in a steely clasp and twisted behind her. Another hand slapped across her mouth.

CHAPTER FIVE

Laura's stomach lurched with fear. "Let me go," she sputtered, twisting away from the hand at her mouth. It disappeared, but the grip on her arm didn't relax. She was dragged along while her captor felt for a light switch, and then she could see.

"You!" Thomas said in disgust, releasing her arm with a jerk. "I thought I might have a murderer in my grasp."

Laura rubbed her aching wrist. "How do you know I'm not? You seem better qualified for the position of murderer than I am anyway," she added tartly.

Thomas didn't answer. He had already turned on another light beside the bed and was leaning over the pillow, concentrating intensely.

"Don't you ever answer a question?" Laura asked in frustration.

Taking advantage of his preoccupation, she went to the other side of the bed to see if the body was still there. It wasn't. Then what was Thomas examining with such fascination? All she could see was a pale object, mostly hidden by the bedclothes.

Thomas pulled the rest of the object out, using a handkerchief, and for the first time Laura saw what it was - the mask of Lottie. A tremor of fear ran through her. It looked pathetic now, like a discarded theatrical prop - which was exactly what it was, except that it was so incredibly life-like.

"Remarkable young chap," Thomas murmured thoughtfully. "So good he fooled himself."

"You mean he didn't realize he was looking at his own mask, not at Lottie's face," Laura answered. She swallowed hard, struggling to digest the unwelcome fact that she had been right. There had been a body, a body with a Cat mask and then Lottie's mask on its face, or else why was the second mask still there? Someone had taken the body away, only the person had forgotten the mask. How horrible to do that, as if the woman's body was no more than a bundle of flesh, to be disposed of like…

Thomas's voice cut into these morbid ruminations. "Exactly. But on the other hand, Nigel doesn't see very well at close range without his glasses, and as Sherlock Holmes, he couldn't wear them."

"He had a monocle," Laura pointed out. "And how do you know that about Nigel?"

Thomas gave her a quick, admiring glance. "You're a good observer. However, as you may also have noticed, Nigel didn't use the monocle to look at Lottie. He put it in his pocket. And I know he needs glasses because he told me when he showed me his studio. He does very professional work, as you can see."

Laura nodded, intrigued despite the feeling of revulsion that came over her every time she looked at the pale object on the pillowcase.

"I wonder how he makes the masks so realistic, and how he learned to make them in the first place," she mused.

"I believe the Baroness taught him," Thomas answered. "She once had something to do with the theater, I think, and knew a lot about mask making."

Maybe that was why the portrait of a younger Baroness had seemed so familiar, Laura thought, because she had been in the theater. The elusive sense of recognition surfaced again, but vanished just as quickly. How frustrating!

Spurred on by her show of interest, Thomas continued his explanation. "Nigel adapted one of her techniques to create a series of face portraits, as he calls them. First, he makes a bust of his subject; then he covers it with fabric – buckram, I think it's called, that conforms perfectly to the contours of the face and head when it's wet. When the fabric dries, he peels it off and has a mask. It's quite flexible, Nigel tells me, and can be kept in place by an almost invisible piece of elastic under the hair. By the time he adds coloring, paints the eyes and mouth, adds hair and eyebrows and all the rest, the results can fool almost anyone, at least in dim lights. I'll ask him to show you, if you want. Or maybe he'll do one of you if you're around."

Laura shuddered. In normal circumstances she would have been fascinated, but at the moment masks made her feel rather nauseous. "Later on, maybe," she answered. "Right now I'd be afraid there would be yet another body underneath."

"So you realized there must be a body, too." Thomas sighed. "Hard to come alive again when you don't have a pulse or a heartbeat."

Laura shivered. "And so cold," she whispered. "The Baroness and Angelina felt her arm, and so did Nigel. Maybe that's why he was fooled. Or not fooled, depending on how you look at it. I wonder what he thinks now."

"That he was wrong and Lottie was alive all the time," Thomas answered. "Or at least I hope that's what he thinks. It's safer."

"Safer?" Laura was startled, and then she saw what he meant. "You mean, the murderer wants everyone to think no one is dead. That was the point of using the masks and then removing the body, so they would think Lottie had been lying here all the time and had recovered."

"As possibly they do, except for you," Thomas observed and Laura thought she detected a note of suspicion in his voice. "You decided to return to the scene of the crime to ask more questions Are you a detective in disguise, like Miss Marple?"

"Not at all," she answered primly. "I came because I was…Well, I was just curious." She grimaced. One might even say, as Donald had, insatiably curious. The tired maxim about cats had inevitably followed. Donald hadn't liked her impulsiveness, either. She leaped before she looked, he said, and she had to admit he was right about that. The fact that she was in this room looking for clues and wrangling with a possible murderer was proof enough.

"You are also not lacking in courage," Thomas said, and this time Laura thought she really did see admiration in his face.

Terrified that she would blush again, she leaned over the bed to hide her face. Her eye was caught by a small red spot on the pillow. Blood, she was sure. Had Thomas seen it? Should she point it out? Was that risky? After all, he could be the murderer.

Thomas's voice made her jump. "As I said before, people do not rise from the dead, not without a pulse or heartbeat, and there's some blood on the sheets as well. The question is, why all the disguises?"

"To give the murderer time," Laura replied promptly. "He, or she, had to wait until everyone was asleep to move the body, but in the meantime he had to prevent anyone from seeing who the victim really was, or even from knowing that there was a victim in the first place."

Her stomach lurched suddenly. She was such an innocent! Maybe that was why Tom Smith was in the green room right now. Maybe he had already removed the body, had come back for the incriminating mask and to make sure no other clues to the murder were left behind. And then she had interrupted him, seen the damning clues. If that was true, she was in a very bad position. She took a few steps backward.

"Good thinking!" Thomas exclaimed. "Now all we have to do is find out how the murder was done. And who murdered her," he added with a note of menace in his voice that startled Laura.

She glanced up at him and caught a look that terrified her with its intensity. His eyes, his mouth, all his features seemed to rearrange themselves into another personality, one that was totally focused on some perceived goal and would use any means to attain it. The look vanished in an instant, but she had seen it.

Laura began to shiver and found to her horror that once again she couldn't stop. Tom Smith looked at her sharply. "You need a strong drink." Grabbing her arm, he hauled her out the door and down the stairs. Laura was incapable of resisting. He poured a generous measure of brandy into a glass and thrust it at her.

"Drink," he ordered. Laura obeyed.

Slowly, the shivering receded, and she felt her courage and her common sense return. What an idiot she was to get so worked up! If Thomas had wanted to murder her, he would have finished her off by now and stashed her wherever the first body was stashed. There had been plenty of time and opportunity. But he hadn't.

"Thanks," she mumbled, not looking at him lest he guess that fears about him had triggered her shivering fit.

"In my opinion," Thomas said, watching her carefully, "you should get out of here as fast as you can. Go on with your walking trip first thing in the morning and don't come back."

Laura nodded, but she had no intention of obeying. The shivering had only been a momentary lapse of courage. She was all right now, and she wasn't going to let him stop her from finding out for herself what was going on.

Thomas looked at her doubtfully but said no more. He took her arm again, more gently this time, and led her upstairs. "Get some more sleep if you can," he urged. "That's what I'm going to do. It's been a very long day."

For the first time, Laura noticed that he was fully dressed. "You haven't gone to bed at all," she said, surprised.

He shook his head. "No, my dearest, I have not." he agreed, looking into her eyes and smiling faintly. He was so close that their bodies were almost touching, and Laura felt an almost forgotten surge of longing rise inside her. It must have showed in her face, for Thomas took it as an invitation. Without warning, he bent down and kissed her on the lips. Laura kissed him back, casting inhibitions to the winds.

Walking into Murder

After a long time that seemed to pass in a nanosecond, she drew away, breathless. She still didn't know if Thomas was friend or foe, but she did know that kiss had felt wonderful. Better than anything she'd felt in years.

2.

Laura stumbled back into bed and to her surprise fell instantly asleep. A few hours later she awoke feeling undeservedly refreshed. The duvet, she decided. It was marvelously sleep-friendly. Or perhaps the second, lingering kiss she and Thomas had exchanged. She had enjoyed that one too, even if he was a villain.

There was no sound from the next room, and she hurried to use the bathroom before Thomas woke up. She wasn't sure she wanted to encounter him again – especially while showering or brushing her teeth - until she'd had a chance to sort out her feelings about him. She liked him, mistrusted him and was frustrated by him in equal measure. Adding to the confusion, she was attracted to him – very attracted. How did one behave toward a man under those circumstances? Twenty years of marriage hadn't prepared her for that sort of dilemma.

The sight of sun outside her window buoyed her mood and she pulled on a burnt orange shirt, a favorite color, and her walking skirt. It was loose enough to sway as she walked but sleek enough not to trip her up, and when she wore it she felt like an intrepid female explorer striding fearlessly across the African savannah.

Breakfast was laid out on the sideboard and Laura helped herself. It was pleasant not to be served, more peaceful. No one else was about, either, which helped a great deal. The Torringtons were not a relaxing family.

Walking into Murder

She had almost finished when Antonia turned up. She seemed distracted. Yesterday, she had been perfectly dressed and coiffed, with carefully applied makeup enhancing her lovely features. Today her makeup was smudged, her clothes rumpled, almost as if she had slept in them. So was her hair. If she had been married to anyone except Lord Torrington, Laura would have surmised that she had come straight from a spontaneous bout of morning lovemaking, but she found it difficult to picture the Lord and Antonia indulging in such play. More likely, he was in the stables conferring with the horses.

"I hope you slept well," she said politely to Antonia, and received a startled look in response.

"Yes, I mean, not so well... It's been a difficult time, and then one doesn't..."

"Yes," Laura answered sympathetically. "I hope some of the problems are resolving themselves. At least Lottie has reappeared."

"Yes," Antonia answered flatly, and excused herself to take dishes back to the kitchen. She didn't reappear.

Laura frowned. How odd that Antonia had looked like that, as if she just got out of bed. It seemed out of character. Where had she been?

The answer came from Lord Torrington. "Antonia's got everything under control," he drawled with robust heartiness as he came into the room. "Got up early, sent the groom out to see if we can get supplies, check the flooding and all that."

So there was a groom! That was interesting news. Maybe Antonia had been with him earlier. An affair with a groom seemed to fit her a great deal better than checking out floods and supplies.

Walking into Murder

Shades of Lady Chatterley, Laura mused, except in that lady's infamous case her lover had been a gamekeeper. She would have to find out more about the groom – and about the colorless cook who had vanished. She was missing, and so was a body, presumably female. Were they the same person?

"I'll be off right after breakfast," she told Lord Torrington. "Thank you for putting up with me in the midst of so many difficulties."

"Not at all," Lord Torrington drawled. "Happy to have you. Char – the Baroness that is, sends her regards," he added hastily. "She is resting but asked me to thank you for your help."

"Please thank the Baroness for her hospitality and tell her I enjoyed meeting her," Laura replied, aware that it was true. The grande dame – and she would always think of her by that name - was a wonderfully invincible character, one she would not forget.

"I'll go check on Thomas," she called back as she left the room, recalling her wifely role. Lord Torrington was already deep in his paper and didn't look up.

Laura knocked on the adjoining door but there was no answer. Could Thomas still be asleep? It seemed unlikely. She eased the door open a crack.

Her mouth dropped in astonishment. The room was in total disarray, with clothes flung everywhere and drawers pulled open. Even the mattress had been pulled askew, the duvet tossed carelessly on the floor.

Thomas wouldn't leave a room like this, Laura thought. Or would he? She didn't really know, but it seemed unlikely. Even she would never make this much of a mess. Instead, it looked to her as if his room had been searched. Was someone else at Torrington Manor curious about Thomas and what he was doing here?

Where was he, anyway? She was surprised that he hadn't communicated with her, since he was so insistent on being her husband.

Laura felt a prickle of anxiety. She ought to find out where Thomas was before she left, at least. Grabbing her suitcase with a vow that next time she would leave half the contents behind, she lugged it down to the hall to be picked up and taken to her next night's lodging.

Thomas didn't seem to be in the house, nor was anyone else about. Laura decided to look for him outside, which also gave her an excellent excuse to poke around the grounds and outbuildings before she left.

She came first to a large tool shed filled with the usual assortment of gardening implements and other outdoor paraphernalia. Nothing caught her eye except a large box of rat poison that made her shudder. She had no way of knowing if this particular victim had been fed rat poison, but she would keep the clue in mind. She went on to a barn-like structure beside the stables. This one was more interesting. Shuffling noises greeted her as she came inside, as if a heavy object were being moved or dragged across the floor. Laura stood still, letting her eyes adjust to the dim light. When she could see better, she moved cautiously ahead, her boots soundless on the hay-strewn surface.

She stopped abruptly and her stomach seemed to drop to the floor. She had found Thomas. He was leaning nonchalantly against the far wall and Antonia was pressed hard against him. Her arms were clasped around him and her lips were raised to his.

CHAPTER SIX

Laura looked away, disgusted. So that was the answer to Thomas's whereabouts. He, not the groom, was the cause of Antonia's earlier dishabille.

How disillusioning. She had expected more of Thomas, had thought him either a real villain or a man of some character, not just a womanizer. That seemed so ordinary, so utterly lacking in imagination and style. Worse, she had fallen for it. Embarrassment flooded her as she remembered how enthusiastically she had returned his kisses. If she hadn't been so exhausted, she might even have jumped into bed with him. She had certainly wanted to. How amused he must have been!

Still not believing he could be quite that callous, she glanced back to verify what she had seen. Thomas was looking right at her but he didn't react at all, didn't even seem to see her. Was he that besotted with Antonia?

Might as well get on with what you came to do and get walking, Laura thought, surprised at the depth of her disappointment. If nothing else, she had looked forward to matching wits with Thomas while she tried to figure out what was going on at Torrington Manor. Now even that was impossible. The spice seemed to have gone out of life.

Head down, she walked rapidly out of the barn and down the driveway. She moved so fast she almost bumped into a burly man with a shovel in one hand and a rake over his shoulder. The gardener, she supposed. Laura said a polite good morning. To her surprise, he didn't answer, nor did he move out of her way. Instead he stood where he was, staring at her suspiciously. Then, seeming to remember himself, he bid her a brusque good morning and let her pass.

He must have been watching her the whole time she had been looking into the barn! Laura felt an unexpected sense of violation. She hurried on, aware that his eyes were on her back, and was glad when the lane turned and she could no longer be seen.

She strode on steadily. It was a beautiful day; sunlight poured down, unexpected but welcome after yesterday's storm, and her surroundings were gorgeous. Wildflowers decorated the fields, birds sang, and the world felt made for enjoyment.

Her euphoria was short-lived. At the bottom of the lane she came to a halt and stared unbelievingly at the water coursing across the road. It looked more than two feet deep. Lord Torrington hadn't made up that flood story up to keep the police away.

Laura hesitated. She wasn't going back to Torrington Manor, at least while Thomas was there; that was certain. Maybe she could find a drier place to cross, or maybe it would be easier to take off her boots and wade.

Reluctantly, Laura bent down to unlace her boots. The sound of grinding gears startled her and she stood up again. A huge truck with wheels that looked to be four feet high was lurching drunkenly through the muddy potholes she had just negotiated.

The vehicle ground to a halt, and a stocky man with a shock of white hair that belied his youthful face jumped out. "Might I help? I'm Adrian Banbury, the local veterinarian. My truck churns through flood, snow and ice, and I should be happy to offer you a lift."

Laura smiled. What a delightful way of speaking he had! A charming country gentleman veterinarian, she decided. And at the moment, a savior.

"If you would take me across this flooded area, I would be delighted," she accepted. "I'm Laura Morland, and I'm on a walking trip in the area."

"Surely, you're not walking alone!" Dr. Banbury exclaimed. "You are American, I believe, and perhaps not familiar with our paths. They can be very confusing, I fear."

Old-fashioned as well as courtly, Laura thought wryly. "I'm quite independent," she answered. "So far I've only gotten lost once."

"I see," he answered, and stared at her intently. Disconcerted, Laura put a hand to her face, wondering if there was mud on it.

"Sorry," he apologized. "I didn't mean to stare. It's just that you remind me of someone, someone quite unexpected."

"That's all right," Laura replied politely, but she was still uneasy. He was the second man to stare fixedly at her this morning. Were Englishmen that unaccustomed to seeing a woman walking alone in the countryside? Maybe it aroused some primitive urge in them, as if she were a cow in heat.

Dr. Banbury's voice distracted her. 'May I help you up into the cab? It's quite a high step." Without waiting for a reply, he grasped her elbow and assisted her up.

"Thanks." Laura hoisted her pack in behind her. "I really appreciate a lift though the water. I was about to take off my boots and wade."

Dr. Banbury chuckled, and she was relieved at the change in his manner. "I have done the same many times," he admitted ruefully. "Lest you be forced into another boot removal, I shall drive you through the next flooded area down the road. It is not as deep but it still impedes foot traffic."

"That would be a great help. I didn't know there was another. I've been staying at Torrington Manor, and Lord Torrington only mentioned this one."

"I have just come from the Manor. Lord Torrington has quite a stable and I'm often there, seeing to one equine ailment or another."

"He seems very concerned about his horses," Laura commented. "The one called Senator was out last evening and he wasn't pleased."

"Ah! I heard about that. A young woman took him out apparently. It does seem odd. She returned him in fine condition, however."

So Cat was a good horsewoman. Laura felt a renewed prickle of curiosity. Who was she, and what was she to Thomas?

"I've an excellent idea," Dr. Banbury exclaimed as the truck splashed through the second flooded area. "Why don't you come for a quick visit? My house is just down the lane to the left, and I have a lovely little art collection I like to show visitors."

Laura hesitated. To get to her next destination in time, she should keep walking. Still, Dr. Banbury sounded so delighted with the idea of a visit that it seemed ungracious to refuse, especially since he had rescued her. The notion of a country veterinarian with an art collection sounded intriguing, too.

"That would be lovely," she agreed. "I'm afraid I don't know very much about art, but I would enjoy seeing your paintings anyway."

"Excellent. It's a pleasant little gallery. Many of my paintings are portraits of the fairer sex. Women make such wonderful subject matter, don't you think?

"Fully clothed, of course," he added hastily, and Laura smiled to herself.

The house was tucked into a gentle hillside and she liked it immediately. It was constructed of the local honey-colored stone and surrounded by flower beds, and farther out, lush pastures.

Dr. Banbury paused in the outer hall to remove his muddy boots, and Laura followed his example. Putting mud on these pristine floors would have been mortifying, and she wondered who kept them so clean.

"My housekeeper insists," Dr. Banbury explained, seeming to intuit her thought. "She scrubs the floors relentlessly and lets me know in short order if I violate the rules."

Laura followed him down the wide hall, past a small but beautifully furnished living room and into a study full of books and leather. "You have a lovely house," she commented appreciatively.

"Thank you. I am very fond of it and it meets my needs admirably. It's a good house to come back to at the end of a day in stables and surgeries and such."

Reaching into his pocket, Dr. Banbury took out a key and unlocked a door at the opposite end of the room. "In here," he said, gesturing for her to precede him. "I keep the room locked at all times, and no one goes in except in my company. Some of the paintings are quite valuable and I do my best to protect them."

Laura felt a small shiver of apprehension. He sounded different again. His voice was possessive now, almost reverential.

He smiled sheepishly. "I know," he told her, returning to his normal tone. "I act as if we were going into a church or some other sacred place. I love paintings, you see, and to have them all gathered here, by my own efforts, is for me almost a spiritual experience. I dreamed of this for many years, and then I finally managed to do it, or to begin the process at least."

Laura smiled back at him, appreciating his honesty, and entered the room. Immediately, she too felt its potency. The lighting was perfect, and the paintings glowed. They looked very old. Many were portraits of women as he had said, but all had a wonderful combination of dark and very complex backgrounds, and brilliant color.

"They are marvelous," she told him sincerely. "They glow, don't they?"

"Yes. Partly it's the lighting, but it's also the paintings themselves. The old masters knew what they were doing."

Laura let her eyes roam around the room. "They are truly beautiful," she said reverently, "especially in a room like this, all together."

"I am very glad you understand," Adrian replied, giving her arm a gentle squeeze. "It means a great deal to me when others understand." He seemed genuinely moved by her admiration and Laura was touched. Adrian was a very unusual man, to combine this strong love of beauty with his more prosaic work with animals.

She gazed around again, taking her time as she surveyed the paintings. There were twenty at least, but they seemed to belong together, as if each had been carefully chosen for a quality that matched the others. It looked like an expensive collection, too, and the more mercenary half of her was curious to know how he could afford them. Veterinarians didn't make that much - or maybe in England they did. She had noticed that in many of the towns around here the clinics for animals were much bigger and more modern than the ones for people. The English took their pets very seriously.

Her eye was caught by a small pair of paintings that looked rather like the ones Thomas had examined in Lord Torrington's study. Before she could examine them closely, Adrian took her elbow and steered her toward another painting.

"This is a painting I especially want you to see," he said, pointing at a portrait of a woman in a long dress of shimmering ivory fabric. She wore a wide-brimmed hat with floating streamers in deep turquoise green that set off her rich chestnut hair and the green tint in her eyes. "She is my favorite, the one I love best," Adrian added reverently. The hushed, almost possessive tone had returned to his voice.

Laura stared up at the painting. The woman seemed to look back at her with wide-open eyes, as if delighted at what she saw. Laura found herself smiling. "She looks pleased with life," she said, feeling a sense of kinship with the unknown lady. "As if she thinks one never knows what might happen next."

"Exactly," Adrian replied. "She is an impulsive creature, don't you think? A curious one as well, who likes to find answers."

Laura laughed. "That sounds like me."

Adrian turned to look at her, and an odd little silence seemed to fill the room. Adrian finally broke it.

"You understood immediately," he said, and to Laura's consternation, she saw tears in his eyes.

"Oh dear, I didn't mean that so seriously," she began, wanting to defuse the situation, but Adrian interrupted.

"That was why I stared at you so rudely," he admitted. "You are extraordinarily like my favorite lady, even to the color of your eyes and hair."

He sounded as if he were in love with the woman in the painting, Laura thought uneasily. She hoped he wouldn't transfer the feelings in her direction. Maybe it was time to get walking again.

She looked at her watch. "Thank you for showing me your gallery, Dr. Banbury, but I must get back on the trail now. I need to get to Stourton, where I spend the night."

"Adrian," he corrected. "No need for formality between us. And may I call you Laura? Such a lovely name. I shall call my lady in the painting Laura after this. A serendipitous meeting indeed."

"Thank you. That is a lovely compliment," Laura said, edging toward the door. "You must know a good deal about art," she continued as he locked the door again.

He smiled at her, looking normal again. "I have always loved fine art and so I have educated myself," he explained. "It is not hard to do when you are motivated. A great deal of information is available."

"Some of the people I met last night also knew a great deal," Laura remarked. "Is that usually the case in this country?"

"Goodness, no," Adrian replied with feeling. "Most people in England can't tell one painting from another. Their ignorance is shocking."

"I feel very ignorant myself," Laura admitted.

"You will learn," Adrian assured her. "Believe me, you will. Art is in you, I feel, and I can usually sense these things in people."

Laura winced. He sounded like Donald now, always sure he knew what was best for her. She didn't much like being *sensed*, as he called it, either.

Adrian opened the front door, and she inhaled the fresh air. Adrian and his gallery had been fascinating, but they both made her feel claustrophobic.

"Can you point me toward Withrington?" she asked. "It's the next town on today's walk, the one before Stourton. It should be along this road."

"Withrington is only about thirty minutes from here on foot," Adrian replied. "I can give you a lift into town if you like," he added hopefully. "I would enjoy the opportunity to become better acquainted."

"You are very kind to offer but I'm eager to walk now that the storm has passed," Laura answered. "Thank you, though."

Adrian looked disappointed but didn't insist, to Laura's relief. Instead, he escorted her down the lane and pointed to a walking path. "That path will take you to Withrington. It's a much nicer way to get there than the road."

Laura thanked him, glad to get away. The path led her up a long hill, and she stopped at the top to admire the view. Stretching beyond her were miles of countryside with small villages of golden Cotswold stone tucked into valleys or perched on hillsides. A field of rapeseed gleamed brilliant yellow below her; other fields lay idle but for cows and sheep and horses munching contentedly. It was like an enchanted world, one that was totally unexpected in such a populous country as England.

A narrow lane with stone walls on both sides led her into Withrington, one of the many market towns that were built at a time when wool merchants made great fortunes and invested them in churches and other town buildings. Laura strolled slowly along, enjoying the antiquity that surrounded her. Some of the houses lining the cobbled street were so old they leaned against each other at odd angles. Glorious riots of flowers spilled from their front gardens and from the enormous pots hanging above them.

It was all so different from her neighborhood, Laura mused, where no one seemed to have time to grow flowers, and even when they did, their gardens didn't flourish as they did here. Houses weren't spread across the countryside as in American suburbs either, but were clustered in villages where people could walk to the butcher, the baker, the vegetable stand and the news agent.

Wishing nostalgically that she could too, Laura strolled on to the marketplace, the oldest structure in the village. It had a thickly thatched roof but no sides. Looking down, she saw that the stones under her feet were pitted and hollowed by the hard boots of generations of farmers and villagers. It seemed to her that she could feel the pulsation of all those lives coursing up to meet her. Not all of them were happy lives, either, she reflected, spotting the old wooden stocks where miscreants had their heads and arms thrust through holes and clamped there. The villagers came to gape or throw rotten produce at their helpless victims.

Fanning out in all directions from the town center were the sheep alleys. Long ago wool merchants had driven their sheep from the surrounding fields through these alleys into the marketplace. Laura ducked into one of them and was immediately enclosed in a tunnel where sunlight never penetrated. The walls on each side rose far above her head, and the alley was so narrow that when a woman came the other way Laura had to squeeze flat against the cold stones to let her pass. Narrowness was the point, she supposed. The sheep had no choice but to head for the other end and whatever fate awaited them.

Time for a coffee break, she decided, and eyed the shops clustered around the square in search of a bakery. Some windows featured fine antiques or gifts; others offered tourist trinkets or more prosaic fare, like the great hunks of meat hanging on hooks in the butcher's window and the rows of beautiful fresh vegetables on the greengrocer stand. There was also an ironmonger's, which turned out to be a hardware store. Remembering her need of the night before, Laura bought a flashlight.

The window next door was filled with mouth-watering pastries and cakes, and the interior looked dim and cozy. Perfect, Laura decided. She regarded her mud-covered boots with disfavor. They weren't fit to go in anywhere, so she took them off and left them just outside the door.

A bell tinkled faintly as she opened the door, and a beaming face appeared from behind a curtain. "Take any table you like," the woman said. "I've just opened, and you're my first customer."

"Thank you," Laura sank down gratefully into a creaky chair. "I've been walking and it's good to sit."

"What can I bring you?" The woman smiled again. "I've just made some scones, if that tempts, and there's clotted cream and jam."

Laura could smell them and was definitely tempted. "I would love some!"

"I'll get them right away. Coffee or tea?"

"Coffee, I think," Laura answered. The woman, whose name was Maude according to the pin on her apron, bustled away and soon returned with a pot of coffee and two of the biggest scones Laura had even seen.

'These look delicious," Laura told her, lathering them with clotted cream and jam, and pouring a steaming cup of coffee.

"On your own, then, are you?" Maude asked comfortably. "Must be peaceful, I should think."

Laura laughed. Yesterday had hardly been that. "Most of the trip has been," she answered, "but I got lost yesterday and that wasn't peaceful at all."

Maude looked alarmed. "Dreadful, I'm sure," she clucked. "But where were you going, to get lost like that?"

"To Torrington Manor. It's a bed and breakfast place."

"No wonder then," Maude said, shaking her head with a knowing look. "It's a hard place to find, down those twisty roads and then that long drive.

"I've heard it's very grand at the manor," she went on. "My girl Daisy used to clean there, but that was when the old Baron was alive."

"The old Baron?"

"Died a few years ago. They had to find the next Baron then, and it took them a while, I can tell you! No sons. All killed in the war, only distant relations left." Maude shook her head again. "Isn't the same, is it, when they haven't lived here all their lives? Mind you, though, the new Baron isn't bad. He's restored the manor and the old church, though if you ask me, it was the Baroness who got him to do it. Still, he loves his horses and that's good."

She stopped. "Here I am, talking away, and you wanting to get on with your scones and all. My Anthony says I talk too much and he's right."

"Oh, but I'm very interested," Laura answered quickly. "The manor seems like such a fascinating place."

"That it is," Maude agreed obligingly. "The family has lived there for hundreds of years, and there's been some interesting stories. Fellow who came here once wrote a book about all the nobility that visited, the rebellions they got involved in and all that. They even built a secret passage back then, the book says."

Laura was intrigued. If she ever got back to the manor, she would look for it.

For the moment, however, she was eager to get back to the present family. "How long has this Lord Torrington lived there?"

"Not quite sure," Maude answered, thinking hard. Her brow cleared. "It was when my Daisy's first was born, that's right," she declared. "Almost six years ago now, it was. Time for another, I'd say, but she won't hear of it. It's different these days, isn't it? Sad, if you ask me. Clothes and such is all they care about."

"Yes," Laura agreed, searching for another way to get back to the manor. "Lord Torrington's wife certainly has beautiful clothes," she remarked casually.

Maude sniffed. "If she is his wife. Common tart if you ask me. Beautiful clothes, but that's about it. Ought to keep them on, that's what I think! You should hear all the rumors. There's that groom, at least that's what they call him, for one thing. Too big for his boots and doesn't know a fig about horses. Comes to town and gives orders like he's a lord himself, and never passes the time of day at the King's Arms. That's the pub down the lane, you know. No pints for him at the bar; drinks wine instead and goes right off to sit by himself in the corner. Never had a groom like that before. But that Antonia likes him, never mind poor Lord Torrington. My Daisy went up to the manor to see if she could do the cleaning again and there they were, big as life, kissing each other and who knows what else – the groom and Antonia, I mean."

Laura's eyebrows went up. Thomas wasn't the only one, then. Did Antonia make a habit of seducing men?

"He's not the only one, either," Maude went on, echoing her thought. "There's another I could name around here who's been taken in by her. Terrible shame, that was, but it's over now I guess."

"Who was that?" Laura asked, intrigued. Surely he couldn't be Thomas. As far as she knew he hadn't been here long enough. Or had he?

Maude hesitated, obviously struggling between discretion and her desire to tell all. For once, discretion won the battle. "That I can't say," she replied primly. "No point raking over old gossip, is there? I mean, it's all over and done with now, poor man." She pressed her lips tightly together, as if to reinforce her decision, and Laura dared not ask more questions. Maude must like the man to keep his secret like this.

"Oh dear, I've been talking out of turn," Maude exclaimed, flicking a cleaning rag over the next table. "What you must think!"

"I'm very interested," Laura told her with a smile. "I wondered about Antonia myself. Do you suppose Lord Torrington knows what's going on?"

"Not a clue, I'd say," Maude replied. "But I'd be willing to wager the Baroness does. She's a sharp one. Baroness in her own right, though I'm not sure quite how that works out, I mean the lineage and all. Never could get it straight. She came when he did, you see, being related."

"How did she get to be a Baroness in her own right?" Laura asked curiously. "Did she marry someone called Baron Smythington?"

Maude frowned, thinking. "Can't rightly say I know," she answered, sounding surprised. "I guess she must have, but I don't know who he was. Never did hear. Odd, now that I think about it. Still, a Baroness is a Baroness and that's what counts."

"If she was a Baroness before she came here, she obviously can't be the wife of the old Baron, then," Laura mused, trying to work out what this fact did to the grande dame's relationship with Lord Torrington and Nigel.

"No indeed, that Baroness died a long time ago," Maude assured her. "This Baroness came with Lord Torrington, and a good thing, too. She's the one who keeps the place going, in my opinion. Doesn't come to town much any more, though – losing her eyesight, they say. Still, people admire her."

"Losing her eyesight?" Laura was astounded. The grande dame had looked as if she were seeing right through each of them.

"You'd never know it, would you? She looks at you so sharp. But they say it's true. Poor lady. Sad." Maude shook her head pityingly.

"Yes, it is sad," Laura agreed. "She seemed to me to be such an impressive person. Even Lord Torrington seemed rather in awe of her."

"That he is," Maude laughed. "She runs the show up there. Of course, she's the one with the money. That always tells."

"The money?" Perhaps that was why the face in the painting had seemed familiar, Laura thought. People with money were always in the newspapers at one time or another, and so were Baronesses, especially young ones.

"Yes, so they say. Lord Torrington was living someplace outlandish like France when they finally found him. Hadn't a penny as far as anyone could see. But she had, mark my word. Must have had, with all that restoration work she's done. Costs a pretty penny to keep up a place like the manor, with taxes and all. That's why they opened it up to the public, I suppose, like all the rest of the big places. Some of them even have zoos."

Maude sighed lustily and began to clear Laura's table. "The old Baron would turn over in his grave if he knew that Torrington Manor took in paying guests, but there it is."

"So Lord Torrington and the Baroness haven't been here that long," Laura mused. "It seems odd. I had the feeling they had been there forever."

"That's the feel of the place I expect," Maude answered, "and they've settled right in. The Baroness used to open the annual fair and all that, but then Antonia came and now she does it. People don't like that at all."

"You mean Antonia came still later?" Laura was surprised.

"Oh yes, she did," Maude said, shaking her head mournfully. "Almost two years ago now, I expect. She's the new young wife, or so it's said." She sniffed disapprovingly again. "Not long after that the groom, if he is one, turned up. Or maybe it was the other way round. I'm not quite sure, really, but the pair of them came right on each other's heels. Fishy, I call it. Brought the child with her too, Antonia did. Angelica, she's called, or some such name that has an angel in it, and if that isn't the limit I don't know what is. She's got a terrible temper if she doesn't get her way. The old lady's the only one who can handle her.

"Mind you," she added with a knowing look at Laura, "there's some as say the Baroness is too stiff, but I'm not one of them. Dignity, I call it, and I like a spot of dignity. Know where you are then, don't you. Some of those royals are too chatty for me. My Daisy used to act like that poor Lady Diana was her best friend. All the girls did. But then, she encouraged it, poor girl."

"What do people think of Nigel?" Laura asked, once again steering the conversation back to the matter at hand.

"He's a good boy," Maude declared firmly, "talented, too. He came in here one day and the bell was broken and he fixed it right up. And those faces he makes! Hard to believe they're not real. Does those tours, too, and they're a real attraction. He's going to do mystery ones next summer, I hear. People like that. Brings tourists into town. Mind you, there's some who criticize him because he hangs out with those hippies that live up in the woods, but I don't pay any attention to that. Not bad kids, just mixed up. There's new ones now, though, I've heard, and people aren't so keen on this next lot. Bit of a bully, one of the kids, so they say."

'How about the gardener?" Laura asked. "He seems a hostile fellow too, or at least he didn't seem to like me."

'You're right about that," Maude agreed fervently. "They hired him to be the butler first. He scared the guests off, so they got another butler and used him as a gardener. I can't think why they didn't just get rid of him instead."

A customer entered and she hustled away. "Good talking to you," she called back as she disappeared behind the curtain.

"Thank you so much!" Laura called after her. "I'll be off now." Leaving a generous tip on the table, she retrieved her boots and found the trail again. The second half of today's walk was easy, the notes said, and she was glad. She felt too full of scones and undigested information to walk fast. Maude had been a veritable goldmine!

Questions poured into her mind. Why had a man as surly as the gardener been hired as a butler and then kept on instead of fired? Had he found out about Antonia's affair with the groom and the other unknown man, and had threatened to blackmail her if she didn't let him stay on? Or did he know something incriminating about the missing cook? Was the body hers? And where was it?

A horn brought Laura back to the present. Without noticing, she had turned onto a narrow road that accommodated only one small car going one direction at best. Both she and a six-wheeled lorry, English for truck, were trying to proceed along it. Worse, a car traveling the other way was fast approaching. Laura stepped into the underbrush. Both drivers waved politely before they sped on at a pace that made her shudder.

Another car approached, going even faster. It was sleek and low, a sports car, a brand new and very expensive one, she suspected. Royalty and rock stars were reputed to live in this area, and she watched with interest as it sped by.

Her eyes widened in astonishment. The man driving it was the surly gardener! How could a gardener afford a car like that? The answer came quickly. The license plate spelled out *Lady T*. It must be Antonia's car. Why was a gardener driving his employer's high-priced car? More blackmail? And if Antonia could afford a car like that, why was Torrington Manor taking in paying guests?

Laura's curiosity deepened. She would never be able to concentrate properly on her walking trip, she realized, until she had gone back to Torrington Manor to look for answers to her questions. But how was she to do that without bumping into Thomas? That she refused to do, at least just yet.

Inspiration struck. She would go on one of the tours they advertised. Viewing Torrington Manor as a tourist would provide excellent cover for snooping around. She wasn't likely to run into Thomas, either. Tours never took people through the occupied parts of the house.

Pulling out the brochure she had picked up, Laura saw that there was one today, another in two days. She would go to that one, she decided. By then Thomas would probably have left. After that, she would get on with her walk and enjoy it as she should.

Re-invigorated, Laura set off briskly for Stourton.

CHAPTER SEVEN

Laura followed the path into a grove of trees. Bluebells made a veritable carpet of azure on the floor of the woods, and their light scent filled her nostrils. All tension spilled out of her as she breathed it in. This was what walking was all about: peace, beauty, the glorious sensation of easy movement, not fast but steady and somehow reassuring.

She passed into a field filled with frolicking lambs and their watchful mothers. Laura threaded her way through them, delighting in their antics. The cows in the next field were less welcoming. They eyed her warily, worried about the tiny calves nestling at their feet. Cows were large and intimidating anyway, but when they had young, they were apt to harass unwary walkers.

Laura turned away from them and skirted cautiously along the edges of the fence. To her relief, they didn't bother her. Emerging in the woods again, she sat down to rest for a moment by a small stream. Propping her back against a tree, she closed her eyes to take in the scents and sounds, and breathe…

A sharp tapping roused Laura, and she looked at her watch. She must have fallen asleep. It sounded as if someone was hammering on rocks, maybe repairing one of the beautiful old walls of Cotswold stone. She decided to watch for a few minutes. They were such marvelous walls, and it was good to know they were cared for.

To her astonishment, instead of workmen and walls, she saw Nigel. Sitting beside him was the green-eyed beauty, far lovelier in person than as a mask. Sunlight glinted off her dark hair, revealing reddish streaks; her skin was translucent, her eyes large and very, very green. She was also more girl than woman, Laura realized. But what were they doing here?

Nigel was crouched over a large piece of gray stone, making precise cuts with well-aimed blows. He was so intent on his task that he didn't notice Laura even when she came up behind him. The girl looked up, startled by Laura's approach, and gave Nigel a gentle poke. "Company," she mumbled, and wandered away.

She behaved like a skittish colt, Laura thought, and decided not to speak to her but to wait for Cat to decide it was all right to return.

Nigel blinked, freeing himself from his absorption. "Oh, hello, Laura," he said, his voice friendly. "Like my grasshopper?"

Laura knelt beside him, awed. It really was a grasshopper, carved in stone. A huge one, but so beautifully made that it looked ready to hop away.

"So you're a sculptor in stone, too," she said admiringly. "I think you are truly the most talented young person I have ever had the pleasure to meet. How did you learn to do things like this?"

Nigel looked embarrassed, but she knew he was also pleased. "Dunno exactly," he answered. "Just comes out, I guess."

Laura smiled at him. "Then we'll all just hope that it keeps coming out," she told him. "You are very good."

"My father doesn't like the idea," he said with a grimace. "He wants to send me to some boarding school. Can't make a living on art, he says."

"How about your mother? Or the Baroness?"

Nigel looked embarrassed. "My mother's dead, has been for a long time," he explained, and hurried on before Laura could frame the conventional murmurs of sympathy. "Antonia, she's my stepmother I guess, isn't too bad about the art stuff, but that's because she doesn't care what I do as long as I keep out of the way." He grinned, taking the sting out of the words. "Gram's the best, though. She's an artist too, and she thinks I'm better off here. Even my father doesn't argue much with her."

Angelina had also called the grande dame "Gram," Laura remembered. Did that mean the Baroness was grandmother to both of them? Or could the term just be a nickname for an older relative?

"I can understand that," she agreed with a laugh. "There is something about the Baroness that precludes resistance."

"You talk like a teacher," a voice behind her said conversationally.

Laura laughed again. "Maybe that's because I am," she answered. "And you sound like an American."

Cat took another step forward but didn't answer. She was very young, Laura saw anxiously, much too young to be the missing wife - unless Thomas was a cradle snatcher as well as a womanizer.

Laura turned back to Nigel lest she spook the girl with too much attention. "Have you done other sculptures in stone?" she asked, settling herself comfortably on a convenient log.

Cat answered for him, which was a good sign. "He's done lots," she announced. "There's a toad - he's my favorite - and a bullfrog, and a lizard of some sort. The grasshopper's the biggest though."

"I've got a whole group planned," Nigel elaborated. His supercilious pose had completely disappeared and his eyes were alight with enthusiasm. "Next I'll do a mouse, because I've found a rock that has a mouse in it. I mean, it's the right sort of rock for a mouse. Then I'll do a cat, staring at it, and I'm not sure what else yet."

"I want my dad to see them," Cat told her spontaneously. "He's very dull because all he cares about is old art, the stuff in museums, but he'd still be a good person for Nigel because he'd know what to do with art, or maybe help him get training.

"But I don't want to be here when he comes!" she added with a dramatic shudder. "He might try to take me home again!"

"Does your father live in England?" Laura asked casually.

Cat rolled her eyes heavenward. "Good grief, no! He lives in New York now, at least I think he still does. I don't see him much anymore.

"I don't want him here, either," she added darkly, "but I wouldn't put it past him to come looking for me. He's always worrying."

A startling idea occurred to Laura. Not a lost wife, a lost daughter, though why Thomas would lie about it she couldn't imagine. She would have to tread carefully if she was right.

"I met a man who was looking for a missing wife yesterday," she contributed in an easy voice, "though he didn't say anything about a daughter. Nigel's father thought he was the thief who's been taking the silver, and that I was his wife, and that we were in cahoots. We managed to convince him that we weren't thieves, but

I'm afraid he still thinks I'm the missing wife." She glanced at Nigel, hoping he would pick up the cue.

Cat looked skittish again, but also curious. "What did he think that for, about the silver, I mean?"

"Oh, that's just my father," Nigel reassured her. "He suspects everyone of everything, but I don't think he cares that much about the missing silver." He gave her a sidelong glance. "As long as nobody takes his horses, he's okay."

"Well, he doesn't exercise them enough," Cat retorted hotly. "He ought to ride them more, or have that groom ride them."

"Stewart's too busy making out with Antonia," Nigel replied without rancor. Laura was startled by his casual acceptance of Antonia's affair, but she tried not to show it. She wondered if Thomas knew.

"Does your father know that?" Cat asked. "Would he care if he did?"

Nigel looked embarrassed again. "I'm not sure. I don't think he knows exactly, I mean. Just as well."

"You've got that right," Cat agreed. "My dad found out that my Mom was having it off with some guy and he went ballistic. Refused to give her money, and got out the lawyers. But she only did it because he was always away on one of his boring cases."

Not all boring, Laura thought caustically, if a woman like Antonia was waiting – if, that is, her guess about Thomas was right. *Cases* sounded interesting too. What kind of cases did Thomas have?

"Mom says he's a bastard," Catherine added, shrugging her thin shoulders as if she didn't care.

"Don't be so hard on him," Nigel objected. "Your dad's okay and he isn't boring. He liked my masks, too, said they were brilliant."

Cat stared at him. "You mean he *is* here?" she squeaked.

"That's what I came to tell you," Nigel answered. "I just hadn't got around to it yet. And I think you should talk to him. I mean, how do you know your mom's telling the truth about him? You ought to find out, at least. He and Laura were both at the manor," he added nonchalantly. "He's the man she talked about, the one my father thought was the thief, but of course Laura didn't know he was your father then."

Laura smiled her thanks. Nigel was very quick. It was a relief, too, to know that Thomas wasn't a cradle snatcher as well as a ladies' man.

"Damn," Cat exploded. "I wish he'd get lost. Does he know I'm here?" She put her hands on her hips in a threatening gesture. "If you told him, Nigel, if you told him…"

"Relax, Cat. I didn't have to tell him. He saw you on the horse."

"Oh God," she moaned. "Wouldn't you know. And my name is not Cat. It is Catherine. I am not a cat! Got that?"

Fiery! Laura thought. *No wonder he's having trouble with her.* About time he came to find her, she thought critically – if that was really why he had come. Catherine needed finding. She looked less like a cat than a stray kitten, with her skinny frame and tangled hair.

"Okay," Nigel said, abashed. "I'll try to remember." He looked at his watch and sighed. "I've got to go.

There's a tour today, so I can't be late. I take them round and explain stuff."

"Your tours sound very enterprising," Laura told him. "I'd like to come on the next one if that's all right. Torrington Manor is fascinating."

Nigel looked pleased. "That would be great. I think you'd like it. Most people seem to. I don't show them the whole place, of course, but there are plenty of rooms to spare. It will be even better when I get the figures into them. Like Madame Tussaud's, you know. Tourists really like that.

"I'm not so sure about the mystery part of it after last night, though," he added apologetically. "Sorry about that. Didn't mean to have you find Lottie. Must have been quite a shock for you. She was really out!"

"It must have been an even worse shock for you," Laura replied.

"It was," Nigel agreed fervently. "Well, I've got to go. See you later, Cat - I mean, Catherine," he amended hastily.

"Good to see you again, Laura," he added politely. "Thanks for what you said about my work." He smiled at her, an unexpected smile that lit up his narrow face, making it almost handsome. He gave a small salute, grabbed the bicycle leaning against a nearby tree and pedaled off.

"He's great," Catherine said, and Laura nodded. To be an entrepreneur as well as an artist – and an actor – was quite remarkable.

"I hope he gets the chances he ought to have," she said earnestly, and wondered if Catherine would find this sentimental.

Apparently she didn't. "Yeah," she sighed, perching near Laura. "I hope he does."

"Not easy," Laura agreed. "Parents are well meaning usually, but they can get in the way. I did, I'm sure."

"You have kids?"

"Two. One just started college and the other just got married," Laura answered. "So they're independent now, or mostly independent."

"I wish my dad felt that way about me," Catherine said forlornly. "My Mom says he thinks I'm too young to be here, just hanging out with a bunch of guys, living in the woods and all that. Wants me to go back to school, but school's boo-ring." She drew out the sound as if savoring the word.

"Mom doesn't mind though," Catherine added more brightly. "She's cool. She doesn't care what I do. Gives her more time to hang out with her new boyfriend."

Laura wished she could give the absent mother a swift kick. Her vote was with Thomas on the school issue. This girl looked barely sixteen. To leave her entirely on her own was simply irresponsible – or uncaring.

"What about your father? Does he have a girlfriend?" she asked, striving for a neutral tone.

Catherine snorted with laughter. "My dad? You've got to be joking. He is the most straitlaced man in the whole world. If he has someone in his life he's going to be married to her. That's why he went ballistic when mom started having an affair. She said he'd have another fit if he knew I was coming here with a bunch of guys."

84

Interesting, Laura mused, though not necessarily accurate. Children seldom knew or wanted to know about their parents' love lives, or thought they were too old to have one. At least Thomas hadn't flaunted his to his daughter - if it existed - as the mother had. She gave him credit for that.

Catherine looked cautiously at Laura. "Not that I… I mean, I'm not what he thinks," she said, and the fierce tone was back. "He just has a nasty mind."

"Fathers do tend to think the worst," Laura answered, remembering Donald "going ballistic" as Catherine put it, when Melinda had started going out with boys. If she'd known then that Donald was having an affair at the time she would have gone ballistic herself. What a hypocrite!

"What does your father do? I mean, for a living," she asked.

Catherine shrugged dismissively. "Oh, he's an art detective, kind of."

Laura was astounded. "An art detective?"

"Old, boring stuff, like I said," Catherine answered. "I think he works for art museums, finding paintings and other stuff that got stolen. That's why he's never home. He's always in Rome or Naples or whatever," she finished vaguely.

"Masterpieces," Laura murmured, trying to take in this unexpected information. "He tries to find missing masterpieces."

The revelation put an entirely different aspect on everything that had happened at Torrington Manor, and her brain worked feverishly to fit it back together again. First, Thomas as art sleuth was less likely to commit a murder, and if he was on a job, there was good reason for his room to be searched. She remembered how he had examined the paintings in the study, asking if they had been cleaned. Had something unusual about them caught his expert eye? On the other hand, he could be at Torrington Manor for the simple reason that he was looking for Catherine and heard she was in the area.

Catherine's voice brought her back to the present. "I guess you could call it that, finding masterpieces I mean," she mumbled. Her expression changed and she looked mutinously at Laura. "And now I guess you're going to tell me to talk to him, too," she said, trying to sneer and failing. "All my teachers do."

"I'm not sure," Laura answered honestly. "I need to know more about him before I can recommend anything. I only met him yesterday, you know.

"I'd need to know if he's a person you can trust," she added, voicing one of her concerns about him. "Parents certainly aren't perfect, but it helps if you can depend on them doing what they say."

"Oh, he does what he says, all right," Catherine responded fervently, sweeping her hands into the air in an exaggerated gesture of horror. "Once, he said if I ever stayed out that late again without calling, he would ground me for three weeks. He did, too. It was brutal!" She made a face, but there was a note of pride in her voice. Laura wondered if it was for her resolute father or her own ability to tolerate so much suffering. Probably both, she decided. Experience had taught her that teenagers often did want a firm hand even if they got furious when it was applied.

"I'm sure it was," she answered mildly, "but he may have had a point. I mean, why were you supposed to call?"

"So he wouldn't worry about me," Catherine replied promptly. "Yeah," she added, her tone grudging, "I guess you're right."

Laura was encouraged. "So I expect he's worried about you now," she said in the same mild tone.

Catherine sighed. "Yeah. He's a terrible worrier." Again, Laura heard that note of pride. So it was for her resolute father. That was a good sign.

Laura decided the small victory was enough and changed the subject again. "How long have you known Nigel?" she asked.

Catherine smiled, and Laura realized it was the first smile she had seen. "Not long," the girl answered. "I really like him, though. It's as if I'd known him forever when we talk. Not like the other guys."

"You don't like them?"

Catherine shrugged. "The girl and most of the guys I came with have left," she said, "and I don't like the others as much. I'll probably be getting out of here soon."

Laura almost held her breath. "Well, let me know if you need any help doing it," she said casually. "I'd be glad to help if I can."

"Thanks," Catherine mumbled. "Got to go now," she added hurriedly. Jumping up, she ran like a colt into the trees. Laura stared after her in dismay. Had her causal offer of help spooked the girl that badly?

The truth was more prosaic. Catherine's ears had heard the approaching footsteps that Laura only now discerned. Three young men sauntered toward her. They were not a prepossessing group. Laura had plenty of scruffy-looking kids in her classes and she gave them the benefit of the doubt until the largest youth spoke.

"What have we here?" he said in a taunting falsetto. "One of those lady walkers? Kind of cute even if she is pretty old, don't you think, guys?" The two others nodded nervously and didn't look at her.

Laura paid no attention to him. She rose without haste and walked toward the trees where Catherine had disappeared. There was no way she was going to leave the girl to deal with this trio alone.

The bully, however, hadn't finished with her yet. He didn't touch her, but he placed himself directly in her path, blocking her. He appealed to his friends. "What shall we do with her, guys," he sneered. "Shall we let her go?"

"Jeez, Buddy, leave her alone," one of them said. "We've had enough trouble."

Laura's ears pricked up. Trouble? What kind of trouble? Probably with the local police. She would use that to threaten them if she had to.

"I'm leaving," she said shortly, and walked around him. The youth called Buddy followed, mimicking her walk and staying right on her heels.

"Cute ass, don't you think guys? A little baggy though." Buddy snickered unpleasantly at his own wit.

Laura turned to face him. "I am leaving now," she told him. "I am also warning you and your friends that if you persist in this obnoxious behavior I will inform the police that you are harassing walkers and that I have decided to press charges against you."

The two youths looked horrified. "Cut it out, Buddy!" one of them said. "Morris would be furious if he heard."

"Coward," Buddy sneered, but Laura saw the flicker of fear in his eyes at the mention of Morris, whoever he was. "Besides, what am I doing except giving the dame some flak? Old ladies like her enjoy the atten-"

He got no further. A dynamo catapulted from a tree and landed on top of him, all fists and legs and chopping hands. Within seconds, Buddy was bent double, clutching his groin. Catherine stood over him, fists clenched.

"Jeez," one of the others ejaculated. "Where did you learn to do that!"

"Shut up," Catherine ordered. "Any more out of you and you'll get the same. Get out, both of you! Now!"

Both young men turned and disappeared without another word, though Laura wasn't sure how far they went.

"Thanks," she said to Catherine. "I guess it's time I learned to do that."

"No problem," Catherine answered nonchalantly, but her voice shook and her face was pale. She continued to watch Buddy closely.

Recovering a little, Buddy made a move to grab her. One of Catherine's knees came up with a jerk. He screamed and fell to the ground, rolling over and over in agony.

"You'll pay," Laura heard him gasp when he got some breath back. "You'll pay. I'll get you one of these days."

"You want more?" Catherine taunted him, but Buddy's threat had frightened her. Laura grabbed a nearby stick, ready to bring it down on Buddy's head if she had to.

"Well done, Catherine," a deep voice said. "I see I'm not needed after all. You and your friend seem to have the matter well in hand."

A man sauntered toward them, peeling an apple expertly with a long knife as he walked. Laura thought he was probably the best looking man she had ever seen. His hair was pale blond, his eyes a brilliant blue, and his features were perfect, so classic they could have come from a Greek statue. His clothes were classic too. A well-cut tweed jacket emphasized his broad shoulders, and the grey flannels beneath them were perfectly pleated. He was older than the others but not more than thirty, she guessed. She wondered how long he had been watching.

"Hello Morris," Catherine said tonelessly.

Laura regarded him with interest. So this was the Morris Buddy's pals had mentioned. She could see why he scared them. Morris was scary.

Morris's eyes slid from Catherine and rested on her. "Want some?" he offered, holding out a chunk of apple.

"No, thank you," Laura said. Morris turned to Catherine and held the chunk out again. She shook her head.

"Too bad," he said, his tone mocking. "Best apple I've had in a long time. The nice woman at the vegetable stand gave it to me. Said she likes to see young people eating healthy food."

Neither Laura nor Catherine answered. He regarded them thoughtfully; then he looked down at the writhing figure on the ground.

"So Buddy has been causing trouble, has he?" he asked, and deftly flipped a curl of apple skin into Buddy's stomach. "I guess I should have known he

90

would," he said with feigned sadness. "Still, he was useful in his way. It will be a shame to have to get rid of him. But that's the way it goes." He sighed.

Laura wondered what that meant. The tone had been gentle, but there was no doubt about the implied threat. She didn't like Morris, though she couldn't have said exactly why. He was just... just wrong.

"I'm glad I found you, Catherine," Morris continued, his voice silky. "I've come to take you to lunch. I think we had a date?"

Laura looked swiftly at Catherine. Her face was pale again, and she hadn't looked up since Morris had appeared. Who was this man, and what did he mean to her? Surely Catherine wasn't involved with him? More likely, he had an unhealthy interest in her. He would be harder to handle than Buddy, too. He was older and very confident. She felt a rush of pity for the girl. Imagine trying to handle the horrible Morris on top of Buddy and everything else!

Laura made up her mind. "Catherine is having lunch with me. We're old friends, you see," she explained to Morris, astonished at how easily she could lie – and at how strong her impulse was to let this man know that Catherine wasn't alone. "We haven't seen each other for a long time and there's a lot to catch up on, so Catherine will be staying with me for a while."

Morris looked at her with raised eyebrows. Laura was sure he didn't believe her but he didn't let it show. "Best to do as the lady says," he told Catherine after only a second's hesitation. "But I intend to have you keep that date," he added, and now there was no doubt of the threat in his voice. He gave Catherine a long look before he turned and walked slowly away.

A hand shot suddenly out of the trees and grabbed the back of his shirt, almost strangling him with his tie. Morris gagged.

Laura's eyes widened in astonishment. Thomas!

"You will leave my daughter alone. Is that understood?" Thomas's voice was steely. He shook Morris for emphasis and then shoved him hard into the trees. Morris stumbled. Pulling himself up again, he fired a look at Thomas so chilling that Laura gasped. Without a word, he walked away.

Thomas turned to face Catherine. "I've come to take you home," he announced flatly. "Now."

CHAPTER EIGHT

Laura winced. Why did fathers have to be so heavy-handed? That authoritarian tone wasn't going to work. Donald had used it all the time and it invariably made the situation worse.

She glanced at Catherine and saw that she was right. A mix of emotions crossed the girl's volatile face. Astonishment was followed by a flash of relief, and then tears threatened. A stubbornly set jaw and fiery eyes followed.

Thomas's face looked just as conflicted. Laura suspected that part of him wanted to hug his errant daughter, another part needed to vent his pent-up worry. Unfortunately, that part got the best of him again.

"Well?" he questioned, glaring at Catherine.

Catherine responded as Laura had predicted. "I was doing fine on my own until you had to come and mess things up!" she shrieked. "Why can't you just leave me alone?"

Thomas opened his mouth, no doubt to remind her that she'd messed things up quite well all on her own. Laura coughed loudly to get his attention. He turned, as if noticing her for the first time.

"Catherine has demonstrated an excellent ability to take care of herself in extremely difficult circum-stances," she lectured him in her best pedantic tone. "However, I believe she might be amenable to a change of scene if you were amenable to moderating your strategy. The one you have chosen isn't wise at all. In fact, it is guaranteed to fail."

Thomas stared at her, nonplussed, and Catherine giggled. Good. She had at least diverted them. Her professorial manner had that effect on people who were overwrought, she had noticed.

"What do you suggest?" Thomas asked finally. He had a large purple bruise on his cheek and looked ghastly.

"I suggest that Catherine is hungry and ready to drop with exhaustion. Shall we walk into town and feed her before further conversation takes place about her future?"

Catherine seized on this suggestion. "Let's go! That's a great idea."

"Am I permitted to come?" Thomas asked, his insouciance returning.

"That is up to Catherine," Laura replied frostily.

"I guess it'll be okay," Catherine conceded. "As long as you don't tell me what to do!" she added vigorously.

"I shall try to moderate my tone in accordance with the professor's wishes," Thomas agreed, barely managing to avoid sarcasm. "But I *am* your father," he added, unable to resist the last word.

Laura glared at him. "We all know that. Now, for goodness sake, try greeting your his long-lost daughter with pleasure, not orders."

Thomas swallowed hard. "I'm glad to see you again, Catherine," he said, and hugged her stiffly, as if uncertain of his welcome.

"Great to see you, too, Dad," Catherine agreed. And then miraculously, they all began to laugh. Catherine's laughter held a note of hysteria, and Laura wasn't surprised. Too many conflicting emotions were thrashing around in the poor girl's head. Food was the remedy, and a safe place to sleep. She hoped the B&B she had for tonight had two beds.

Laura led them back through the woods and its bluebells to Withrington. She decided to go to one of the pubs instead of the tea shop. Maude would be too curious and she had the feeling that a nice dark pub would enclose itself around them and help both Catherine and Thomas to relax.

"We'll go in here," she said firmly before Thomas could come up with a possibly unwelcome suggestion of his own. "Pubs are wonderful for hot drinks and nourishing hot meals."

The pub was all she had hoped for. Its dimness was welcoming, as were the dark wooden benches covered by ancient cushions and the low, beamed ceilings. Three men at the bar nodded at them politely as they entered, then went back to their pints. Otherwise, the place was almost empty, and Laura was relieved. Despite the season, a gas fire burned in the grate at one end of the room, and she headed for it. Perfect, she thought, as they settled themselves at a table facing the fire.

"What would everyone like?" Thomas rose to go to the bar and give their order. Laura ordered a pot of tea; Catherine decided on hot chocolate.

"I'll go look at the menu and then we can decide what we want to go with it," Laura told Catherine. "It's written out on the boards beside the bar."

"I'll come." Catherine jumped up, showing a resurgence of energy at even the thought of food. "Oh, cottage pie," she said immediately, seeing it on the board. Laura and Thomas chose the soup of the day, leek and potato, which came with a hunk of crusty homemade bread. Thomas stayed to give the order at the bar while she and Catherine went back to their corner.

For a time they were silent, a silence that felt companionable to Laura, and she was glad. When she did speak, she purposely chose a neutral subject so she wouldn't destroy that fragile sense of companionship.

"You were fantastic back there," she told Catherine. "I've been meaning to take self-defense classes but haven't got around to it yet. I worry that I'm too old, too, that I'd do myself more harm than good."

Catherine shook her head. "You can do it at any age," she said with confidence. "It's tae kwon do, and lots of older people do it very well."

"How long have you been taking lessons?" Laura asked, wondering if she really looked that old or if anyone over thirty qualified as "older."

"About three years," Catherine answered. "It's the thing I miss most about not being at home," she added. "You have to work really hard at it."

"I bet you do," Laura said. "That feels good sometimes, though."

"I love it," Catherine said fervently. "I mean, it's not that I like hurting people," she amended, making sure Laura understood. "I don't like hurting anyone, even someone like Buddy, but it makes me feel good to be able to take care of myself.

"You have to, these days," she added darkly.

"I imagine it hasn't been easy for you," Laura agreed, "having to be always on guard. Buddy and his pals are horrible. Morris is even worse."

Catherine's face twisted, and she looked ready to cry. Laura looked down at her teacup while the girl got herself back under control.

"I think Morris scares me even more than Buddy," Catherine said when her voice was steady again. "Buddy's a nuisance, but Morris is creepy."

Laura nodded. "I'm not surprised he scares you. He scares me, too. But how do you know him? I can't imagine Morris living in the woods."

"Oh, he doesn't," Catherine answered. "I'm not sure where he lives but I bet it's a lot fancier than the woods. He's only been coming around for the last week or so. That's when I decided to leave as soon as I could. You've got to have money to leave, though, and I'd run out."

Laura was shocked. "Doesn't your mother send money? Or your father? Surely, if he's worried about you, he must."

Catherine shrugged. "My mom is supposed to, but she doesn't always remember. She's always had plenty of money, and I don't think she knows what things cost every day. I mean, you don't when you've always been paid for, do you? My dad would help, I think, but he's already paying my mom for what I need, so..."

"Well, I know what things cost," Laura interrupted hotly, abandoning the effort to give Catherine's mother the benefit of the doubt, "and I'm going to see to it that you have enough to go home if that's what you want to do. I will not see you stranded here."

Thomas, showing an admirable sense of timing, set down a tray. "Hot chocolate for the champ, tea for the professor," he announced.

"Did Catherine tell you she won second place in the international tae kwon do championships?" he asked Laura as he handed her the tea. "That's why she's the champ."

"That's fantastic, Catherine." Laura smiled at her.

"Thanks." Catherine managed a smile before applying herself diligently to her hot chocolate. Laura heard her foot tapping nervously under the table.

Thomas sat down across from Catherine and looked at her anxiously from time to time, as if struggling to come up with a good way to approach her.

Catherine rose abruptly. "Going to the WC… ladies'," she mumbled. "Back in a minute." Grabbing her pack, she fled.

Laura sighed. Something had to be done to get Catherine out of here, but so far she and her father seemed barely able to talk to each other.

Thomas's bruised face was grim. "We've really made a mess of it, haven't we?" he said. "Her mother and me, I mean."

Laura saw no point in prevaricating. "I think she's too young to be here on her own. And she has to have at least one parent she can trust."

"Damn the woman," Thomas said fiercely. "She couldn't even remember to send Catherine's money." He must have overheard at least some of the conversation, Laura realized. It was probably just as well.

"Why didn't you come before this?" she asked, wanting badly to know.

Thomas's answer surprised her. "I didn't know Catherine was here until a week ago. Her mother never bothered to tell me. Once I knew, I came as soon as I could, but it took me a while to find her. I was getting frantic."

Laura was startled. "Does Catherine know that?"

Thomas shook his head helplessly. "I don't know. My ex-wife probably forgot to mention that she never told me. She's like that."

"Well, tell Catherine now. It's important," Laura said. "She needs to know."

They saw Catherine emerge from the bathroom. "I will," Thomas promised. "But first, I need to ask for your help. I've got to get Catherine in a safe place right away but for reasons I can't explain at the moment, I can't take her with me tonight."

"She can come with me," Laura said immediately. "I'd already planned on it and I would love to have her. It might be better for her to be with someone outside the family right now anyway." She grinned. "She can teach me some tae kwon do."

The bartender appeared holding their laden plates. Catherine's eyes lit up and she almost ran back to the table. The cottage pie was a steaming mix of minced lamb topped by mashed potatoes, and Catherine ate it as if she hadn't seen food for days.

Thomas waited until she had finished most of her meal before he spoke. "I would have come before now if I had known you were here," he began tentatively. "I thought you were still in Virginia. And I did try to call."

Catherine whirled on him. "You didn't know? But she said she'd tell you."

Thomas shook his head. "Your mom didn't tell me until last week and then I came right away. Did she say she had told me before that?"

"She just said you were off on some trip and you probably wouldn't like the idea anyway, so for me to go ahead and she would tell you later where I was. And anyway, I guess I thought I didn't want you to come, but..."

Catherine gulped. "Oh, well, it's good you came now," she managed to say. "I mean, I guess this isn't really working out any more."

"I would agree with that," Thomas said grimly. "I can't tell you exactly what the right solution is at this moment, Catherine, but between us we ought to be able to find one that will suit you."

A weight seemed to lift from Catherine's thin shoulders. "I guess we could," she agreed. "But what about now?" she added in a small voice. "I mean tonight..."

"I meant what I said to Morris," Laura assured her quickly. "I've got a B&B nearby. You can come there with me tonight, maybe the next night if that's best."

Catherine frowned. "Is that really all right with you? I mean, you're on a walking trip and all that, and now I come along..."

Laura reached over and took Catherine's hand. "I will enjoy having you with me," she said sincerely. "I really will. It will be like having Melinda back, my daughter. We used to travel together all the time. Once we went to Greece and drove all over in a bright red car we'd rented. You'd have loved it."

Catherine brightened. "That sounds cool. I wish my Mom liked things like that."

"Well, your dad does," Thomas interjected, "and he will." He sighed, rubbed his forehead and looked at his watch. "Unfortunately, I have to leave now. I will call later, though, if Laura will provide the number at your B&B."

Catherine seemed suddenly to notice his bruise. "What happened to you?"

"I seem to have walked into a door," Thomas said smoothly.

Catherine raised a skeptical eyebrow. "Which means you don't want me to know," she said resignedly. "I just hope you didn't lose your temper with someone." She grinned. "Truce, okay?"

The words seemed to be a private code because Thomas grinned back. "Truce," he agreed. "And now I'm off but I promise I will call later. Maybe we can all have dinner together later. I'll pick you up at the B&B."

Laura rummaged in her pack for the number and the address, scribbled it on the bar bill and handed it to him. "It's the Fairfax House in Stourton."

"If you haven't heard from me by seven o'clock, call me at Torrington Manor. Phone's fixed now," Thomas said as he headed for the bar to pay the bill.

"All right," Laura agreed, wondering why he was going back to Torrington Manor and didn't want Catherine with him. Was it because he was involved with Antonia? Or something to do with his art work?

Another unwelcome thought intruded. As an art detective, it would be easy for Thomas to play both sides of the game – looking for stolen masterpieces and at the same time scouting for good fakes to sell to unsuspecting buyers. The art world was full of that, she had read. Maybe he and Antonia were working together.

She turned back to Catherine, who was eyeing the desert card. "What would you like?" Laura asked, taking the cue.

"Maybe some vanilla ice cream if they have it? It's the best I've ever tasted over here. Oh, I forgot you're paying," Catherine added, chagrined. "I guess I won't." Laura ignored this and ordered the ice cream.

"How *did* you manage living up there?" she asked Catherine curiously when the desert arrived. "I mean, manage to eat without any money and sleep with Buddy around, and then Morris turning up?"

Catherine patted her flat stomach dramatically. I haven't been eating much recently, that's for sure," she answered, "As for sleeping…" She broke off, looking embarrassed, and Laura didn't press her. It was none of her business really.

"It's not what you think," Catherine protested. "It's just that I'm not supposed to be at Torrington Manor and Nigel didn't want me to get in trouble, so he said just to use the stable. I don't go in the house," she added hastily, "just the stable."

"But if they found out, wouldn't Buddy or Morris go there too?"

"No way," Catherine's grin was triumphant. "They're too scared."

"Scared of Nigel's father? Or the groom?"

"Nope, of the dogs. They're big, I mean really big, and they patrol the place at night," Catherine explained with a grin, and went back to her ice cream.

Catherine was delighted with the quaint B&B when they arrived. She ate ravenously of the small cakes provided for them and laughed happily when Laura explained that if she pulled on the string hanging by the bathroom door, the shower would produce marvelously hot water in which she could luxuriate for as long as she liked. Then she sank down with an ecstatic sigh onto one of the twin beds.

"I haven't been on one of these for ages," she exclaimed, and when Laura looked over at her again, she was fast asleep.

Laura took a turn in the shower; then she settled on her bed and tried to decide what to do next. Nothing seemed to make sense to her now – not the body or the missing cook, not Nigel and his masks, not Antonia and her car or Thomas and the big bruise he had acquired. It was all just too complicated. Sighing, she let her eyes close.

She woke suddenly, aware that it was getting dark and that she had forgotten something. The phone; that was it. Thomas had said to call if they hadn't heard from him by seven, and it was already seven-thirty.

Laura dialed the number for Torrington Manor. A voice she didn't recognize told her that Mr. Smith had left, that they had no idea where he had gone and didn't have a forwarding number for him. She asked for Lord Torrington or the Baroness next and was told that Lord Torrington had gone away for a few days, taking Nigel with him, and the Baroness was out at the moment.

Laura's attention was diverted by Catherine. She was sitting bolt upright in bed, lips trembling. Tears were welling up in her eyes.

"Thank you for trying," Laura said quickly, and hung up the phone. "What is it, Catherine?" she asked in concern. "What's the matter?"

"He didn't come here to look for me, like he said," Catherine replied angrily, struggling to suppress the tears. "I thought he had but he didn't."

"What makes you think that?"

"Because he only uses the name Smith when he's on a job," Catherine hissed. "His real last name is

Langley. So he came on an art job, not for me. I should have known when I saw that bruise, but I didn't want it to be true."

I have three names, Laura remembered Thomas telling her. *Thomas, Langley and Smith.* He hadn't exactly been lying, she supposed.

"Maybe he is on a job, but he was looking for you, too," she assured Catherine quickly. "I know that's true because he told me, while you were in the bathroom. He was frantic to find you after he heard where you were."

The words seemed to comfort Catherine, and her anger turned to fear. "He hasn't called," she said anxiously. "It's way past seven and he hasn't called."

"Does he usually call when he says he will?"

"Always, unless he's in some kind of trouble, like his car broke down or some case gets really weird. That happens sometimes."

Laura sat back against the headboard and tried to think clearly. It was certainly possible that Thomas was in trouble. His room probably had been searched, and whoever had given him that bruise might have tried to silence him more permanently.

There was only one way to know for sure, she realized, and that was to go back to Torrington Manor and find out.

She turned to Catherine, who was watching her carefully. "I have to go out for a while," Laura said, trying to keep her voice neutral. "Why don't you just relax and go back to sleep, call for some food if you want -"

She got no further. "No way," Catherine said defiantly.

Laura stared at her, startled. Catherine's tears had dried up, and her face wore a look of steely determination. "There is no way I will stay here," Catherine repeated emphatically. "I can tell you're worried about my father and are going to look for him. I'm coming with you. If you don't let me, I'll look for him by myself."

Laura considered. Catherine clearly wasn't going to stay here, and she was more likely to get into trouble looking for Thomas on her own. If she came along, she could at least be watched – and hopefully be protected from finding out that her father could be a crook himself or be having an affair with Antonia.

"All right," she agreed. "You can come. In fact, I'll be glad to have you."

Catherine grinned triumphantly. "Lead on," she said, grabbing her jacket and swinging it twice around her head. "Lead on and I shall follow!"

Laura grinned back. "What do you say to a spot of housebreaking?" she asked, grabbing her own jacket and slinging her pack on her back. "Or manor breaking, I guess I should say."

CHAPTER NINE

Laura consulted her map. It was torn and smudged from so much intense use but she managed to pick out a pub that wasn't too far from Torrington Manor. A cab could take them that far, they could get some food and then walk the rest of the way.

The pub was satisfyingly dim and smoke-blackened. They ordered a platter of bread and cheese and more tea and hot chocolate. They ate quickly; then, feeling like a pair of conspirators, they set off on foot along a narrow country road that Laura knew would soon intersect with the lane leading to the manor. The sky was completely dark now, and no lights showed anywhere around them. They almost missed their turning but at the right moment a car came by. Its headlights showed a one-lane track rising steeply on the left. Trees and vine-encrusted bushes on both sides made it even harder to see, and they kept stumbling over unexpected obstacles as they climbed. Laura switched on her flashlight and saw with relief that they were almost up. She switched it off again quickly, lest someone see. She was just in time.

"A car," Catherine whispered as they reached the top of the hill, and Laura heard the sound of an engine laboring up behind them. Headlights appeared around a curve, and they ducked behind the bushes. The vehicle crested the hill and sped down the other side, going much too fast for the twisting, narrow lane. It hit the deep hollow at the bottom of the hill with a wrenching bounce and a heavy splash. It slowed briefly, but picked

106

up speed again and disappeared around a sharp bend in the road.

Not a car but a delivery van. Laura was surprised. Why was a van speeding down the lane to Torrington Manor at this time of night? The lane went nowhere else, so it must be going to the manor.

The question vanished from her mind when they reached the hollow and saw that it was still underwater. Laura had no idea how deep it was. Did she dare risk the light again to find a way across?

"Over here," Catherine murmured. "Not as deep." She must have eyes like an owl's, Laura thought with envy, ears as well. Catherine had heard the car well before she had. Maybe camping in the woods had sharpened her senses. Or maybe it was just youth. Laura sighed. Age didn't come in an onslaught; it crept upon one with tiny changes that were barely noticed until younger people made the deficits impossible to ignore.

Water sloshed around their feet as they waded through but didn't come over the top of their boots. Laura was grateful. Wet feet all night held no appeal. They climbed another shorter hill, went around the bend, and saw the manor ahead. It was the first time Laura had seen it from a distance, and she was impressed by its bulk. The large central portion of the house was flanked by two long wings, and at the end of each wing was a high round turret. Lights shone in one of the turrets and a few windows.

"I wish Nigel was here to help," Catherine whispered. "You said he'd gone with his father. I hope they aren't at that horrible school. Nigel would go crazy there."

"I doubt he could be made to stay," Laura whispered back. "We'll find out about that later but right now we've got to decide what to do next. Maybe we could go to the edge of the lawns behind the house, hide in the trees there, and watch for a while. We might see your father through one of the windows."

"Okay," Catherine agreed. Together, they crept up the rest of the lane and slithered into the woods beyond the house. Laura made out the dim outline of the barn where she had seen Thomas and Antonia, and beyond it the stable.

Abruptly, she remembered the dogs. "What about the dogs?" she asked with a flicker of alarm. "They might give us away if they're out."

"Leave them to me," Catherine said confidently. "They might still be in their run beyond the barn, but usually they're let out as soon as it's dark to guard the place. I'll go see."

She was gone before Laura could object. One short bark interrupted the stillness; then frantic yipping, and then whining sounds of joy. Catherine reappeared out of the gloom. Two huge dogs pranced behind her. They looked more like ponies than dogs, and Laura stepped back a pace. Great Danes, she thought but wasn't sure.

"This is Laura," Catherine told the dogs sternly. "Laura is a friend, so you mustn't growl at her."

She turned to Laura. "Hold out your hand," she instructed in a low voice. "Let them sniff all they want. They're big babies, really. All they want is love. And food." She placed a hunk of bread into Laura's hand as the dogs sniffed eagerly. One of them took the bread delicately, wagging its tail in appreciation; Catherine supplied another hunk and the second dog repeated the maneuver.

"They're very polite," Laura observed. "Are they always this nice?"

Catherine laughed softly. "No. They can scare people half to death. The guys in the woods and most of the locals won't come near them. Still, once you get to know them they're okay. They slept with me in the stable every night, so they got to know me pretty well. Anyway, dogs like me; I'm not sure why, but they always have."

"No doubt hunks of bread help," Laura said dryly.

Catherine grinned. "All animals like a treat," she replied, "so I always keep one handy. I grabbed a few extra pieces at the pub, just in case.

"Good boy, Jasper, good girl, Lucy," she praised, as the dogs snuffled at Laura's hands to see if more bread would materialize. "No more now, and we have to stay here very quietly and watch."

The dogs seemed to understand because they sat down nearby, their great heads resting on their paws, but Laura was certain they were very alert. Their ears were pointed up and turned from time to time as they caught a sound, and their noses quivered eagerly.

One of them whined suddenly, a soft whine that seemed to Laura to signify distress, as if they wanted to explore a sound or scent but weren't sure they ought to.

Catherine turned to them. "All right," she said softly. "Go see." The dogs sprang up and disappeared into the darkness.

"The van again," Catherine whispered. "That's what they heard. It's coming back here. Must have been at the front of the house."

Laura nodded. She heard it too, the van backing up and turning on the gravel drive. It came slowly around the side of the house. The dogs ran beside it eagerly.

To their astonishment, Morris emerged. The dogs stalked toward him, growling low in their throats. "They hate him," Catherine whispered. "I never worry about Morris when I'm in the stable. He won't come near me."

Morris edged toward the back door. "Damn!" he said. "Get away from me, you brutes!" The dogs advanced, their growls louder now, and he leaped back into the van. With a furious squeal of tires, he propelled it closer to the back of the manor. In response, a door opened, emitting a flood of light. Antonia started to come out but retreated quickly when she saw the dogs.

"I told you not to let them out," Morris hissed at her.

"I didn't," she said, watching them fearfully. "Maybe the latch came undone."

Laura glanced at Catherine, who was grinning widely. "I let them out," she murmured. "I thought they might come in handy."

"Well, throw them some food so I can get in," Morris snapped at Antonia. "And make sure you throw it well away from the door."

Antonia complied, but her aim was imperfect, and the dogs were snapping at his heels before Morris got to the door. He closed it hard in their faces, and Laura heard the faint sound of a key turning in the lock. With a last threatening bark, the dogs turned to the food. When they had gobbled it all up, they trotted back to Catherine, looking very pleased with their performance. Catherine was pleased too and praised them lavishly.

110

"I wish we could hear what they're saying," Laura murmured. "Maybe Morris is in on this, too, whatever it is your father is investigating."

"Wouldn't be surprised," Catherine answered. "If you'll wait here for a minute, I'll get us in."

Laura was astonished. "But how? I heard Morris lock the door. And we can't get in the front way because the butler will give us away. He's automatic."

"Not to worry," Catherine assured her. "See that window up there?" She pointed at the end window on the second floor. "That's Nigel's room. He told me if there was ever an emergency to come in that way. There's a trellis, and lots of vines and stuff. It's perfectly safe. I'll go up and then sneak downstairs and open the back door for you."

"The window looks very high, and Morris is inside," Laura objected, but Catherine had already reached the trellis. The dogs loped after her eagerly.

"Stay," she told them in a stern whisper, and began to scramble up the trellis with the ease of a monkey. Laura watched, torn between admiration and anxiety. Catherine disappeared over the window ledge. Visions of Morris confronting the girl flew through Laura's mind. She shuddered, and had almost made up her mind to knock boldly at the back door when it opened.

Catherine beckoned. "All clear," she hissed. "They're in the drawing room."

Laura hesitated again, wondering if it was irresponsible to go on with this crazy escapade, especially if it endangered Catherine, but curiosity and concern about what had happened to Thomas won her over. She just had to make sure neither of them was seen. She slid inside.

"Not yet," Catherine told the dogs as they trotted hopefully to the door. "I'll let you in later." Their tails went down in disappointment, but they obeyed and sat down outside the door to wait. Morris would get a nasty surprise when he came out again, Laura thought with satisfaction.

"We can hide in the hall just outside the drawing room," she said softly. "It has long curtains and we can stand behind them."

Noiselessly, they crept through the kitchen area and along a passage to a door that Laura thought must open into the front hall. She was right, she saw with relief as they opened it cautiously. They heard Antonia's voice and slid behind the thick curtains. They were very dusty, and Laura concentrated on trying not to sneeze.

"I wish you'd leave, Morris," Antonia was saying, with more spirit than Laura had expected from her. "You know Bark doesn't want you here."

"And when your lord and master speaks, you listen, eh, Antonia?" he asked casually. "No place for me at the inn. How very sad."

"You know that's not true," Antonia snapped. "He's put up with you for more than a week already for my sake, and now he's fed up."

They sounded as if they knew each other well. Laura frowned. Surely, Morris wasn't another lover? More likely, he was a co-conspirator.

Morris seemed unperturbed. "Our lordly Bark seems to be feeling quite flush lately," he remarked. His tone was casual, but there was a double meaning in the words that Laura didn't understand.

"That's not true," Antonia said defensively. "What gave you that idea?"

112

"I keep my ears open, and my eyes," Morris answered, and Laura was certain that his words had some special meaning for both of them.

"You should never have come here," Antonia said, sounding defensive. "Everything was going along well until you came along."

"Stewart seems to think I've been a great help," Morris replied. "After all, someone has to do the dirty work when unexpected problems arise, and your darling would rather keep his hands clean. "Bit of a coward, I fear," he added musingly.

"That's not true either," Antonia objected. "He's just…just not very…" Her words trailed off shakily, and Laura was sure the slight had upset her.

"Drink?" Morris asked. Antonia made no answer. Laura heard the clink of a glass being set down and then a drink being poured. "Here's to all our health," Morris said, his tone mocking.

"You've got to go," Antonia said urgently. "They could be back any moment. I don't know what Bark will do if he finds you still here."

"All right," Morris agreed equably. "I'll be off in a minute. Don't want to ruffle the lord and master's feathers. But first, Antonia darling, I have one more small matter to discuss with you. Very boring, I fear, since it has to do with me needing a spot of the ready, and with a certain young la-"

His voice broke off abruptly as the dogs began to bark hysterically. Laura felt Catherine's hand on her arm. "Car," she mouthed.

Laura nodded. Even she had heard the sound of tires on gravel under the dogs' fierce barks, which came now from the front of the manor.

Walking into Murder

The barks changed into whines of pleasure, and she heard Lord Torrington's booming voice. "Come to greet me, have you?" he told them cheerfully. "Didn't think Antonia would let you out. Glad she did, eh Jasper? Down now, Lucy, that's a good girl. Come on, both of you. Inside for a drink and some food."

"I'm off," Morris announced softly from the drawing room. "Tell you the rest later, darling."

Laura heard his steps glide past the curtains toward the kitchens. He wasn't quite fast enough. Just as Morris opened the door to the back hall, Lord Torrington came through the inner door. The polite voice instructing visitors to leave their cards and progress to the drawing room was no match for his bellow.

"What the hell are you doing here?" Lord Torrington demanded. "I believe I made my position quite clear, Morris, and if you come again I'll call the police. Now get out!" He sounded much less gentlemanly than usual, Laura noticed with interest. Even his accent sounded different.

Morris didn't argue. "Yes, Sir," he answered, mockery strong in his voice. His footsteps receded slowly down the long passage to the kitchen. Laura sighed inaudibly, sorry the dogs were no longer there to greet him.

To her horror, they trotted over to the curtains and began to sniff eagerly at her feet. She held her breath.

"Damned mice, they get in everywhere," Lord Torrington grumbled to himself. "Walls are full of them. Or maybe rats, damn them."

Rats! Laura stiffened. A whole family of them could be hiding behind the curtain. She wanted badly to look down at her feet but dared not move her head or anything else.

"Stop snuffling at those damned curtains," Lord Torrington muttered impatiently to the dogs. "Can't get at the damned creatures anyway." Jasper and Lucy ignored him. Exasperated, Lord Torrington snapped his fingers. "Come," he ordered sharply as he went into the drawing room. The dogs hesitated, and he called them again. "Come on, you great brutes."

They obeyed this time, their nails clicking on the stone floor as they followed him. Laura let out a sigh of relief and then realized she was going to sneeze. She should have known better than to hide behind dusty curtains. She squeezed her nose hard in a desperate effort to hold the sneeze back, but the impulse was irresistible and it emerged anyway. The sound was muffled but still audible.

"What was that?" Antonia asked sharply.

Laura held her nose again as another sneeze threatened. The dogs saved her. One of them sneezed, too, a loud wheezing sound that utterly obscured her next sneeze. Maybe they were allergic to dust too, she thought gratefully.

"Dogs," Lord Torrington answered briefly. They heard the sound of a drink being mixed; then there was silence - a very uncomfortable silence. Laura waited with interest to see what would happen next.

She jumped when the butler's voice sounded again. Another person came through the two doors. The footsteps were lighter than Lord Torrington's heavy tread.

"Nigel," Catherine mouthed, and Laura thought she was probably right. The feet crossed quickly to the main staircase and mounted the steps.

Lord Torrington's angry voice broke the silence. "Why is that devil still hanging around? I thought he'd left!"

He didn't wait for an answer. "Where's Angelina?" he asked sharply. "Don't like her here when Morris is around. Too friendly with her by far. Don't trust his motives."

"I sent her to stay with my mother," Antonia replied. "I thought it best. Besides, Lottie has gone away for a few days."

"Damned right it's best," Lord Torrington grunted. "I just hope your mother can hold on to her. Last time the silly child ran away from her and we had the deuce of a time finding her. She's a clever little creature, but she doesn't know what's good for her.

"Morris doesn't either, since he's still here," he went on furiously. "He's a loose cannon and I don't want him around. And you didn't answer me. Why the hell is he still here? You knew I wanted him gone."

"He came back on his own," Antonia said, sounding defensive again. "He said he was helping Stewart with something." She began to weep. "I can't stop him," she wailed. "He's always been like that, doing what he wanted no matter what. If he gets an idea in his head he just does it…"

The weeping came to a halt. "He scares me, Bark, truly he does. Ever since I've known him, he's had that awful fascination -"

"There, there, m'dear, not your fault," Lord Torrington soothed absently, as if to a child. "He's a bad one, though, no way around it, and he's got to go. I'll make sure he does," he added grimly. "That's -"

He broke off as the dogs sprang up, barking loudly. A buzzer sounded in the hall near Laura.

"Who could that be?" Lord Torrington asked irritably. "Have we got guests for tonight? If we have, I suppose we'll have to let them in. But who the hell is going to cook for them? Why did that cook vanish anyway? You've got to learn to cook, Antonia," he went on with a return to his former truculence. "Don't know why you never have. Can't be that hard."

"Perhaps you should give it a try, then." Antonia's voice dripped with ice and sweetness. She really did have claws, Laura thought, and was pleased. Lord Torrington positively exuded male chauvinism – a tendency of quite recent origins, despite what most people thought. Until patriarchal religions had come storming along, females had been in charge, and about time they were again, too.

Lord Torrington merely grunted, and Antonia sighed. "Charlotte put a piece in the local paper, an advertisement for another cook," she told him. "It came out today. I imagine that's someone applying for the post."

Laura frowned. Who was Charlotte? The name sounded familiar, but she didn't think she knew anyone called Charlotte.

"At least we might get some dinner in the future," Lord Torrington replied, sounding more cheerful.

"Not if those two beasts greet her," Antonia retorted sarcastically. "Most people don't like being drooled on or knocked over."

"I suppose you're right," Lord Torrington agreed grudgingly. "I'll put them out the back door and you get the front."

He whistled to the dogs, hustled them past the curtains, where they tried hard to linger but without success. Lord Torrington grabbed their collars and shoved them through the door that led to the kitchens.

"Out!" he told them firmly, opening the back door. "Go take a pee."

Antonia went to the front door. Laura and Catherine heard her greet the newcomer over the butler's ubiquitous voice and then two pairs of footsteps came into the hall and passed by the curtains into the drawing room.

"Do forgive our automatic butler," Antonia was saying with a mix of humor and condescension that perfectly suggested the trials of parenthood. "Master Nigel, Lord Torrington's son, created him when the real butler left. It's become rather a joke with all of us, but there are times when I wish I knew how to turn him off. One of these days I must ask Nigel about it."

Antonia had morphed from weeping wife to sarcastic one and then to indulgent stepmother in two minutes flat, Laura thought in astonishment. The woman was a chameleon! But then, all of them seemed to have the ability to switch roles suddenly. Lord Torrington was no exception. When he returned to the drawing room his truculence had evaporated, and he was the perfect jovial host and prospective employer.

"Good of you to come, Mrs. Murphy," he said, after Antonia introduced him and explained that Mrs. Murphy was indeed interested in the position of cook at the manor. "Let's have a chat, find out if the position will suit. Then I'll take you up to meet the Baroness in her sitting room upstairs. We work at these things together, you know. All quite informal."

"Thank you, sir," Mrs. Murphy replied primly. "That will be fine."

Catherine gave Laura a poke. "Nigel?" she mouthed, pointing upstairs. Laura nodded. There was a surprising amount of traffic at the manor tonight, and they might not get another chance to leave their hiding place undetected. Lord Torrington would soon bring Mrs. Murphy out to meet the Baroness, too.

"Back stairs," Catherine mouthed. Laura nodded again. Catherine led the way up to Nigel's room, the last on the main hallway, and they knocked softly at his door. The sound of another door closing and soft footsteps farther down the hall sent them piling into the room without waiting for an answer. Nigel wasn't there.

Catherine's face fell. "I wonder where he's gone," she whispered.

"Maybe to his grandmother's room," Laura suggested. "But we can't go there." She peered around the room. She dared not turn on a light, but two large windows let in some moonlight. The bed looked as if a tornado had struck, but the rest of the room was very neat. Masks hung in well-spaced rows along the walls.

The dogs began to bark hysterically again, and they went to the window to see what had disturbed them. Surely, the prospective cook wasn't leaving already?

An engine sprang to life and she saw the van, with Morris driving, backing toward the barn. It stopped, the engine idling. Laura fought down a laugh. How was he going to manage the dogs this time?

To her disappointment, he didn't try. Instead, he waited in the van while a darker man she didn't recognize called softly to the dogs and opened the back door to let them in again. Jasper and Lucy bounded through, delighted to rejoin Lord Torrington.

"That's Stewart, the groom," Catherine whispered, as the dark man went back to the van. "I wonder what they're doing."

Once the back door had closed behind the dogs, Morris climbed out. The two men opened the back doors of the van and then went into the barn. After a while, they came out, carrying a bundle that looked like a rolled-up rug. It must be very heavy, Laura thought. They were both straining to hold it up. An oriental carpet perhaps? Could they be stealing it?

Catherine gasped. "Look! Look at the end of it!" Laura looked, and saw shoes protruding from one end of the rolled-up rug.

"My dad's shoes!" Catherine moaned, grabbing Laura's arm. "They're my dad's shoes. I'd know them anywhere. Laura, my dad's inside that rug!" She turned to Laura, her face frantic with terror.

Unbelieving, Laura stared at the rug. Surely, that couldn't be true. Then she saw the shoes and recognized them immediately. Thomas had worn those shoes the night they had been at the manor together. She had noticed them because they were so perfectly polished. Her stomach tightened with fear.

Catherine gasped again. "It's him! It really is him!" Laura saw it too, just a quick glimpse of Thomas's face sticking out at the other end of the rug. Then the two men dumped him unceremoniously into the van.

CHAPTER TEN

"What have they done to my father?" Catherine whimpered. "Is he dead? Laura, what should we do?" She looked like a panicked child, all pleasure at their escapade erased from her face. Laura tried o reassure her.

"I doubt he's dead," she answered, pretending an assurance she didn't feel. "I mean, why would they bother to wrap him up in a rug if he was?"

Even to her, the argument hardly sounded convincing, but Catherine seemed to accept it. "We have to rescue him," she whispered. "We've got to get to him fast if he's still alive. Hurry! Follow me!"

She ran to the other window, which had the trellis underneath, put one leg over the sill and began to descend. Laura peered down to make sure Catherine hadn't fallen and immediately felt dizzy. She had never liked heights. Did she really have to go down that way? Maybe she could run down the back stairs and go out the back door, or maybe alert the others, explain what was happening…

"Come on," Catherine hissed. "There's no time. Hurry up!"

Laura took a deep breath. Catherine was right. If Thomas was still alive, they had to get to him fast. There was no time for the stairs or to find help. No one would believe them anyway, and she couldn't let Catherine face the two men alone.

Gingerly, she lowered herself onto the trellis, clutching the window as she felt with her foot for a secure toehold. There weren't any. The trellis was fragile, and the vines swayed dangerously under her grip. She forced herself lower anyway. How had Catherine done this so easily?

She was halfway down and Catherine had just reached the bottom when the van doors slammed. The unexpected noise made Laura flinch, and she grabbed at the vine to steady herself. The engine revved, spewing gravel, and the vehicle sped away. She craned her neck, trying to see where it was going. As she did, the piece of vine she was holding swung away from the trellis, taking her with it. Swinging wildly, she clung desperately to the branch and struggled to rein in her feet. One toe hit a branch; she shoved the rest of the foot into it, then the other foot and waited for her heart to stop pounding so violently.

"Hurry up!" Catherine's voice was impatient and lashed with terror.

Laura obeyed. She couldn't stop now, so she might as well get down as fast as she could. Gritting her teeth, she willed her hands, her feet and toes and fingers, and even her elbows and shoulders to find a piece of wood or a bit of vine, anything that would hold her up until she could find the next precarious perch.

The strain on her arms had become intolerable, but she dared not look down to see how far she had come. Then she would definitely fall. Even thinking about it made her dizzy. She dislodged one foot tentatively from its perch; then a branch cracked sharply and her other foot went out from under her. Grabbing frantically at vines and trellis, she plummeted toward the ground and landed with a thump. After a stunned moment, she moved an arm and a leg and realized to her astonishment that she was unhurt – aside from the fact that she would be a mass of scratches and bruises tomorrow.

She got shakily to her feet. "You did great," Catherine hissed. "Follow me!" She ran into the darkness before Laura could object. She trailed after Catherine, hoping the girl knew where to find a car. But when she caught up with Catherine again, she was opening one of the stable doors.

Laura's stomach dropped to her boots. Surely, Catherine didn't expect her to go after Thomas on a horse? She hadn't ridden a horse for forty years, and that was only a pony led by some long-suffering adult in endless circles around a dusty ring. She had not enjoyed the experience. The pony had bitten her, she remembered, when she was finally able to get off.

"Good boy, Senator," Catherine crooned. "Good boy." She hauled out a saddle and the cloth that went under it and approached the huge horse.

"Hold this strap," she commanded, handing Laura a long leather strap attached to the horse's head. Laura obeyed, keeping as far as she could from the prancing forefeet, and the teeth.

"Hold still, boy," Catherine told the horse, who nuzzled her gently before he turned his attention to the stranger. He snuffled Laura expectantly, and then blew hard out of his nose in her direction. It felt like a fluttering wind on her cheek, and she felt almost pleased. Maybe he liked her.

She was quickly disillusioned. Senator whipped his head in the other direction, then plunged it up and down in rapid succession and pawed at the ground. His eyes began to roll wildly, and he snorted harder.

"Steady, Senator," Catherine soothed. "Steady now. We're going for a ride, isn't that great? You don't get to go out at this hour very often, do you?" Catherine went on talking, her voice low and steady, and the horse gradually stilled. Every once in a while, though, he rolled his eyes at Laura, as if he expected her to perpetrate some dreadful assault on him.

"No need to worry about me, horse," she told him, trying to mimic Catherine's soothing tones. "I am highly unlikely to get any closer to you than I can possibly help, so you see, you have all the advantages here." The horse seemed to listen with interest, so she kept up a stream of similar nonsense while Catherine got him ready.

"Great," Catherine said finally, slipping a metal object in Senator's surprisingly receptive mouth and adjusting the last strap. "You're really good with horses, you know. He didn't even spit out the bit. Too mesmerized by you. Anyway, he's ready to go."

She led Senator outside, and Laura followed at a safe distance from his long legs and hard hoofs. Somewhere off to their right, they heard the sound of the van, laboring once more up the long hill.

Catherine's taut shoulders slumped in discouragement. "What if we can't catch up?" she asked. "What can we do then?"

Laura tried to think of another way to reassure her. Without Catherine, this rescue would never get off the ground.

"We have one advantage," she pointed out. "They have to use lights. We should be able to spot them once we're on the top of the hill." She wasn't sure there was any truth in this claim, either, but Catherine nodded, intent on the chase again.

"I'll get on first and calm him down while you climb up behind me," she explained. Laura's jaw dropped. She was supposed to get on too? But how? Senator's back was higher than her head.

Catherine forestalled any objections she might have made. "See that mounting block?" she asked, gesturing at a solid-looking hunk of wood. "Stand there, and when I'm in the right position, climb aboard."

With a leap that astonished Laura, she propelled her slender body into the saddle, adjusted herself against it and grabbed the reins.

Recovering her wits but little of her courage, Laura climbed up on the block and waited with a sense of impending doom. This was impossible, surely. She was bound to fall off the back of this creature. Senator sloped down at quite a sharp angle at that end. She watched warily as he pranced in nervous circles around her.

Catherine soothed him expertly, seeming hardly to move in the saddle as Senator snorted and danced skittishly. "Over there," she told him when he had settled a little. Firmly pulling at the reins, she guided him toward Laura. He complied, his big feet mincing delicately in the required direction.

Catherine held him still as Laura struggled to heave a leg over his back. This was a great deal harder than going over a windowsill, she decided, and wondered how she could get some leverage. Finally, she clutched the back of the saddle, gave a great leap and found herself perched on Senator's buttocks with one leg dangling almost to the ground on the other side. Catherine leaned over and pulled her back so that her legs were evenly distributed on both sides. Slowly, Laura levered her hips forward until she was pressed against the hard saddle.

She winced. The horse – not to mention the saddle - would give her some nice bruises, too, but in much more delicate places.

"Quite a leap," Catherine observed. "Now, hold on tight. We're off!"

Laura clung tenaciously to Catherine's waist as she urged the horse forward, first into a trot, and then into a canter. The latter was faster and more frightening, but Laura almost welcomed the shift. Catherine managed to raise herself up and down with graceful regularity as Senator trotted, but Laura bounced so hard with each step that she knew she would be unable to walk for at least a week.

Their pace slowed to a walk when they came to the stream at the bottom of the hill. The horse splashed through it unconcernedly. Laura was pleased to note that she was so high up that the water couldn't reach her. Senator's tail, however, could. It whisked back at her face with maddening regularity as they proceeded. Laura tried closing her eyes, but that was worse. Total darkness was unnerving as well as unbalancing, she discovered, when one was bouncing up and down in unexpected patterns.

Catherine urged Senator into a trot as they ascended the hill, but then he lurched to a stop. Laura peered around Catherine's back. The moon was bright enough so that she could see across the hills on both sides of the road. On one of those hills a pair of lights bobbed up and down.

"The van," she murmured, and Catherine nodded.

"There's an old shed up there," she said. "That must be where they're taking him. It's on an old farm track. Pretty muddy and rough for a van, but I guess they can make it." She steered Senator gently to the left, looking for the turning.

"There," Laura whispered, pointing at an almost invisible pair of tracks. Catherine turned into them, keeping Senator to a walk on the uneven terrain. Laura was relieved until she realized that his walk was almost harder to endure than his other gaits because it swayed her back and forth at the same time that it bumped her up and down. She was about to ask Catherine if she could get down and walk, or even run if that was necessary, when she saw the van turn, and the headlights came toward them. Why were they coming back already? Had they just dumped Thomas up there, or was he still in the van?

"Off," Catherine said, to Laura's infinite relief. Uncaring of Senator's potentially murderous hoofs, she slid off his back and landed in an inglorious heap.

Catherine dismounted with far more grace and led the horse quickly off the road and into the bushes. Laura followed as fast as she could, surprised that she could walk at all. Fear was a great motivator, she realized.

They reached cover just in time. Within minutes the van shuddered past them. Its tires churned deep into the mud as it bounced and clattered, but somehow it kept crawling forward. Laura and Catherine ducked down to hide their pale faces.

"Should we follow them or go up to the shed?" Catherine asked, panicky again.

"Go up to the shed," Laura answered with a confidence she didn't feel. "I'm pretty sure your Dad's up there. I'll go the rest of the way on foot," she added. "I'll never get back on the horse without that block thing.

"Besides," she added fervently, hoping to cheer Catherine up, "I don't intend ever to get on a horse again for the rest of my days."

Catherine giggled. "I'll walk too," she offered. "This is bad terrain for a horse in the dark, so I'll lead Senator. Lord Torrington would kill me if he got injured."

"I am far less worried about Lord Torrington right now than about the pair of thugs that just left," Laura retorted, and immediately wanted to take back the words. There was no point in reminding Catherine of what they might find when they reached the shed. It was better to keep her positive.

They trudged up the slope, and sooner than Laura had expected they saw the old building just in front of them. Catherine slung Senator's reins loosely across a fence; he lowered his head placidly and began munching on grass.

Cautiously, they approached the shed and peered into the dark space. The rug had been dumped in a heap in one corner but it was too dark to see anything else. Turning on her flash-light, Laura splayed it around the small space to make sure no one was there, and then she dared to let it rest on the rug. The shoes were still visible but not the head. There was no movement inside it. They crept closer, terrified to look and terrified not to. Finally, unable to wait any longer, they began to unfold the heavy carpet.

"Dad!" Catherine whispered in horror as the man's head reappeared. His eyes were closed, his face deathly pale. Catherine dropped to her knees beside him and clutched his hand. "Dad! What have they done to you?

"Laura, is he dead?" Her young voice was filled with terror.

Laura sank down beside her and picked up the other hand. "He's alive," she assured Catherine quickly. "He's warm, and there's a pulse."

"Not for long, I fear." The deep and cultivated voice came from the door. Morris stood there, fingering a long knife nonchalantly. "First, I have a few questions to ask him. So far, he's refused to answer but now he might reconsider. After that... Well, we'll see, won't we?"

Terror rose in Laura's chest. Morris must not have left with Stewart. Why hadn't she thought of that? He must have been watching them all along, waiting, biding his time. And now he had Catherine to use as a threat to make Thomas talk...

Still fingering the knife, Morris sauntered toward them. Laura's arm shot out to pull Catherine behind her, but her gesture came too late. Catherine had already sprung. Lowering her head, she rammed Morris in the belly, knocking him backward, then kicked him hard, aiming for the groin but getting his chest instead. The double blows knocked the wind out of him. Gasping, he struggled to his knees. Catherine faced him defiantly.

Laura looked around for a weapon of some kind - anything she could use to defend Catherine. A long wooden object lying near Thomas caught her eye. Grabbing it, she hurried to Catherine.

Morris stared at them unblinkingly while his breathing steadied. His eyes were narrowed with rage. Laura shivered. Never in her life had she seen eyes that were so totally devoid of human warmth – and so

129

mesmerizing. She felt incapable of movement, held in place by the sheer force of that malevolent gaze. Catherine too seemed unable to move. Laura could feel her terror.

"You are going to pay," Morris said, his voice icy with threat. "You can be sure of that. No one barrels into me like that without paying very dearly."

With the agility of a cat, he sprang to his feet, raising his knife to strike. This time, Laura knew, he didn't mean to be deflected.

CHAPTER ELEVEN

Laura screamed at the top of her lungs and then screamed again, in the vain hope that someone would hear her. The scream resounded deafeningly in the small space. Before the noise died down, she grabbed Catherine's hand and charged for the door of the shed, swinging her makeshift weapon wildly at Morris as she went. Her tactic worked; they raced past Morris before he could react.

Dragging Catherine behind her, Laura ran. She headed for the track, but then thought better of the tactic. Morris was probably faster and their only hope might be to hide in the bushes and take him by surprise. Catherine at least had some ability to defend herself, and she still had her long stick. She veered down the slope toward the bushes, still pulling Catherine behind her. If only the moon would go behind a cloud so he couldn't see them!

Morris was catching up. She could hear his thudding footsteps. He was running with incredible speed for someone who had been flat on his back only moments ago, as if rage had given him unnatural strength. Madmen were supposed to be unnaturally strong, weren't they?

She heard other footsteps, different ones, and tried to think what they were. The horse. The horse was coming after them too.

Morris was almost upon them now; she saw his knife flash in the moonlight, and then Catherine's hand was wrested away…

Laura stopped, searching the gloom for the girl. There she was, only a few steps behind her. Morris was right beside her, and this time Laura was certain she saw the knife flash. She leaped toward the two figures, brandishing her stick.

A terrified whinny followed by another scream, a scream of pain this time, brought her to halt once more. Catherine was still in the same place, but Morris was lying on the ground. Had Catherine managed to knock him down again?

"Senator," she heard Catherine whisper into the sudden silence. "Oh, Senator." The horse nuzzled her gently, and she threw her arms around the huge neck and began to sob, long, painful gasping sobs.

Laura was beside her in seconds. "It's all right, Catherine," she soothed. "It's all right. We're both all right."

"He was frightened," Catherine sobbed. "He heard me scream and he saw Morris running after me with the knife, acting so crazy. And then Morris ran in front of him, trying to get me, and he reared...."

Her voice dwindled away. Senator nuzzled her again, a little harder this time, and Catherine held on to him as if she would never let go.

Laura bent over to look at Morris. He wasn't a pretty sight. Senator's hoofs had caught him mostly in the arm and shoulder, but in the semi-darkness it was hard to tell about other injuries. He was still breathing, but he looked badly hurt. They would have to get help for him as well as Thomas.

The knife, knocked from his grasp by the horse, was lying on the ground nearby. Laura went over and picked it up, wincing with distaste as her fingers touched the cold steel. As cold as its owner's eyes, she thought irrationally. She wrapped it carefully in the bandanna

132

she always brought with her and slipped the bundle into an outside pocket of her pack.

Catherine's sobs diminished. Laura put a comforting hand on her arm. "We need to get help," she said. "We'll check on your father and then maybe you can ride Senator back and alert someone at the manor."

Catherine looked at her in confusion. "But who do I alert?" she asked in a voice that bordered on hysteria. "Stewart and Morris brought Dad here, and that means… that means they could all be in it…"

Her voice trailed off. She was right, Laura realized. Stewart must be involved in whatever was going on at the manor and Antonia probably was too. For all she knew, all of them were, and she wasn't going to let Catherine ride unsuspectingly into a den of thieves.

Laura sighed and decided to concentrate on Thomas for the moment. "We'll go check on your father. That's the first step," she told Catherine.

Reminded of her father, Catherine sprinted to the shed. Laura followed as fast as she could. Still, she heard Catherine's joyous exclamation well before she managed to catch up. "Dad! Dad! Are you okay? Oh, Dad! I was so scared…" She started to cry helplessly, like a child.

Relief shot through Laura when she saw Thomas sitting up. He looked dreadful in the glow of her flashlight, but he was definitely alive. He even tried to smile when she came in. His arms were clasped around Catherine, who was still sobbing.

"I am very glad you're alive," Laura told him, barely controlling the tremor in her voice.

"Alive, yes," he replied, putting one hand up to rub his head while he stroked Catherine's back with the other one. "The rest is up for grabs. I should have stayed unconscious a while longer. No one could sleep through that racket, though. What happened?"

Catherine stopped crying. "I rammed him," she said with a trace of pride. "Aren't you glad you paid for all those lessons?"

Thomas looked appalled. "Rammed who?"

"Oh, I forget. You were knocked out. Morris. He had his knife and he was going to use it on you. He said he wanted to ask you some questions, so I had to do something. He was real mad at you for telling him off in the woods."

Any color that had been left in Thomas's face bleached out. "You rammed Morris?" he asked incredulously. "*I* wouldn't dare do that even if I could. Nor would anyone else I can think of."

Laura grabbed his shoulders and eased him back to the floor. "It's all right now," she assured him hastily. "Morris is out cold. The horse knocked him out, not us."

Thomas gaped at her. "Oh, Lord, here I thought I was leaving Catherine ensconced in your safe hands and now it sounds like all hell's broken loose instead. I should have known better than to put you two together."

Laura bristled. Why couldn't the man say something appreciative instead of criticizing them for what they'd done? She had suffered a lot of discomfort on his behalf and Catherine had displayed extraordinary courage.

"Catherine was perfectly safe, we both were," she protested indignantly, "until we saw you wrapped up in the rug and decided we ought to rescue you. We didn't have a car so we came on Senator. You wouldn't have liked it much if we hadn't come, so you could at least be grateful."

Thomas took a deep breath, which seemed to hurt a lot. "Blasted ribs," he muttered. "No, I wouldn't have liked it if you hadn't come," he conceded, "and I am grateful. Thank you, Catherine. Thank you, Laura."

His face changed again and he regarded his daughter sternly. "I do appreciate what you've done for me and I admire your courage, but I still intend to take you out of here at the earliest possible opportunity."

"Okay, Dad," Catherine agreed meekly. "But first we've got to find out why they brought you here. I mean, rolling someone in a carpet and lugging them way up here is a really strange thing to do."

"And I want to know why you didn't call," Laura inserted.

Thomas considered. "Well, I was looking around in the barn and I guess someone snuck up behind me and coshed me," he said. "Then Morris asked me questions but I was too groggy to understand, which really made him mad so I guess he hit me again. That's about all I remember. I guess they wrapped me in a rug after that, though why a rug I can't imagine, except maybe to hide me." He managed a smile at Laura. "Hard to make a call when you're knocked out and wrapped up."

"What were you looking for in the barn? And why did someone hit you over the head in the first place?" Laura pressed, determined to get as much out of him as she could while he was in a confessional mood.

To her chagrin, Thomas was once again saved from answering, this time by Senator, who distracted all of them by poking his head through the door and eyeing them quizzically, as if he too wanted some answers.

"Look, Senator wants to come in!" Catherine chortled, running outside to join the horse and rub his velvety nose. Laura smiled, glad to see Catherine enjoying Senator's antics after all that trauma.

Thomas's low voice brought her back to reality. "They hit me over the head because they don't like me interfering, and I was looking for clues in the barn because I am paid to interfere," he said quietly, so Catherine wouldn't hear.

Laura's eyebrows went up in surprise. He had actually answered her!

"And I believe they brought me here because this is Morris's favorite spot for questioning," Thomas added caustically. "Nice and remote. No interruptions."

"Morris is an appalling man, and I am very glad he didn't have the chance to question you again," Laura agreed. "However, he was badly hurt when Senator came to Catherine's rescue and he needs a doctor. Do you by chance have a cell phone?"

Thomas rummaged in his pocket. "I did, but I don't seem to now. They must have taken it. Cell phones don't work well up here, or for that matter, anywhere in England except London, so they're not much use anyway."

His expression changed. "What's that in your hand?" he asked, pointing to her makeshift weapon.

Laura looked at the object closely for the first time. "It's a walking stick, I think," she answered, pleased with her discovery. "It has carvings on it and some kind of metallic handle."

Taking it from her, Thomas examined it carefully. His face was set in tight lines. "Where did you get it?"

"It was on the floor near you, and I grabbed it when Morris turned up," Laura explained. "Why? Do you know something else about it?"

"I know the person who owned it," he answered grimly, and his eyes flashed a warning message toward Catherine. "She was a colleague of mine and she always had it with her. She had it made to her specifications." He flipped it over from end to end. "The top can be a club, and I believe there's a retractable knife in the other end. Though how one would get it out in time I can't imagine," he added in a faint attempt at humor. "I've never been able to make gadgets like that work."

Laura regarded the walking stick with renewed respect. Maybe she would keep it. It would be useful next time she encountered a sadistic fiend like Morris. Or even a bully.

"I'd better see what else is in this shed," Thomas said wearily, getting to his feet. He swayed unsteadily and began to crumple.

"No, you won't. I will," Laura told him firmly, and helped him to sit down again. Leaving the stick with him, she roamed around the shed, shining her flashlight as she went. A pile of what looked like crumpled cloth caught her eye and she went over to examine it more closely.

"There are some clothes here, and some papers under them," she reported in a low voice. "I'll bring them over."

She picked up a jacket and saw with a jolt of fear that it was dotted with rusty stains. Blood? Under it was a manila envelope, a very old one. It looked ready to fall apart with age, as if it had spent long years in an attic.

Walking into Murder

The attic at Torrington Manor? She made a mental note to search it.

More clothes lay in a pile nearby, contemporary ones – jeans and a gray t-shirt and similar items. She took them wordlessly to Thomas. She had little doubt that they had belonged to the missing cook.

"That could be blood on the jacket," she murmured, wanting to prepare him. "Doesn't look good for whoever owned it."

"The aforementioned colleague, I expect," Thomas told her grimly. "She came here posing as a cook." His face twisted with grief and anger. "Bastard," he murmured under his breath. "She didn't deserve this."

Laura shuddered and tried not to not to think about what her fate must have been, especially if Morris had her up here. "I'm sorry," she murmured, feeling helpless in the face of his obvious distress.

She turned with relief to the envelope and undid the clasp, anxious to see what was inside. She didn't find much, just a photograph and an old newspaper clipping. It seemed a pathetic bundle of clues.

"A newspaper clipping," she reported. "An old one. And a photograph. Do you think your colleague was collecting clues about whatever was going on at Torrington Manor?"

"Could be," Thomas replied absently. He had picked up the clipping and was frowning over it, perplexed.

Intrigued, Laura trained her flashlight on it and began to read herself. Her bewilderment grew as she scanned the article. It was about a long-ago society wedding in France. How did that fit into the puzzle? There were no photographs of the bride and groom and no names either. The whole top of the article, where presumably photos and names would have been, had been torn away, which was interesting in itself. The article did say that the groom was a Baron, though, and she immediately thought of the grande dame. Was this how she had become a Baroness? But why would the art detective posing as cook want to know about that?

She turned to the photograph. That made more sense. Three paintings were lined up side by side, and they were exactly alike.

"Three photos of the same painting or three paintings?" she asked Thomas.

"Three paintings," he answered with only a cursory glance. He didn't sound surprised, and Laura wondered whether that was because he already knew making forgeries was part of this scam or because he was part of it. She still couldn't quite get that thought out of her mind.

"How does someone make such exact copies?" she asked curiously. "And surely the fakes don't fool the experts."

"They can and they do," Thomas answered, sounding implacable again, which had the effect of persuading her that he wasn't part of the scam, after all.

"In one easy lesson," Thomas went on, perking up at the prospect of a discourse on art, "three major types of forgeries exist. The first is a copy of a masterpiece sold as the original, which can and often does fool the experts if the techniques are right. The second is a pastiche, a painting of typical scenes copied -"

A loud whinny and the sound of pawing hoofs cut off his words. Catherine's agitated voice followed. "Come quickly! Morris is talking and he's got Senator all upset. He wants to go down there and I'm not sure I can hold onto him. Hurry!"

Laura grabbed the walking stick and ran outside. Senator really was upset. His eyes were rolling wildly and his big head jerked up and down as he tried to pull away from Catherine's tenacious hold on his reins.

Gathering her courage, Laura walked slowly toward the agitated horse, murmuring soothing words as she went. Senator seemed to calm a little, and she put her hands on the reins just below Catherine's. Together, they managed to haul Senator up the hill away from Morris. Catherine took a deep breath.

"Thanks. He was just frightened. I think he'll be all right now. It was Morris. He's mumbling and cursing. Maybe we'd better look at him."

"You stay with Senator and I'll go to Morris," Laura instructed. "If you keep the horse calmed down, I'll calm Morris down. He hasn't got four lethal feet," she added in an effort at humor. Catherine looked much too pale and strained.

She was rewarded with a weak smile. "Sounds like a good deal to me," Catherine agreed, rubbing her face against Senator's neck.

Laura approached Morris with caution. "Knife, need knife," he muttered viciously. "Get them; I'll get them." He tried to sit up but fell back with a gasp. "Damned horse. Get him too."

Laura tried to soothe him. "Lie still," she ordered. "I'm going to send for the doctor. He'll take care of you soon."

"No doctor," he said distinctly. "All right."

"No, you aren't all right," Laura replied firmly. "You are badly hurt and you must not move or try to talk."

Morris opened his eyes. They stared up at her malevolently. "The bossy lady. Who the hell are you, anyway?"

"It doesn't matter," Laura soothed. "You need to rest."

"Antonia," Morris ordered. "Bring Antonia. Have to talk to her. Important. Very important." His eyes were apprehensive now as well as threatening.

"As soon as I find a doctor I will tell Antonia what happened to you," Laura promised. "She can come to the hospital, I'm sure."

Morris shook his head. The gesture made him wince in pain. "No hospital," he gasped. "No bloody hospital. Antonia. Just Antonia."

"You must have known Antonia a long time," Laura ventured, trying to understand his insistence.

Morris frowned. "Your idea of a joke? Not funny."

This wasn't getting her very far. Laura decided to try a more direct approach. "Not a joke," she assured Morris. "I have no idea why you have known Antonia for a long time." A new thought came to her, and she gave a muffled gasp. "Is she your sister? Is that it?"

Morris gave her a contemptuous look and closed his eyes. "Leave me alone," he said. He didn't speak again.

He didn't need to. Laura was certain she was right and wondered why she hadn't seen the resemblance before. Antonia and Morris looked very alike, with their blondness and their classic features. She didn't much like Antonia but having a brother like this must have been a sore trial.

In the meantime, however, *she* seemed to be stuck with Morris. She had to find a doctor somehow.

She frowned in frustration. Morris could be bleeding to death in front of her eyes, Thomas desperately needed medical attention too, and there was no way to get help because phones didn't work up here even if she had one, and she didn't know who to call anyway because she didn't know who to trust.

An unexpected sound caught her attention and she whirled, her heart beating hard with panic. A vehicle was coming! She could see its dark bulk straining slowly up the track. It sounded exactly like the van Stewart and Morris had used. She could see the lights now too. What if Stewart was coming back? He might have heard her screams earlier and wondered what was going on. He might even bring reinforcements in case there was trouble.

A cold frisson of fear crawled up Laura's spine. Now what was she to do?

The walking stick. She had that at least. If she could just figure out how it worked, quickly. Laura bent over it, straining to see.

There was no time. The vehicle ground to a halt and she heard the sound of someone jumping out. Only one person? Excited yaps came next. Dogs! Had Stewart brought the dogs?

Laura clutched her stick with both hands, raised it high and waited.

CHAPTER TWELVE

"Might I help?" The polite voice came out of the darkness below. Laura jumped; then her body sagged with relief. Dr, Banbury! It was only Adrian Banbury. What was he doing here at this time of night?

She lowered the stick and realized that she was trembling all over. The art-loving veterinarian might make her uneasy, but he was definitely her savior. This was the second time he had appeared exactly when she needed him.

"Good heavens, it's Laura!" Adrian exclaimed when he was close enough to see her. "But what are you doing up here alone?" He closed the remaining distance between them. "I am so sorry if I startled you," he went on apologetically. "When I took the dogs out for their last walk of the day, I thought I heard someone scream. We don't usually get screams on the moor, so I put the dogs in the truck and came up to investigate.

"But I'm rambling. Are you all right? That's the main point. It simply isn't safe for a woman to be up on the moor by herself at night. And was it you who screamed?" He came up to her and took her hand, looking genuinely distressed by her plight.

Laura almost laughed. How courtly he was! Despite what had happened tonight, the moor was probably a great deal safer at night than the city she routinely traversed to teach. "I'm fine," she assured him, aware that her hands were still shaking, belying her words, and that he must feel them. "I'm afraid I was the one who screamed, though. And I'm not up here by myself. I've got two wounded men and a young friend with me."

She stopped, wondering how on earth she could explain why she and Catherine were up on the moors with a horse that didn't belong to either of them which had injured a man who had gone after them with a knife, as well as a man who had been rolled up in a carpet unconscious and brought to the shed to be tortured for information by the man with the knife.

The task was clearly impossible. "It's a long story," she apologized, "but I really could do with some help. That's the most important part right now. We need a doctor for this man, for one thing." She pointed at Morris.

"I should say you do," Adrian agreed, bending over the prone body. "What happened to him?"

"I'm afraid it was the horse," Laura explained. "He was defending my friend. The man, his name is Morris, came after her with a knife. I guess that's when I screamed. It all happened so unexpectedly, you see."

Catherine appeared beside her and took over smoothly. "You see," she explained, "the horse, Senator, got loose, and we saw him heading up here. Maybe the groom forgot to latch his door, or something like that. Laura and I followed him as fast as we could, but it's quite a long way. I guess this man must have frightened Senator – he's normally very gentle, but he doesn't like people who lunge at him unexpectedly. Anyway, he must have been terrified, or he would never have lashed out like that."

"Lord Torrington's horse, I see," Adrian observed, stroking Senator's neck gently. "I know him well, and I don't consider him dangerous, not at all. What do you think frightened him so badly?"

"I wondered if the man had been drinking," Laura contributed since Catherine seemed to have no ready answer this time. "We saw him come out of the shed just before this happened, and he seemed almost demented. He was running around with a knife in his hand, and then he started chasing us," she added, warming to her story. "The horse felt threatened, I guess, or maybe he felt we were being threatened. Anyway, he reared and lashed out, and the man was right in front of him, trying to get at Catherine."

"I see," Adrian answered thoughtfully.

"Well, let's have a closer look at the man," he went on briskly. "Could you shine my torch on him while I examine him?"

Recalling that "torch" was British for flashlight, Laura took it and shined it obligingly on Morris. "Looks remarkably like the fellow who posed as butler up at the manor," Adrian murmured, as if to himself.

"You mean *he* was a butler there?" Catherine was astonished. Laura was even more surprised. Morris must be the butler Lord Torrington had fired. She had never thought of that. Adrian's choice of words was striking, too. *Posed as butler,* he had said. How interesting.

"Yes, I saw him at the manor a couple of times when I came up to look at the horses," Adrian replied. "Didn't last long, though, not even as long as the last one." He gazed searchingly into Morris's face and then began to examine him with professional-looking fingers. Morris groaned.

"Dr. Banbury is the local veterinarian," Laura informed Catherine hastily to distract her. She was looking rather green. Probably she hadn't seen Morris clearly until now. He wasn't a pleasant sight.

145

"Nasty," Adrian commented, and Laura had the odd feeling that he was talking about Morris as well as his injuries. "Not a good idea to get in front of a frightened horse, is it? We'll have to get him to hospital as soon as we can."

"That would be wonderful," Laura agreed. "I'm very glad you came up to investigate. This is the second time you've rescued me and I'm grateful."

Adrian bowed graciously. "I am delighted to be of service to such a lovely lady. It is indeed my pleasure."

He turned to Catherine. "Well, young lady," he said genially, "I think I should take you and Laura back to my housekeeper, who adores looking after people. You can rest while I make arrangements to have Morris picked up. You've had quite a shock, you know. The horse can come too. We'll stable him at my place until morning. I'll let Lord Torrington know so he won't worry."

He frowned. "It seems strange that Senator is saddled," he commented. "Do you suppose Lord Torrington meant to ride him later?"

"He must have, I guess," Catherine replied, all innocence.

Laura decided to change the subject. "I'm afraid we have another casualty to see to," she reminded Adrian. "He's in the shed. I think Morris must have hit him over the head."

"He's my dad," Catherine explained. "We found him already up here."

"Well, let's have a look at your father, too," Adrian said agreeably. "One day, however, I would appreciate hearing the real story," he added. "You two seem to have had some astonishing adventures."

Laura could think of no response, so she started up the hill for the shed. "This way," she told Adrian loudly, hoping Thomas would hear and have the wits to hide the evidence they had found. How would she possibly explain the bloody clothes?

To her relief, there was no sign of the manila envelope or the clothes when they entered the shed. She wondered where Thomas had stashed them, and then she saw her bulging backpack. She shuddered. She would hand the grisly bits of clothing over to Thomas at the earliest opportunity. They were evidence, after all.

"This is Dr. Banbury," she told Thomas. "He has kindly offered to rescue us. He can arrange to have Morris taken to the hospital."

Thomas surprised her. "Dr. Banbury and I met briefly a few days ago," he told her. Laura noticed that he looked faintly alarmed.

"Aha! The gentleman who was looking for his daughter," Adrian exclaimed. "It seems you've found her. Excellent! Mr. Smith, isn't it?"

Catherine stared at her father. "So you did come to look for me," she said softly. Her smile lit up her face, but then confusion replaced her obvious relief. "But then why did you say you were looking -"

Thomas cut off the rest of her sentence. "Yes, I did find her, I'm glad to say," he replied heartily. "Good to see you again, Banbury. You've come along just when help is urgently needed. We are most grateful."

Catherine and Laura exchanged a baffled look. Why had Thomas switched from missing daughter to missing wife?

Adrian's voice distracted them. "I'll go back to the truck and bring it closer," he offered, reverting to practical matters. "Then we'll get you into it."

"Thank you, Adrian." Laura smiled at him. She tied the walking stick to one of the straps on her pack and hoisted it onto her back. It felt very heavy.

"I'll help you stand up," she told Thomas. "Do you think you can walk?" He nodded, and Catherine came to help. By the time Adrian returned with the truck, they were waiting for him and ready to go.

"Will Morris be all right up here?" Laura asked worriedly. "It seems awful to leave a wounded man up here alone."

"I've already radioed for help and told them exactly where to find him," Adrian reassured her. "They'll be here in a matter of minutes and get him right to hospital. We can wait if you like, though."

"Let's get Thomas into the truck and then see," Laura answered. They helped Thomas into the front seat; Catherine clambered into the back of the truck with Adrian's dogs, which Laura was delighted to see were a great deal smaller than Jasper and Lucy. She squeezed herself between the two men – a position that reminded her she was very sore indeed.

By the time the truck had lumbered down to the first curve, lights were already visible coming the other way. Adrian stopped to confer with the hospital attendants, and then they set off again. Laura gave a long sigh of relief. Morris at least was taken care of. And she was going to have a restorative drink if Adrian would provide one.

She shifted uncomfortably, trying to brace herself against the bumps. Adrian noticed her discomfort and gave her an inquiring glance. "The horse," she explained. "I hadn't been on one for forty years or more and found it a remarkably uncomfortable experience to get on one again."

She clapped a hand to her mouth in consternation, remembering too late that Catherine had said they'd followed Senator on foot.

Dr. Banbury chuckled, but she had no doubt he had taken note of her slip. He was too polite to mention it, however. "I'll give you some of my miracle liniment," he said instead. "It smells terrible, but it is purported to work."

After that, none of them tried to talk above the grumble of the engine and the crunch of tires. Laura was grateful for the silence. It was wonderfully peaceful just to sit there and try not to bounce, and to know that for the moment at least, she didn't have to rescue anyone.

Adrian seemed to understand. Not until he had them ensconced in chairs by a warm fire with a small tumbler of brandy for her and for Thomas, as well as a frothy cup of hot chocolate for Catherine, provided by his housekeeper, did he ask any questions. "Now," he said, "what were you and Catherine really doing up on the moors with the horse? You are both excellent storytellers, but I still know a story when I hear one."

Catherine looked insulted, but Laura laughed. "I thought we were quite creative," she answered, "but I guess I gave us away by mentioning that I'd ridden Senator. In fact, we were trying to help Catherine's father. He'd been hit over the head and taken away, we assume by Morris, though I'm not sure why." She stopped, trying to think what else she could say without giving too much away - or alarming Catherine, who still

149

knew nothing about the missing and presumably dead cook, the masks and various other pieces of the complicated story.

Thomas came to her rescue. "I've been told you have a fine collection of paintings, Banbury. I would love to see them one day."

Adrian looked annoyed. "I will be happy to show them to you, but first I would like to find out what two unsuspecting women were doing on the moor at this hour of the night. I gather they were looking for you, but I might ask what you were doing there."

Thomas nodded agreeably. "I fear I annoyed Morris, and he lashed out at me when I was in the barn at Torrington Manor. Or perhaps I frightened him. He's a volatile fellow. At any rate, he picked up a stick and clubbed me. Rather a nasty blow. I'm afraid I passed out for a time, and the next thing I knew I was up at the shed and these two were trying to ward off Morris themselves."

He shook his head gravely. "Why he took me up there I cannot imagine, except that I have begun to think the man is mad."

Laura was impressed. What an accomplished liar the man was! Much better than her. A pretty good actor, too. Was that all part of his job?

"We saw Morris taking my dad away in the van and we didn't have a car, so we rode up here on Senator to help," Catherine contributed with the blandly innocent face Laura was coming to know.

Adrian looked baffled. "There's no doubt Morris is volatile," he agreed. "But I would never have thought him capable of this!"

"I hadn't known he was Antonia's brother," Laura put in, just to see how the others would react.

Thomas looked at her with respect; so did Catherine. Adrian's reaction was different. "Yes, I suspected they were brother and sister as soon as I saw him," he replied with an almost condescending nod. "I am rather a student of faces and they have the same classic features, same fair hair and blue eyes – and the same deficits of character."

His voice became harsh. "Antonia certainly can't be trusted. She puts on an excellent act as the lady of the house but -" He stopped abruptly, as if ashamed of revealing emotion.

"I noticed that, too," Laura observed. "She does seem to be acting all the time. She's good at it too."

"Too good, I fear," Adrian agreed.

Laura remembered Maude's remarks about the other man Antonia had seduced. Could he have been Adrian? He would be no match for her, with his old-fashioned notions about women.

Catherine yawned hugely and covered her mouth with her hand. Laura wondered if she had done it on purpose to suggest that the interview come to an end. Regardless, the yawn gave her a perfect opportunity to move on.

"I think I had better get Thomas and Catherine back," she told Adrian. "Thomas should probably see a doctor, and Catherine is exhausted. So am I, for that matter. We don't have these sorts of adventures normally."

"I trust you will avoid any more of them," Adrian said reprovingly. "From what you have told me, the situation with Morris could get unpleasant, and I hope you two will let Catherine's father handle any further developments. I shall of course look into things myself, as I know most of the people involved, but I assume you and Catherine will have the sense not to become any more entangled."

How incredibly pompous the man could be! Laura held on to her temper and merely nodded, trying to look serious. Thomas, she noted, was trying not to laugh. His levity was irritating, but she was glad to see some of his normal insouciance returning. He hadn't sounded like himself without it.

"Now, where can I take you?" Adrian asked, resuming his brisk tone. "I assume that you, Mr. Smith, are staying at the manor."

"Catherine and I are staying at the Fairfax House in Stourton," Laura told him. "It would be wonderful if you could take us there. And I really am sorry to cause you so much trouble."

Adrian repeated the formal little bow he had displayed earlier. "It is indeed my pleasure to be of service to a pair of such gallant ladies," he replied.

Thomas uttered a choking sound and clutched his chest. Not a heart attack, Laura was sure, just more suppressed laughter, which undoubtedly played havoc with ribs that had recently suffered a vicious kick.

Still with a hand on his chest, he rose slowly to his feet. She and Catherine each took an elbow as they trooped back to the truck. Thomas wobbled between them, but seemed to regain strength as they approached Torrington Manor.

"Perhaps it would be easier for you, Banbury, if you dropped us at the Manor," he suggested smoothly. "My car is there, so I can take Laura and Catherine on to their lodging."

Laura had no intention of letting him drive, but to her surprise, Adrian agreed to the plan. Maybe he'd had enough of these strange beings called Americans who were always getting themselves into trouble.

"I'll drive. You're not fit to," she said firmly after Adrian had left them. "Why don't I drop Catherine off at the B&B and then take you to the hospital so they can have a look at you? You've probably got a broken rib or two as well as a concussion."

"I'm feeling a great deal better now," Thomas assured her. "You can drive, but I'll skip the hospital. There's not much they can do anyway."

Laura didn't argue. She was too tired. What energy she had left had to be devoted to staying on the correct side of the road. She never had been able to tell right from left with any accuracy, so it wasn't going to be easy.

"I want to know why you said you were looking for your wife at the manor, but told Dr. Banbury you were looking for me," Catherine asked from the back seat.

"I saw Banbury before I realized there might be an art fraud going on at the manor," Thomas answered, and in the rear-view mirror Laura watched Catherine's face light up with relief. "After that, it seemed prudent to keep your name out of it so no one could use you to get at me if they found out that I was an investigator.

"And then Laura materialized out of the mist like the proverbial answer to a prayer," Thomas added, "so I found myself a wife instead. Best idea I ever had."

"Well, don't let them get hold of her, whoever they are," Catherine admonished sleepily. "She's part of the team. We need her." She yawned. "A bed sounds wonderful," she admitted. "The stable was nice with the dogs but it's itchy too. And there are rats. I saw a lot of strange activity, though. It's interesting there at night."

Thomas turned toward her sharply. "What did you see? Besides rats."

"Well, a truck drove up a couple of times and parked outside the barn. A bunch of guys were there, and they were loading stuff into the truck, just like they did tonight. Only then it was paintings, at least that's what they looked like. I didn't dare go close enough to see who the men were, though."

"Did you see anything else?" Thomas was fully alert now.

"Not much else except Antonia getting it on with Stewart," Catherine answered. "I guess they do that a lot." She wrinkled her nose in disgust.

Thomas blinked. "Antonia and Stewart," he murmured tonelessly.

Laura wanted to laugh. If Thomas *was* having an affair with Antonia, that bit of information would certainly rankle.

"She's not your type, Dad," Catherine declared. "I told Laura that when she asked."

Thomas's face was a study in astonishment and Laura suspected her own was a study in embarrassment. She hadn't really asked that, had she?

Thomas gave her a curious look. "I've been meaning to ask you how you met Adrian," he said, changing the subject completely.

"I met him when he gave me a lift over the flooded road at Torrington Manor," Laura explained. "He was kind enough to show me his gallery," she added, feeling she should say something in Adrian's defense.

Thomas's eyes widened. "That really is a coup! I've been told that he only lets a few chosen people go in there, and so far I'm not one of them."

"I think he asked me because I look a lot like one of his portraits," Laura said thoughtfully. "At least Adrian seems to think so."

"He fancies Laura," Catherine told her father from the back seat. "That's why he asked her. He can't take his eyes off her. Haven't you noticed?"

"No, I can't say I had," Thomas answered, sounding disgruntled.

He turned to Laura. "Why did you ask if I was involved with Antonia?"

"I didn't quite ask that," Laura replied, "just if you were the type to have affairs." She hesitated and then plunged ahead. "I was curious because I saw you in that clinch with Antonia in the barn."

Thomas confounded her again. "Clinch? What clinch?" He sounded genuinely astonished.

Laura squirmed in her seat, a motion she immediately regretted. "Well, I went to look for you this morning to say I was leaving, and Antonia's arms were around you, and..." Her voice trailed off, and she felt her face flush.

Thomas shuddered. "They were? No wonder I felt so horrible. That's like being embraced by a viper. Damned woman must have doctored my morning coffee as well as knocking me on the head. I haven't been able to clear my brain all day."

Laura blushed even harder. That didn't sound like a pretense. Obviously, she had jumped to the wrong conclusion. Thomas saw her face redden and grinned. "You are charming when you're that pinkish color, especially when your hair is decorated with twigs and leaves, and the rest of you with dirt."

"I am sorry if my appearance disturbs you," Laura answered stiffly. "I shall try to moderate it in the future."

"That was a compliment," Catherine corrected sleepily.

"A compliment?"

"My mom spends hours getting her hair right, and her nails and her clothes and her face and everything else," Catherine drawled. "It's pretty boring, so you're a relief."

Laura wasn't sure being a relief was a compliment, but she let it ride. At least she'd found out something about Thomas. He wasn't keen on women who fussed over their appearance. In her case, that was a pretty good start.

Catherine suddenly sat up. "You know what?" she exclaimed, tapping her father on the shoulder, "I think Laura is really Miss Marple in disguise, except she's much younger and prettier. He loves Miss Marple," she explained tolerantly to Laura, and stretched out on the seat again.

"Much prettier," Thomas agreed. "In fact I would say she's the prettiest detective professor – or should it be professor detective - I have ever had the pleasure of meeting."

"As well as the smelliest," he added sotto voice to Laura. "That liniment Banbury gave you is horrendous. I bet he did it on purpose so he can have you all for himself."

Laura glared at him. "You are impossible!"

Thomas smiled broadly. "If we ever get to know each other really well, and I sincerely hope we do, I shall strictly forbid smelly liniment of any kind."

"And I," Laura responded through gritted teeth, "will never, ever again come to your rescue on a horse."

She brightened, considering another possibility. "For that matter, maybe I'll just use the liniment as my special perfume when you're around instead."

CHAPTER THIRTEEN

When Laura came down to breakfast the next morning, she was greeted by an unwelcome piece of news.

"That poor child's been kidnapped," her landlady informed her excitedly as she brought in some freshly baked muffins that smelled gorgeous. "The one at the Manor, you know. She's an odd little thing but still..."

Laura was horrified. "You mean Angelina?"

"That's the one," her landlady agreed. "Vanished, she has. She was staying with Lady Torrington's mother, but now she's run off, or more likely been taken by one of those horrible child molesters. They've got everyone they can find out looking for her."

"Now, now, my dear, nothing to worry the guests about," her husband rebuked as he brought in Laura's pot of tea. "The child will turn up safe and sound just the way she did the last time she disappeared.

"She's a one for tricks, Angelina," he explained to Laura. "The last time she persuaded a friend to invite her to stay for the night but she never told her grandmother or anyone else. She likes getting everyone all excited."

He was right, Laura reflected, remembering how Angelina had stood in the middle of the drawing room and announced dramatically that the woman on the bed really was dead. She felt a sudden pang of fear. Who else had Angelina told? Whoever had killed the cook might view the child as a threat. He or she had gone to great pains to hide the fact that a death had even occurred.

Laura drank her tea gratefully but found the rest of her breakfast hard to get down, despite the truly superb muffins.

"Lord Torrington was worried about Angelina running away again," Catherine commented when she came down for breakfast. "I guess she did. She sounds like one determined kid."

"She is that," their host agreed, appearing with the coffee pot this time. "They'll find her, though, just like the last time," he added confidently.

Laura wasn't comforted. Angelina hadn't seen a dead body on that occasion and had been no threat to anyone. Thomas was another concern. He had driven himself off last night, saying not to worry about him because he might have to be away for a few days, but how were they not to worry?

"I feel badly about leaving you with Catherine," he had apologized, "But I can't think what else to do. I never thought when I came here that I would get embroiled in this blasted case. I really did come here to look for Catherine, you know, and one day I will be able to explain what happened. For now, I can only ask for your help.

"But please don't let Catherine get into any more dangerous situations," he had begged. "Things could get really nasty. I don't want her hurt, or you for that matter." Impressed by his serious tone, Laura had promised.

She looked at her watch. Thomas had also said he would try to call in the morning, but so far he hadn't. Was that because he didn't have access to a phone or because he was incapacitated? There was no way to tell.

The weather didn't help, she thought gloomily. Rain slashed at the windowpanes and poured from the gutters in gushing torrents. Laura dashed out to get some cash after breakfast with the vague idea that she might need more money now that Catherine was with her. If she didn't hear from Thomas soon, she decided when she returned to the hotel, she would call a cab and go to Torrington Manor on her own. Perhaps she and Catherine could help to look for Angelina, and in the process, check on Thomas.

She waited for another half hour; then she and Catherine put on their rain gear and loaded their packs with essentials in case they had to roam the countryside searching for Angelina. Laura was just about to call for a taxi when their host knocked at the door.

"Gentleman to see you," he said cheerfully.

"I wonder if it's Adrian," Laura said as they went downstairs. "He must know about Angelina, too. Maybe he wants us to help."

Instead, a burly man holding a very wet cap was waiting in the hall. The hostile gardener, she realized, except he looked friendlier now. He even attempted a smile.

"Dr. Banbury sent me to fetch you," he told them politely. Laura was even more astonished. Why would Adrian send this man?

"I thought you were the gardener for Torrington Manor," she objected, aware that that the thought of getting into the car with this man made her uneasy.

"I'm gardener and chauffeur in both places," the man answered in the same polite tone. "Dr. Banbury would like to meet you at Torrington Manor."

Laura felt deflated. She'd made a mystery out of nothing. He had been driving Antonia's Mercedes because he was also her chauffeur.

"Why does Dr. Banbury want us to come?" she persisted.

"He didn't tell me that," the gardener replied, and she heard impatience in his tone. Still, he was trying to be pleasant, and she decided not to antagonize him by asking more questions. Surely, Adrian wouldn't send him unless it was all right. Besides, he would take them to Torrington Manor, which was where they wanted to go.

A remarkably sleek-looking car stood at the curb. Adrian must do very well indeed as a vet, Laura thought, impressed. She wished he had used this car last night. Her derriere might feel a good deal better.

The gardener cum chauffeur opened the back door for them, closed it carefully and slid into the driver's seat. The car's engine purred to life.

"I dunno about this," Catherine whispered. "I think he's one of the men I saw loading paintings. And why would Dr. Banbury send him?"

"He's his chauffeur and gardener," Laura explained in a low voice. "Same at Torrington Manor, so it should be all right."

Catherine was looking out the back window. "We're being followed," she reported nervously. "There's a dark car right behind us."

"You've watched too many TV shows," Laura said with a laugh that sounded forced even to her own ears. Her uneasiness increased. Was this really the way to the manor? The road didn't look right to her, and they hadn't passed the pub where the taxi had left them last night.

She leaned forward. "I thought we turned left back there for Torrington Manor," she told the gardener, and wished she had asked for his name.

"Have to go around the back way," he replied. "The other road is under water still with all the rain."

That sounded reasonable to Laura. "I don't know your name," she commented, trying a friendly tone. If she could butter him up a bit, she might learn something useful.

"Roger," he answered shortly.

"Have you worked for Lord Torrington and Dr. Banbury long?"

"No," was the curt reply. Roger cut the wheel abruptly to avoid a hole, as if to emphasize that he had to concentrate on driving, and Laura subsided into the back seat. There seemed nothing else to do. If the man really was trying to take them somewhere they didn't want to go, they could always open the doors and leap out. The car was moving very slowly, due to the rain and the muddy road, so it should be possible. Or was it? She tested the door handle and found it was locked. The various buttons and knobs she tried failed to release it.

"Car's still with us," Catherine reported softly.

Laura didn't respond. She was suddenly filled with misgivings. Catherine was her responsibility and she had promised Thomas to keep her out of danger. They should never have got into this car.

Unexpectedly, Roger pulled over and the car stopped. Laura stared out the window and saw nothing but trees and bushes. This couldn't be Torrington Manor.

"Out," Roger said. "We walk from here."

"Where are we?" Laura asked. "I'm not getting out until I know where we are and why we have stopped here."

"Please yourself," Roger replied with a shrug. Laura didn't believe him. His tone was light, unconcerned, but his eyes told another story. They were mocking, even triumphant, and her stomach tightened with fear. He didn't mean them to have a choice. Why had she ever got into this car?

She knew she was right when the car behind them turned around in a farm track and pulled up facing their car. Stewart climbed out. When she looked back at Roger, she saw a gun in his hand.

"Uh, oh," Catherine muttered. "A different duo. Armed, at that."

"Yes," Laura agreed, horrified that she had got Catherine into this. She wished fervently that she had the cook's walking stick, but Thomas had kept it as evidence.

Maybe she could bluster their way out instead. "Put that damned gun away," she snapped irritably to Roger. "This isn't cops and robbers, and it makes me nervous."

It was the wrong thing to say. Roger's face darkened with rage. He pointed the gun at her. "Out," he snarled. "Now!"

Laura knew that this time he meant it. The mockery had left his eyes, and she saw only implacable dislike.

Catherine took her hand. "I guess we get out," she said.

"Stick together," Laura told her in a whisper as they left the car. "Hang on to each other and don't let go. They might try to separate us to get the advantage."

""Do you think Dr. Banbury really sent him?" Catherine whispered.

"I doubt it, but we can't be sure. He could have," Laura replied grimly.

Stewart started up the road he had used to turn the car around, and Roger gestured with the gun that they should follow. He came behind, his heavy footsteps squelching into the wet earth. The track led up a long hillside filled with sheep, then curved down between two hills. It was a lovely place, or would have been in any other circumstances, with fine views in all directions. Laura was glad she had her pack. Her compass and maps were in there; if she could get to them, she would try to orient herself.

The rain had eased during their drive, but now the clouds opened again, quickly turning the farm track into a quagmire. Stewart slipped with every step. His shoes were more suited to London sidewalks than a rough track, Laura noticed, and he had no rain jacket. Both seemed odd for a groom who presumably spent most of his time out of doors. Laura examined him as he struggled through the ever-deepening mud. He was handsome in a macho way, with almost Grecian features and a sturdy build. He wasn't a type that appealed to her, but she could imagine that Antonia might find him sexy, with his curly dark hair and stubble, at least in comparison to Lord Torrington's country gentleman looks, which didn't seem Antonia's style.

"Stop," Roger ordered behind them, and Laura's stomach tightened again. Were they going to be shot in this remote place?

Stewart disappeared up the track, and Roger trained the gun on them. He appeared to be waiting. Laura and

164

Catherine watched him, their muscles tense with readiness in case a chance came to escape.

Incongruously, the playful whistle of a steam engine cut into the silence.

"It's the kids train," Catherine murmured. "Runs near here."

Laura nodded. She had seen the tracks on her map, and the local shops were full of posters and brochures advertising the little steam engine and its glorious ride. The contrast between her present situation and the innocent tourist attraction was ludicrous. Here she was with a gun in her back, and a short distance away, eager children and their indulgent parents steamed happily through the countryside.

Silence fell when the train had passed. Laura wondered what would happen if she and Catherine dived simultaneously into the bushes. Before she had time to evaluate this possibility, Stewart returned. He nodded at Roger, communicating a message of some kind. Roger motioned with the gun for them to continue along the track.

"At least he didn't shoot us there," Catherine whispered jauntily.

"Right you are," Laura agreed, feeling her spirits rise a little. She had a lot to learn about courage from Catherine.

They rounded a corner and saw a low stone cottage. Built against the hillside, it was surrounded by a clearing that must once have been a garden. A few roses and a border of bright flowers still sprawled haphazardly across the earth. Laura would have found the setting charming if she had come across the place in an innocent ramble. Then she noticed a disturbing anomaly.

All the windows were boarded up. She felt a thud of panic deep inside.

She turned to face Stewart and Roger. "Where are we, and why have you brought us here?" she demanded. Neither man answered, but she noticed that Stewart looked tense and miserable, even afraid. Aha, she thought. He might be the weak member of the team. The knowledge could be useful.

Stewart pushed open a door at the back of the cottage. He didn't look at either of them. "In there," he said with a swift gesture. He had unexpectedly delicate hands, and there was paint under his fingernails, Laura noticed, surprised by both facts. Had he been interrupted in some painting job to come here?

She was about to refuse his order with the vague hope that he might intervene on their behalf, but a glance at Roger's face stopped her. He looked as if he would welcome an excuse to shoot. Stewart's eyes, in contrast, were almost pleading. Was that because he didn't want to see them shot, or was there another reason?

She and Catherine went through the door and found themselves in a tiny kitchen. To their astonishment, it was well fitted out with appliances, pots, pans and everything else a kitchen might need. There was even some food stacked on the counter - cans of soup, packets of tea and coffee, a loaf of bread and some cheese. The lights were on, too. How extraordinary! This must be a holiday cottage, for people to rent. Why had they been brought here?

She took another step into the room and heard the door close behind her. She whirled, but knew immediately that she was too late. A key turned in the lock, and a bolt scraped noisily as it was driven home on the outside of the door.

"They're locking us into this place!" Laura said in disbelief, and felt an irrational urge to laugh. She had been expecting a bullet, or at the very least a dark and smelly cellar inhabited by rats and lacking food or drink. Instead, she was being locked into a well-stocked cottage.

"This is ridiculous!" Catherine muttered with an hysterical giggle.

Her face sobered instantly. "Look!" she exclaimed in horror, pointing at a row of boots at one end of the room. Laura followed her gaze but it took her a moment to see the significance. One pair of boots was very small. They were also pink.

She had seen them before, on Angelina.

2.

Laura stared in horror. What were Angelina's boots doing in a boarded up cottage? Had she been kidnapped, or worse? Surely, no one would harm an innocent child. Things like that didn't happen in these sleepy villages and gentle hills, did they?

"Why would anyone bring Angelina here?" Catherine asked softly. Her face was stiff with fear.

"I don't know. You wait here while I look for her," Laura answered, not wanting Catherine to see Angelina if anything dreadful had happened to her.

Cautiously, she ventured out of the kitchen, through a small living room and into the bedroom. Catherine paid no attention to her order and followed her. The bedroom was darker, but there was enough light to see that Angelina was lying on one of the beds.

Laura bent over her and felt her body crumple with relief. Angelina was all right. She was only asleep, not unconscious, or worse. Her breath rose and fell at comforting intervals, and there were no visible injuries.

"Angelina's all right," she assured Catherine shakily. "She's just asleep."

They stared down at Angelina. Her face was tear-streaked, her dress dirty and torn, and even in sleep her hands clung to a bedraggled bear. She looked forlorn and pitiful, and Laura's heart ached for the child.

Catherine sighed behind her. "Poor kid," she said softly. "She must have been here all this time by herself."

"That's awful," Laura whispered angrily. "How could anyone be so cruel?"

"At least she hasn't been hungry," Catherine commented with a touch of macabre humor. She pointed at a large pile of candy wrappers beside the bed. "Probably thought she was in heaven while they lasted."

"Probably got sick, too," Laura said wryly, "if she ate all those. Better to let her sleep while she can," she added, leading Catherine out of the room. "In the meantime, we can evaluate our position. This is a pretty upscale prison, but we're still locked up, and that makes me mad. Let's see if there's a telephone first."

There wasn't. It hadn't even been pulled out of the wall or anything dramatic like that. There just wasn't one. "I don't know who we'd call anyway," Laura said gloomily.

"So what do we do?" Catherine asked.

"We get out of here somehow," Laura replied. "We have to let someone know that we've found Angelina and that she's all right."

"We've got to get out so we can make sure my dad's all right, too," Catherine said, her voice shaky. "I'm worried. Why didn't he call this morning?"

Laura's stomach twisted. What was she going to tell Thomas this time? She had promised to keep Catherine safe. Worse, she might never get the chance to explain.

"Two excellent reasons to escape as quickly as possible," she told Catherine, determined to keep their spirits up. "There's a way out, we just have to find it."

The thought seemed to energize Catherine. "At least there's a bathroom," she commented as she went into the next room. "It's pretty luxurious too."

Laura joined her. "That's good to know," she said, surveying the antiquated but well polished fixtures. "The proverbial bucket in a corner in novels never did have any appeal."

Catherine wrinkled her nose. "Smelly. Now what?"

"I'll check out the closets," Laura suggested, "see if there's anything useful like tools. A hammer would be great."

"I'll try the basement," Catherine volunteered. Grabbing a flashlight from her pack, she wrenched open a creaky door and disappeared down the steep stairs.

Laura turned her attention to the closets. She found a few items – a plunger that might do duty as a battering ram, a long unused wrench, a screwdriver but no hammer. The fireplace yielded tongs and other heavy implements. If they could open a window and knock the boards off from inside, they could escape that way.

She examined the windows in the living room, which were big enough to climb through if they could get the boards off, but sealed shut by layers of paint. She chipped at it with a knife from the kitchen.

An outraged voice made her spin. "You don't belong here!" Angelina yelled at Catherine, who had just emerged from the cellar.

The child had an obsession about who belonged where, Laura thought with exasperation, and then she softened. Maybe the child's need to have everyone in the correct place was a way of putting her small world to rights, despite the inexplicable actions of adults. How very sad.

Catherine wasn't perturbed. "No," she agreed. "I don't belong here. You don't either, though, so I guess we're even."

Angelina looked mutinous. "You were in the green room," she said, her tone accusing, "but I don't know who you are."

"Aha!" Catherine exclaimed. "I beat you on that because I do know who you are."

"No fair!" Angelina objected and opened her mouth wide to scream.

Catherine forestalled the explosion. "I bet you can't guess how I know," she challenged.

Angelina was stumped. "I'm hungry," she announced crossly.

"You sure can eat a lot of chocolate bars," Catherine told her. "Where did you get all those?"

"Morris gave them to me," Angelina confided. "He said I could eat all of them if I wanted to." Her small face looked suddenly pathetic. "He said he'd be right back, but he didn't come. Nobody came and I couldn't get out. The door wouldn't open, and anyway it was dark, and I didn't like being here all alone. It's horrible."

Tears welled up in her eyes. She squeezed them shut tightly, determined not to let anyone see her cry. Laura resisted an unexpected impulse to hug her.

"That's why we came," Catherine told her, "so you wouldn't be alone any more. And now that we're here, we are going to stick to-gether!" She spaced out the word with dramatic emphasis, and Angelina giggled.

Catherine grinned back at her. "Did Morris bring you here from your grandmother's?"

Angelina nodded. "But then he went away again and he didn't come back. I didn't like it here then."

"That wasn't very nice of Morris," Catherine responded.

Laura frowned, wondering why Morris had brought Angelina to the cottage. Was it possible he had hoped to extract money for her safe return? She remembered him telling Antonia that he needed "a spot of the ready," which she assumed meant cash. Would he really try to pry money out of his sister by kidnapping Angelina?

Laura flinched. How horrible! If she was right, Antonia must be crazy with worry. No mother deserved that. Lord Torrington and the Baroness must be frantic by this time, too.

Angelina's voice interrupted. "Morris said we were going to come here together and have a party and play games, but he didn't play any and I don't like him anymore," she said, with a charming pout of her rosy pink lips that Laura suspected was a well-rehearsed moue designed to win sympathy.

"Pierre ne l'aime plus, lui non plus," Angelina added in French, addressing the ragged-looking bear that now hung limply from one hand. *"Il est mechant, Maurice, n'est-ce-pas, Pierre?"*

171

Laura's jaw dropped. The child was full of surprises. She spoke French as easily she spoke English.

"C'est vrai," Catherine replied in passable French; then lapsed back into English. "I'm not surprised that Pierre doesn't like him anymore, either."

"I bet you'd like us to take you and Pierre home again now," Laura put in.

Angelina thought about that. *"Peut-etre*; I guess so," she commented with a Gallic shrug. Laura repressed a smile. No doubt Angelina was weighing the possibility of games and candy in the cottage with Catherine against the familiarity of home.

Catherine compromised. "We're going to be here together for a bit; then we'll take you home," she told Angelina. "Now, let's see what we can find to eat."

Catherine was a master at this, Laura thought admiringly. Where had she learned to deal with small children so well?

Angelina settled for chicken soup, since there was no more candy, and bread with lots of butter. Laura made herself a cup of tea while Catherine and Angelina talked.

"I'll give you a clue about how I knew who you were," Catherine said. "It's a person who lives in your house and plays games with you there."

"Nigel?" Angelina looked delighted.

"You've got it," Catherine told her with equal delight. "Nigel is a friend of mine and he told me all about you."

"Nigel knows someone named Cat," Angelina announced. "Is that you? You look like that, sort of."

"My name is Catherine, not Cat," Catherine told her firmly. "I told Nigel to call me Catherine, too. Cat was a kind of baby name. Like you being called Angie."

Angelina digested this information; decided it was satisfactory, and turned to look at Laura. "What about her?" she inquired doubtfully.

"Laura's a friend, too," Catherine assured her.

"She wouldn't let me look at Lottie," Angelina accused. For the first time, Catherine looked stumped.

Laura decided to intervene. She didn't want Angelina focusing on dead bodies right now, or Catherine for that matter. "We're going to have an adventure," she announced. "You and me and Catherine."

Angelina was dubious. "What kind of adventure? Do we have to go outside again? I don't like to go outside when it's raining."

Not a good start, Laura thought. The great difficulty might not be getting out of the cottage but getting Angelina down the muddy track.

"We'll be like Indians, sneaking along so quietly that one sees them," Catherine explained. "First, though, you have to help us find a way to get out of the house because some nasty person has locked us in."

Angelina looked interested. "I'll help," she offered, jumping up.

"Good. I need someone to help me get a window in the cellar open so we can escape," Catherine told her. "I hope you're not scared of cellars."

Angelina looked as if she was scared of them, but she shook her head bravely and followed Catherine down the hall.

"Are there spiders?" she asked nervously as they started down the steep stairs. Catherine assured her that there weren't. Spiders were much smaller than people, she added, so they were the ones who ought to be scared.

Laura listened to their voices recede and nursed her tea, knowing she should get up and help, but wanting to think. If only she knew what this was about, what role the diverse characters played in the plot, and who was in charge, she could make more sensible decisions about what to do next. All she knew so far was that Thomas was an art detective and that paintings were involved, but in what way remained a mystery. She also had the strong feeling that some person who remained hidden from view was manipulating everyone else, an unseen puppeteer who pulled the strings, making people conform whether they wanted to or not. She wondered if she, too, was being subtly manipulated by those unseen hands....

The sound of a car brought Laura out of her reverie. She dashed to the cellar door. "Car's coming," she yelled.

She ran back to the kitchen, thinking fast. It could be someone coming to rescue Angelina, but more likely Roger and Stewart were returning. They had to get out of here quickly, or hide at least, until they knew who it was. What might they need? Anything she could take, she decided, and grabbed her pack, Catherine's, their rain gear, the little pink boots and the forgotten bear, some biscuits and what was left of the bread and cheese, and hauled them down the cellar steps. She ran back up and closed the door hard behind her. It didn't open easily and that might give them an extra minute or two.

"Can we get out the window you found?" she gasped. "It could be Roger again. I've brought our packs and rain gear."

"If we can get it open enough," Catherine replied calmly. "It's tiny but at least it's at ground level and didn't get boarded up. I've got it part way open with this." She held up an iron spike. "Help me wrench it up more. Then we'll get our coats and boots on and give it a try."

Opening the window proved easier than getting Angelina dressed. She took a dim view of the pink boots and an even dimmer one of the coat. "It crackles," she objected, "and I can't get my arms in."

Laura shoved the arms in anyway. "Remember about the Indians," she urged. "They don't get caught if they're quiet."

Angelina nodded eagerly and put her finger against her lips. Laura made a final adjustment to the coat, noticing as she did so that the child had an unusually pointed chin. Where had she seen a chin like that?

Catherine's voice interrupted. "I'll go first," she whispered, "then send Angelina through before you come." She inserted her lithe body into the narrow opening easily and wriggled outside.

"Okay, your turn," she whispered to Angelina.

Angelina balked. "I'll get my party dress dirty," she wailed. Laura forbore to point out that the dress was already filthy and fastened the raincoat firmly around the child's belly instead. It was decidedly tight. Angelina had her mother's blue eyes, but lacked her slender physique.

"Now the dirt can't get in," she assured Angelina, and hoisted her into the window frame. "Off you go!"

she hissed. Angelina opened her mouth to scream but thought better of the idea when she saw the forbidding expression on Catherine's face, and wiggled through instead. Laura followed with difficulty, wishing she had been less enthusiastic about buttered scones.

Rain greeted her, but it was gentler now and didn't obscure her vision. Catherine had chosen well, she saw. The window opened onto the side of the house opposite the back door through which they had entered, and thick bushes grew in front of it, blocking them from sight. Just to their left was a small copse of trees. Incongruously, the children's train chose that moment to release its series of shrill whistles.

"If we can get to the trees, we should be all right," Catherine whispered when the sound finally died away. "They're still in the car, I think. I don't hear them, anyway, although no one can hear much over that racket."

"You go first with Angelina, then I'll come," Laura suggested. Catherine nodded. Grabbing Angelina's hand, she sprinted for the trees.

Laura heard the ominous sound of the noisy bolt being drawn back on the kitchen door. She ran. "Let's get out of here," she gasped when she reached the others. "When the car leaves, I'll angle toward the track to see who it is."

"Can I go first?" Angelina asked in a loud whisper. Catherine nodded and pushed the child in front of her as they walked cautiously through trees. Absorbed in the game, Angelina was mercifully quiet, as was the train.

Laura listened for the sound of a car returning. After what seemed like a long time, it came. She veered closer to the track and peered through the bushes. It was the same car that had brought them here, and she thought Roger was driving, with Stewart beside him, but the windows were fogged up and she couldn't see clearly.

She hurried back to Catherine and Angelina. They were sitting side by side on a log, and they looked up at her trustingly, waiting for her to tell them what to do next.

Laura felt a surge of panic. She was responsible for their safety, only there wasn't any safety. Someone – perhaps that unseen guiding hand she had sensed – wanted them out of commission and wouldn't give up until they were. At the same time, she had to get Angelina back to her family, and she had to find out what had happened to Thomas, for Catherine's sake even more than her own. That meant she had to go back to the manor – the most dangerous place they could be. On the other hand, she mused, it was probably also the last place anyone would think to look for them.

An idea began to form in Laura's mind, an idea that grew until it actually began to seem possible. True, it involved some risk, but mostly to her, and with some help she was sure it could be managed. Surely, someone would be willing to help them. But who?

The familiar faces of everyone she had met since she had come paraded through Laura's mind. One at a time, she dismissed them for even the possibility of collaboration, as in Dr. Banbury, or a tendency to talk too much, like Maude. Secrecy and the ability to act decisively were crucial to their success.

When she had finished her assessment, only two names were left: Nigel and the Baroness. Both were too intelligent not to be aware of any underhanded activities going on at Torrington Manor, but she didn't think either of them would be an active participant in anything illegal. Nigel would help them to the best of his ability, but he was also very young, too young to be saddled with so much responsibility. She needed someone older, someone with authority. The grande dame was the only logical choice. Surely, a woman of that caliber wouldn't condone the virtual kidnapping of her own granddaughter. The grande dame had too much integrity.

Catherine touched her arm lightly, jerking Laura back to the present. "Where to now?" she asked.

Laura grinned. "Somewhere unexpected," she answered. "Somewhere no one would ever think to look."

CHAPTER FOURTEEN

Laura and Catherine and Angelina sat in the front seat of the first car behind the small steam engine. With an ear-splitting whistle and a noxious emission of black smoke, the train started off. Angelina hung on tightly to the railing, her face ecstatic. Behind her, rows of similarly entranced children were perched in their seats, surrounded by watchful caretakers.

"You're right. No one would ever think to look for us here," Catherine remarked as she removed her hands from her ears and the scarf from her face. It hadn't been clean to begin with, but now it was black with soot. The train had a roof, which mercifully protected them from the continuing drizzle, but the sides were open. This had the effect of letting in uninterrupted fumes and noise as well as unrestricted views.

Laura laughed; then her face sobered. "I hope no one will think to look for us at our next port of call, either. It's an unexpected place to go, certainly, but a lot will depend on luck."

She had consulted the map and worked out a route to their next destination, Torrington Manor. As she had hoped, her memory had been accurate. The children's train wound along a curving track from a station near the cottage until it reached a similar station to the east; then it turned and went back to its starting point. Passengers could get on and off at either station, and the second station was less than a mile from the manor. They could walk from there.

Laura's lips tightened. She still thought the manor was the last place anyone would think to look for them,

179

but it was also the place where their enemies gathered. She comforted herself by recalling that the house was very large and there must be plenty of empty rooms to hide in, if they could just get to them unseen. Besides, if her plan worked, no one would recognize them anyway.

Catherine's voice broke into her reverie. "This was an inspiration!" she yelled as the train gathered speed, clattering noisily along its tracks after another deafening series of whistles. "Angelina lives up to her name in this setting."

Laura smiled. It was true. Angelina's face was transfixed with delight. The poor child probably didn't get to indulge in children's activities very often. It was hard to imagine Antonia or anyone else bringing her here, yet the little train was only a few minutes drive from Torrington Manor.

"Thanks," she yelled back, pleased that this part of her plan was a success. As well as providing much needed transportation, the promise of a train ride had been the only way to persuade Angelina to keep walking. The major problem now, Laura realized, would be persuading her to get off the train again when they reached the halfway point.

Her assessment was correct. Angelina put up such a fuss when the time came that people began to stare. Fearful of attracting unwanted attention, Laura decided this was not the moment to press home lessons about how tantrums did not get the desired results. Instead, they embarked on a second trip, and when Angelina still showed no signs of cooperating, on a third. They had to wait until evening to put the rest of the plan into operation and this seemed as good a way to spend the time as any other, Laura reasoned, although distinctly dirtier.

"We've only got a short walk and then we're there," she said brightly when they finally extracted Angelina from the train after the third ride. Laura hoped she was right. She didn't want to walk on the roads for fear of being seen, so she had decided to travel cross-country, using map and compass for direction. It didn't look very far, but with no clear walking path it was hard to tell.

Angelina regarded them mutinously. "I don't want to walk anymore," she stated, and sat down on the station bench, hands firmly clenched around its slats. Catherine sighed, unable to think of a solution. Laura remembered early hikes with her own children and had an inspiration.

"Do you have M& M's or anything of that sort?" she whispered to Catherine.

"Only an old chocolate bar somewhere in my pack," Catherine answered. "Why?"

"When my kids were little, I bribed them with M&M's at intervals, to keep them going," Laura answered shamelessly. "We had to get them to the campground for the night, and that was the only way they were going to move any further."

Catherine laughed. "Not so different than carrots for a horse or chunks of bread for the dogs," she said. "I think it's a great idea."

She went back to Angelina. "I know you don't want to walk any more," she said, "but I have another game. It's called the chocolate game. Every time ten whole minutes have passed, you get a chocolate reward if you keep walking all that time."

Angelina hopped off the bench. "I bet ten whole minutes have already passed since we got off the train," she ventured.

"But you haven't been walking," Laura countered. "Let's get started right now, and then the ten minutes will be up even sooner."

Angelina began to flag after five minutes but walked on gamely until the time came for the reward. Catherine reached into the depths of her pack and pulled out a squashed candy bar. Angelina wrinkled her nose dubiously.

"Is it good?"

"Marvelous," Catherine assured her, and broke off a generous chunk.

Even a triple bribe, however, failed to move Angelina when they came to a thick swath of gorse and blackberry bushes. Laura could hardly blame her. The child's legs were bare. Sighing, she heaved Angelina onto her back. The trouble with using a map and compass as guides, she realized belatedly, was that they had to walk in a straight line, and that could be downright hazardous. In the absence of a path, there was nothing gentle about this countryside.

Angelina was a solid child, and Laura was glad to put her down again when they reached some fences. She was also an unpredictable one. She scrambled expertly under the fences, looked appraisingly at the trickling streams that ran through the marshy ground ahead, and announced that she wanted to walk now. Splashing happily, she managed to get all of them very wet.

"As long as water doesn't come in the form of rain, it's acceptable," Catherine commented in exasperation. "Where are we, anyway?"

Walking into Murder

Laura consulted her compass. They still seemed to be on course. "The manor should come into sight just over that next hill," she answered with a confidence she wasn't sure she felt.

They trudged up the hill; then staggered down unexpectedly steep cliffs on the other side, hanging on to trees or sliding on their backsides so they wouldn't fall. At the bottom of the hill, they dragged themselves under yet another barbed wire fence and set off across the field it enclosed. A group of cows trotted over and stood blocking their way. The chimneys of Torrington Manor loomed tantalizingly beyond them.

Angelina approached a cow and stroked its nose. The animal put its head down, swiped it sideways in a sudden movement, and knocked Angelina off her feet. "Stupid bloody cow," she screamed. "You're not supposed to do that. Cows are supposed to eat grass!" She pushed the cow full in the face with a clenched fist. It turned and fled. The other cows followed, their hoofs thudding into the soft earth.

"I don't like cows any more," Angelina announced.

Catherine gulped. "I'm not sure I liked them all that well in the first place," she admitted. "I think you were very brave, Angelina."

Angelina looked surprised. "I was?" She considered the matter. "Since I was so brave, will you give me a piggy-back this time?"

Catherine consented, and sprinted to the next fence. The manor was just ahead now, and Laura's nervousness increased. Maybe it had been a terrible idea to come here. What if the wrong person saw them or they couldn't get in? And how were they to keep Angelina quiet while she figured out their next move?

Catherine proved equal to that task. "This is like one of Nigel's mystery games," she told Angelina. "We have to sneak around and not let anyone see us. We might even try to sneak into the house without anyone seeing us!"

"I know how to do that," Angelina said confidently. "Nigel showed me. You have to go in through the cellar. It's nasty down there."

Laura was startled. That was an unexpected boon, if it was true.

"I bet your cellar is no worse than the one at the cottage," Catherine said. "Besides, we'll be there, too. We can all go together."

"Okay," Angelina agreed. "We have to go in there." She pointed at an old-fashioned folding door that lay at an angle against the side of the house at ground level. Each side of the door had to be lifted up and then folded to the side to reach the cellar below. They would probably creak, Laura thought, and looked around nervously. No one was in sight, but someone could appear at any moment.

"Worth a try," Catherine whispered. The sound of a car coming up the road decided them. Together, they scuttled to the house and heaved the heavy doors open, revealing a set of steep stairs. Holding Angelina between them, they went cautiously down; then reached back to pull the doors closed behind them. Immediately, the darkness was absolute. A musty smell so strong they had to struggle for breath enveloped them. Gasping, Laura fumbled for her flashlight and switched it on.

Angelina seemed unaffected by the dank atmosphere. "I want to hold the torch," she stated, and held out her hand.

"You can if you promise to shine it all around," Laura agreed. Angelina complied, moving the thin beam in a wavering circle. The cellar seemed to go on forever, stretching into the blackness like some medieval dungeon. And perhaps it was, Laura thought. Torrington Manor must be very old.

Catherine brought out her own flashlight and shone it more methodically around the huge space. On the far wall, rows and rows of slatted shelves held moldy-looking wine bottles that Laura suspected were magnificent vintages. She hoped they weren't too old to drink. What a waste that would be!

A huge structure that looked like a trouser press except larger loomed against one wall. "Do you suppose it irons sheets?" Laura whispered.

"If people actually iron sheets," Catherine replied, displaying a cavalier ignorance of how the sheets on the bed she had slept on last night had acquired their pristine smoothness. "There have to be stairs around here someplace," she went on, moving her light around.

Laura saw a number of doors, some open, some closed, and wished she could search the rooms behind them. They might hold all manner of clues as well as junk. Later, she would come back and look into all of them.

Angelina corrected Catherine's idea. "It's not stairs, it's a tunnel and then stairs," she told them impatiently, as if they really ought to know. "You have to go through the tunnel first."

A tunnel! Laura was thrilled. Maybe the manor really did have a secret passage, as Maude had suggested, built during one of the rebellions so the inhabitants of the house could hide or escape from their enemies. In books at least, there was often a door concealed in the paneling of one of the rooms from which steep stairs or a ladder led to the underground passage. Sometimes the passages led all the way from the house to a concealed exit in the rocks or some other secluded place.

"That's pretty neat," Catherine said enthusiastically. "I think a tunnel's a great idea. Show us the way, Angelina. Let's go!"

Gratified by their excitement, Angelina proudly led the way across the room, shining the torch in front of her. "You have to pull that away," she told them, pointing to a large and very old chest of drawers. It looked as if it had stood undisturbed for hundreds of years, but when Catherine shone her light on it, Laura saw clear handprints in the dust on each side of the massive piece. Nigel must have moved it, so perhaps it wasn't as heavy as it looked.

Beside it, looking distinctly out of place in this ancient setting, was a gleaming white freezer chest. A long extension cord snaked across the floor, suggesting that it was in use. Laura frowned at it, offended by its modernity, then turned her attention to the big bureau. Placing their hands firmly against its sides, she and Catherine managed to pivot it slowly out of the way. Behind it was a hole about four feet high. Laura's enthusiasm waned. Did she really want to crawl through that? She had never liked being confined in small spaces.

Angelina darted into the hole and sped along, waving the torch wildly ahead of her. Catherine slipped off her backpack and followed at a slower pace, since she had to stoop and shove her pack in front of her.

Laura had no choice but to follow. The others had the flashlights, and being left alone in this huge dark cellar was definitely worse than squeezing through a hole.

"Wait for me!" she called. The sound reverberated along the muddy walls but no answer came back. Bending over as far as she could, Laura crept into the dark space in a vain effort to catch up. She bumped her head hard, pulled it lower and bumped her back instead, and she kept tripping over her backpack. Her elbows scraped painfully against the sides of the hole, which was rocky as well as narrow, much too narrow to turn around in. Laura felt the beginnings of panic. There wasn't much air in here, either. Almost none, in fact. It was already getting hard to breathe.

"Wait," she called breathlessly. "I can't see. You've got the lights." This time there was an answer, and some of her panic receded.

"Sorry. I'll try to shine mine back." Catherine's answer seemed to come from a great distance. A feeble glow lit up the ground ahead of Laura's feet. She lumbered toward it, trying not to think about spiders or rats.

"This is horrible," she muttered as she bumped her head for at least the tenth time. Dropping to her knees, she tried crawling instead, but that was worse since her knees and hands suffered as badly as the upper part of her body. She raised herself stiffly again and scrambled on, feeling like a stiff and exceptionally clumsy crab.

Catherine heard her labored breathing. "Almost there," she said comfortingly. "It opens out up here."

"If I could I'd go backwards," Laura rasped. "I don't think I can stand much more of this."

Fortunately for all of them, she didn't have to. As Catherine had said, the passage opened out, revealing a ladder that led straight up into the darkness. It was a very old ladder with rungs that looked as it they could crumble at a touch. Laura eyed it warily.

Angelina scrambled up like a monkey; so did Catherine, which didn't surprise Laura. Hesitantly, she put her foot on the first rung, tested her weight, tried the next rung and the next, all the while concentrating on not looking down, or up for that matter.

"We'll keep going. There's not enough room for all of us on this ledge," Catherine whispered from above. "I'll shine the light down for you, though. Isn't this exciting? Imagine - a real secret passage!"

"Exciting is one way of describing the experience," Laura agreed caustically, but Catherine had already disappeared into the darkness above her.

The ledge to which Catherine referred was indeed small, but what came after it was worse. Steep and very narrow circular stone stairs wound up and up and up some more. Even when Laura craned her neck backward, she couldn't see where they ended.

A spell of dizziness assaulted her, and she focused intently on the steps in front of her. They were very old, hollowed and pitted in the center, making them so shallow her boots wouldn't fit. What had once been a handrail had rotted away. Laura wedged the tip of one boot against the first step, raised herself carefully, and tried the next step, pressing against the cold stone wall of the turret for balance.

Faint noises above reminded her that the occupants of the house could be nearby. "Wait until I get there before you do anything," she called softly. An image of

Angelina and Catherine bursting into Lord Torrington's bedroom flashed into her mind.

There was no answer. The light Catherine had been shining down for her suddenly disappeared, and Laura almost screamed. "I can't see," she muttered irritably instead, struggling to keep her nerve in the darkness. This wasn't just horrible. This was a nightmare!

Catherine's whisper finally came. "Sorry. Someone was in the room. We come out in a closet, so it's okay to come on up now." She shone the light toward Laura.

Laura scrambled up as fast as she dared. When she reached the last step, she saw a small hole above her. It was barely big enough for her head, never mind the rest of her. She managed to squeeze one shoulder through, then the next, and Catherine hauled the rest of her out. The sharp edges of the hole made an audible ripping sound as they tore her shirt, and when she tried to stand she stumbled ungracefully over a box. If anyone was in the room beyond, the person must realize by now that something unusual was happening in the closet.

Angelina made that particular fear irrelevant. Twisting impatiently from Catherine's restraining grasp, she opened the door of the closet and walked out.

"I don't like the closet," she explained. "It's dark in there."

Laura sighed. So much for secrecy. She should have known it wasn't possible with Angelina in tow.

She might as well go out too. The closet was extremely dusty, and she would soon give them away by sneezing, anyway. Dusting themselves off, she and Catherine followed Angelina into the room.

At exactly that moment, a door on the other side of the room opened and the Baroness walked in.

CHAPTER FIFTEEN

Laura repressed a desire to laugh hysterically. This was like a replay of her first entrance into the manor.

"Hi Gram," Angelina said. "We came through Nigel's secret passage and I escaped from the cottage with Laura and Catherine, but it was pretty boring in the woods, so then we took a train ride and that was fun. They made me get off again, though, and we had to walk some more."

The Baroness took a deep breath, visibly steadying herself. "Hello, Angelina, my dear." Her voice shook despite her effort to control it, and for once the emotions in her eyes were clear and unguarded. The grande dame was immeasurably grateful, and almost unbearably relieved.

She must have aged a few years from worry and fear while Angelina was missing, Laura thought. Despite the child's obstreperous ways, Angelina was obviously precious to the Baroness.

Except she hadn't aged. Instead, the grande dame looked younger, more like the woman in the painting. Laura frowned, trying to identify the change.

"Excuse me for a moment," the Baroness said, and disappeared into an adjoining room. The sound of running water suggested that it was a bathroom. No doubt she was composing herself, Laura realized. Seeing the missing Angelina suddenly pop out of her closet must have been quite a shock.

When the Baroness returned, she looked just as she always had, not really old, but not young either. Perhaps, Laura thought, the unexpected look of youthfulness had been a trick of light. Anyway, there were more important issues to think about right now, and time was short.

"Now, child," the Baroness told Angelina calmly, "come with me and wash your face and hands. Once they are clean, you may play with the face paints while I talk to Mrs. Morland and her companion." She led an astonishingly unresisting Angelina into the bathroom.

"That's Catherine. Her baby name was Cat, but she doesn't like people to use it now," Angelina explained with dignity as the Baroness handed her the soap. "She's nice and plays games with me."

"Good afternoon, Catherine." The Baroness inclined her head in welcome, as if seeing a strange young woman emerge from her closet was an everyday occurrence.

"How do you do," Catherine replied with equal composure.

Laura looked around the room curiously while they waited for the Baroness to finish with Angelina. A few sculpted heads were set on a table; under it were large bins that held plasticene or clay. Two half-finished wax figures stood near a window, and masks in all stages of completion hung on hooks or lay flat on other tables. In one corner, wigs and hairpieces spilled from a box, and racks of costumes lined the walls.

This must be Nigel and the grande dame's workroom, Laura realized. It was very professional, as Thomas had said. She had hoped to find a few theatrical supplies and some clothes here, but she hadn't expected all this. Now she wouldn't have to use all that cash to buy what she needed to put her plan into effect.

Walking into Murder

A much cleaner Angelina erupted from the bathroom and ran eagerly to a dressing table covered with an enormous variety of jars and pots, all presumably containing makeup. Laura was amazed. She hadn't known so many kinds of makeup existed.

The Baroness's voice recalled her. "Now," she said, settling herself on a chair and indicating two others. "Sit down and tell me what has happened."

Laura took a deep breath. "First," she began, "I will say that I am glad you are the one who found us. I had hoped that either you or Nigel would be the ones to do so. I would like to tell you what has happened in the last few days, what I am worried about, and what I hope to do about it, which will necessitate your help if you are willing."

"And I want to know where my father is," Catherine put in. "We haven't heard from him and I'm worried."

"That would be Thomas Smith?"

"Yes. Do you know where he is?" Catherine's eyes lit up with hope.

The Baroness considered before she answered. "I am not sure where he is at this moment," she said finally, "but I can tell you that when I saw him this morning he was all right despite a knock on the head."

"Another one?" Catherine was appalled.

"I believe there have been two, maybe three so far," the Baroness replied with a straight face. "He seems to have a very tough skull." Interesting, Laura thought, that she knew so much. Did that mean Thomas had confided in her? Either that or she had eyes everywhere, which for the Baroness wouldn't be surprising.

Some of the tension left Catherine's face. "If he was all right this morning, I guess he's okay," she conceded. "But he should have called."

"When last I saw him he did look a little the worse for wear, as if he'd been rolling about in the dirt," the Baroness added, surveying Catherine and Laura with mischief in her eyes.

Laura flushed, suddenly aware of her disreputable state. Her pants were once again covered in mud, her shirt was torn and filthy, her face and arms streaked with cobwebs and dirt, and she suspected that her hair was fast reaching the dreadlock phase.

"I'm sorry we're so grubby," she apologized. "We climbed through a window and walked through a lot of mud, and we don't have any other clothes."

"Nor does Angelina, I can see," the Baroness answered with a more pronounced twinkle. "Still, she is safe and that is all that matters. Thank you for bringing her back." Once again, emotion suffused her face. She controlled it quickly.

"It was all a bit accidental," Laura demurred. Feeling like a schoolgirl reciting her lessons, she launched into her explanations, trying to include everything that might have significance. It was quite a long story, and by the time she had finished, the Baroness looked dazed. She was silent for a time, thinking hard. Then her face cleared and to Laura's astonishment she began to laugh. It was a warm, rich laugh that seemed to Laura to have retained the exuberance of youth.

"Most ingenious," the Baroness said, still chuckling. "Most ingenious indeed. And yes, I will be happy to help. I have some experience in these matters and will do my best to make the plan a success."

Amazing, Laura thought. No questions or comments, just a quick assessment and an offer of help.

"We will get to work as soon as you have cleaned up," the Baroness continued in a businesslike tone. "To save time, I want to visualize the effects I wish to achieve and do the preliminary work tonight. I will do most of the actual restructuring in the morning."

She stopped, considering them. "First, however, you need sustenance. Nigel will be back soon and can get food for you. Tonight, you will stay in a room we do not usually use for guests. It will not be quite as comfortable as some of our other rooms, but no one will go there. I would prefer that you do not leave it. I will keep Angelina with me; tomorrow I will send her to a trusted friend for a few days. She will be quite safe there. Do these arrangements sound satisfying?"

Laura nodded, too overwhelmed by the older woman's efficiency to think of an appropriate answer.

"Good. There is a washbasin and a shower in the bathroom, with all the supplies you will require to clean up. When you have finished, please put this on." She opened a drawer and handed each of them a garment that looked like an over-sized hospital gown. "In the meantime, I will excuse myself to make arrangements."

Catherine and Laura took turns in the bathroom, and by the time they had finished, the Baroness had returned, with Nigel behind her, carrying a tray bearing a pot of tea, some orange drink and four portions of fish and chips wrapped in newspaper. Laura wondered where they had come from and hoped the new cook, if she had been installed, hadn't produced a meal like this. They were horrendously greasy and not very hot, but she consumed her portion with relish anyway.

Between bites, Catherine told Nigel what had happened to them, with Angelina's noisy help. Nigel was enormously pleased to see the child again, and kept staring at her as if to confirm the fact that she really was there. Laura was touched at his devotion, but Angelina, alternating happily between stuffing fish and chips into her mouth, interrupting Catherine, taking large gulps of orange drink and applying still more make-up to her now very greasy face, was oblivious.

As soon as they had finished, the Baroness stood up. "We had better do the preliminaries before the food, if one can call it that, puts both of you to sleep. Who would like to go first?"

"I believe Angelina has already appropriated that honor," Laura replied, regarding the child with amusement. Her lips were deep red, her skin olive, at least in the patches where grease hadn't turned it still darker, and a black wig hung lopsidedly on her head. She was at that moment penciling her eyebrows to match her new hair color.

Catherine grinned. "So that's why she didn't object to washing up."

"Makeup does not adhere well to dirt, as Angelina knows," the Baroness explained. "Grease, of course, is quite different," she added gravely.

Her face sobered as she turned her full attention first to Catherine, and then to Laura. Presumably, Laura thought, she was doing her visualization. The critical gaze seemed to peel layers from her face and even her mind, and she shifted uneasily. It was liked being examined under a microscope.

Finally the Baroness nodded. "I believe I have it," she said, and her lips curved in an almost diabolical smile. "You may not like the results, but I assure you, the transformation will be complete."

2.

Laura stared at the woman in the mirror. An expensively dressed but harassed-looking woman she didn't recognize stared back. She looked French, perhaps German, but she was definitely not American. Perhaps it was the cut of her clothes or the way she wore her hair, twisted expertly into a severe bun at the back of her neck. She wore a lot of discreetly applied makeup and elegant tinted glasses, and held a fashionable purse. She had a slight frown that seemed permanently fixed to her face. She was not a very pleasant woman, Laura decided, nor was she a happy one.

Her gaze shifted to the girl standing beside her. She was about fourteen, and her pale face had a scrubbed look, as if she had just been ordered to wash it thoroughly. Dark pigtails hung down her back, and she wore a schoolgirl skirt and blouse, white socks and lace-up shoes. Her hazel eyes were sulky, and her mouth had a petulant look – or it did until she started to laugh.

"You look like the ultimate conservative worried Maman," she chortled to the mirror. "Ghastly! I bet you've never unbent an inch in your life!"

"And you look like the ultimate spoiled and bratty schoolgirl," Laura shot back.

"I look *horrible*," Catherine agreed, giving the word a French accent. "I'm going to act *horrible* too. I shall make your life a misery."

Walking into Murder

"Moi aussi," Angelina agreed, getting into the spirit of the game. *"Je suis un enfant terrible!"* Suiting action to words, she flung herself onto the floor and began to scream and pound her fists.

"Mon dieu!" Laura exclaimed in mock horror, turning to the Baroness. *"Qu'est-que vous avez fait, Madame? Deux enfants terribles?"*

Her French came out easily, she was glad to note. She'd read Levi-Strauss in French in graduate school, so it ought to. She hadn't agreed with him in French any more than she had in English. Anthropologists at that time were invariably men, Victorian ones at that, and they saw what they expected to see in other cultures, like dominant men and subservient women, and prostitutes instead of priestesses. Thank heaven all that nonsense was finally discredited.

The Baroness raised her eyebrows expressively, a gesture Laura was coming to know well. "You will pass as Madame Merlin. Your French is quite good," she approved.

"When people fail to recognize themselves, I know I have succeeded," she went on with a ghost of a smile, "but you must keep looking at yourselves so you know who you are now. Then it is easier to act the part."

Obediently, Laura and Catherine stared at themselves again. The Baroness hadn't let them watch while she worked on them, and the results were still a shock. Laura was astonished at what makeup could accomplish, at least in expert hands. The slight tilt at the end of her nose had been eliminated by putty so that the nose now looked long and pointed; her cheeks were flatter, her mouth thinner and framed by deep lines. As a result, her whole expression had changed, or she hoped it had changed. She wouldn't want to look like this all the time. There was plenty of self-absorption but little humor in the woman in the mirror, nor much generosity, if she was any judge.

"If I wish to do a total transformation," the Baroness had said, "I take what is least characteristic of the individual and make it obvious. When I succeed, the person is almost unrecognizable, even to themselves."

That was certainly true of Catherine. All her lightness and fluidity were gone, her bravery and her rebelliousness. She looked stolid, uninteresting, and not very bright. In part, that was because her distinctive green eyes were concealed behind brownish lenses, but changes in the shape of her eyes and face had an even greater effect. There was nothing cat-like about Catherine now, and Laura wished she could have the old one back. She was much more fun than Patrice would be.

Angelina had insisted on being transformed, too, before she went to visit what Laura gathered was a favorite playmate, and her grandmother had complied. She had elaborated on Angelina's earlier efforts, though removing the worst excesses, and the child was now a small boy with olive skin and long dark bangs that fell into his eyes, conveniently concealing their blueness. He wore a navy sailor suit with short pants.

The Baroness rummaged through a cardboard box and came up with a hat to match. It had an elastic band that went under the chin. "There," she said, placing it on Angelina's head and affixing the band. "Now the wig will stay on better, too."

Angelina snapped the band experimentally. "That hurts!" she wailed.

"Then don't do it again," her grandmother replied calmly. "You can look in the toy bin now. A boy in a sailor suit should have some toys."

Angelina was the only one with a wig. For Catherine and Laura, the Baroness had simply dulled the existing color, so that Catherine's hair no longer had reddish highlights, and Laura's was now a flat, uniform brown.

"It is better to make small changes, but important ones," the grande dame had explained as she worked. "Take out the gleam if it is there, in personality or hair, put it in if it is not."

"This is going to be fun!" Catherine said enthusiastically.

"That was Catherine talking," the Baroness reproved. "You are no longer Catherine. You are Patrice. She is seldom enthusiastic about anything. Patrice seldom talks, either. She looks sulky instead. That is convenient, since your French is not as good as Laura's, so you will have to keep quiet."

Catherine looked chastened and practiced looking sulky. It wasn't hard. The Baroness had somehow made her whole face exude sulkiness.

The Baroness continued her lecture. "You must *be* what I have made you, move like that person, think like her, and then you will be all right. Now, move for me as that person would move."

Laura and Catherine began to walk around the room, trying to think how Madame Merlin and Patrice would move. She would be stiff and upright, Laura decided, and straightened her spine. Catherine decided Patrice would be clumsy and immediately tripped over a box.

"Excellent," the Baroness said approvingly. "That looks just right."

Angelina played her role with no effort at all. She strutted up and down, boy-like, whipped a few toys around her head and made a great deal of noise steering trucks around the floor. She looked supremely happy.

Watching her, Laura remembered Antonia. The Baroness seemed in no hurry to tell her that Angelina was safe. She had promised to take care of the matter, but as far as Laura knew, she had not yet done so. Her delay seemed strange. Surely, Antonia had a right to know.

They were interrupted by light knock on the door, and Nigel entered. He stared at them in disbelief. Angelina was practicing horrid faces in the mirror, an activity Laura suspected she would do in both characters.

"Angelina?" Nigel asked tentatively.

"Je ne suis pas Angelina. Je m'appelle Henri," she said without turning, and began to talk to her image in voluble French. Swear words predominated.

"Arrete-toi, Henri!" Laura snapped without thinking. *"Tu es mechant!"*

Nigel's eyes turned to his grandmother, and a slow grin spread across his face. "I have never seen anything as good as this," he told her. "You must have been truly inspired."

The Baroness inclined her head graciously. "From you, that is great praise indeed. I believe your talents have almost surpassed my own."

"Sorry I couldn't be here earlier," Nigel mumbled, looking embarrassed as he always did when praised. "They wanted me to help in the barn, and I couldn't get away." An unspoken message passed between them, as so many messages seemed to between people in this house, Laura reflected.

Nigel bent down to hug Angelina. She squirmed in his grasp. "You make a great little boy," he told her. "And I really am very glad to see you again. We've been worried about you."

His eyes returned to Laura. "Thanks again for rescuing her."

Angelina stamped her foot imperiously and glowered at Nigel. *"Je ne suis pas* little," she objected strenuously, using a mix of French and English in her agitation. *"Je suis* big *et tres* strong."

"How did you learn to speak French so well, Angelina?" Catherine asked.

Angelina looked surprised. "I didn't *learn* it, silly," she answered. "I just speak it. Everyone does in France."

"Angelina lived in France for a time when she was younger," the Baroness explained, and Laura realized that this was the first time she had ever heard that venerable lady explain anything. She must know what was going on at the manor, at least some of it, but despite Laura's list of suspicions and questions, she had volunteered no information, only offered to help.

"There is time for a short rest now," the Baroness she said, glancing at her watch. "I shall have Nigel bring up some breakfast about nine o'clock. You will feel more alert after that." Laura certainly hoped so. She felt limp with fatigue. Last night, the Baroness had worked on them until almost midnight, and she had woken them before dawn this morning to continue. Transformations take time, she had explained.

"Please wear this while you rest," the Baroness went on, handing each of them an odd-looking object made of thin netting.

Catherine stared at it distastefully. "What is that thing?"

"A makeup preserver," the Baroness answered with a straight face, but a gleam of mischief appeared in her eyes again. "Put it over your head, like this." She drew the net over her head and face, demonstrating.

"Yuk," Catherine responded. "Do I really have to wear it?"

"It will help preserve your new identity while you sleep," the Baroness replied. "There won't be time for much repair work before the tour. It starts at eleven o'clock, and you must be prompt."

Laura immediately felt nervous. To go on the tour as herself was one thing, but to go as Madame Merlin, with Catherine alias Patrice as her daughter, was another. The idea of maintaining a new persona in French with other people watching was daunting.

Still, she had to do it. Tonight, she planned to search all of Torrington Manor, and the tour provided an excellent opportunity to grasp the layout of the house. She hadn't confided the search plan to the Baroness, however, or to anyone else.

Reluctantly, Catherine pulled the net over her head when they reached their room. Flinging her skirt and blouse onto a chair, she flopped on her bed and promptly went to sleep again. Laura took off her suit and hung it up carefully, rescued Catherine's clothes and hung them up too, so they wouldn't look rumpled for the tour. Then she put on her own net and sank into the other bed. Thoughts tumbled through her mind and dissolved into meaningless pictures, until finally she fell into a troubled doze.

Angelina, still dressed as a boy, awakened her. "I'm going to see some newborn puppies," she crowed importantly. "Mrs. Paulson is going to take me to her sister's to see the puppies, and she's going to give me tea with lots of scones and jam and cake. I'm to stay there all day and even the night. Gram says so." She ran off.

Laura struggled up through a fog of sleep and hauled herself out of bed, wishing she could wash her face in cold water and shock herself awake. She felt much too groggy to go on a tour, especially as Madame Merlin. Dutifully, she donned her costume, shook Catherine until she got up, and headed for the workroom.

Nigel appeared with coffee and tea and croissants. "The cook worked for some French people once," he told them, "and she's decided to offer these for breakfast instead of cold hard toast. I can get eggs and all the rest, though, if you want them."

"This is perfect," Laura assured him, happy to forgo a large English breakfast. The fish and chips still sat heavily on her stomach.

Nigel turned to Angelina, who had followed him into the room, eyeing the tray greedily. "Mrs. Paulson is downstairs," he told her, "and she says to hurry because the puppies are eager to see you."

"I will take you down," the Baroness said, holding out her hand. Angelina took it and skipped eagerly out of the room.

The Baroness reappeared just as they were finishing their meal. She looked more relaxed, as if she were a little less anxious about Angelina now that the child had been safely delivered to friends by her own hands.

"You must get back into character and not get out of it again," she told Laura and Catherine sternly as she administered some corrective touches to their faces. "It is best to remain in character even when you are alone. The tour participants will be here for dinner tonight, and if you revert to Laura and Catherine, becoming Madame Merlin and Patrice again will be harder. I have also invited Adrian Banbury, who is an old friend and often comes to our dinners. Guests enjoy meeting a country veterinarian."

Laura was alarmed. Dr. Banbury wasn't off her suspect list yet. Still, the Baroness must trust him to ask him to dinner, so he was probably all right. He wouldn't recognize her anyway if she played her part well.

"I wish I didn't have to go," Catherine grumbled. "Formal dinners are awful, and it will be hard to act like Patrice with everyone watching."

"Why don't you take a break and join Angelina and Mrs. Paulson?" Laura suggested. With Catherine gone, her search tonight would be much easier.

"They could take you to see the new puppies," she added as extra incentive. "You could even stay for the night if you want."

Catherine's face lit up. "I would love to do that," she said. "But I don't want to leave you if you need my help."

"All I'm going to do is take a long rest and practice thinking in French," Laura assured her. "So there's no need for you to be here."

"An excellent suggestion," the Baroness agreed. "I will ask Mrs. Paulson to pick Catherine up after the tour."

Catherine looked vastly relieved. "Great. Angelina will like it too. She's had a hard time, poor kid."

The Baroness returned to her lecture. "You must be especially careful if you see anyone who knew you before," she told them. "Antonia speaks fluent French and will detect a false accent in a moment. She is more perceptive than she seems."

She looked straight at Laura as she spoke, and Laura was certain she saw a warning in those penetrating eyes.

"I see," she said slowly. "Yes, I think I see." Her stomach gave an odd little lurch. The Baroness was giving her a clue; she was certain of it. She was saying: *be careful not to underestimate Antonia.*

Laura sighed, wishing the Baroness would simply explain what was going on. Still, there must be a good reason why she did not, so she would just have to find out for herself.

CHAPTER SIXTEEN

The tour participants gathered near the front door at eleven. There were five others: a stout German couple with a grown but still gangly daughter, a middle-aged Englishwoman in sensible tweeds, and a tall, stooped Scotsman with a thick beard and ginger hair. Laura was glad none of them were French. Even if she spoke the language well, she wouldn't fool a native for very long.

While they waited for Nigel, she tried to get into character mentally. *Think like Madame Merlin and you will be her,* the Baroness had told them. Catherine seemed to have managed the task already. Her shoulders were slumped, her mouth slightly open, her eyes pointed toward the floor. She kept fiddling with her hair, pulling strands in front of her face as if she were searching for insects.

Laura was irritated. "Arrete-toi!" she hissed. "C'est insolent!"

Catherine glanced at her, dropped her eyes again and shrugged. Really, Laura thought, she was almost too invested in her role.

Nigel began to speak, and after that she barely noticed Catherine, or Patrice. He was an excellent host. He knew the history of every piece of furniture, every object on walls and tables. He even talked about the floors and rugs. Laura listened avidly and had to rouse herself to remember that she was here to learn the layout of the house, and which rooms might be worthy of further searching. She also needed to look for escape routes and hiding places – and to remember that she was Madame Merlin, though Patrice made that fact difficult to forget. She was as obnoxious as possible, and Laura found herself reacting exactly as Madame Merlin would have reacted without even trying. Really, the girl was a trial! She realized that the thought had come in French, and was comforted. Perhaps she wasn't such a bad actress after all.

To her delight, Nigel even took them up to the attic. "This is called a box room," he explained as they entered a low-ceilinged room filled with old trunks, old pieces of furniture and children's toys in various states of disrepair. "Most old manor houses had one, and everything went into them in case the next generation had any use for them. There is probably more history here than in any other part of the house." He seemed to regret the statement as soon as he made it, and Laura eagerly added the box room to her list of places to search.

At the end of the tour, Nigel asked if anyone would like to see the cellar. Patrice held up her hand but didn't speak. Laura decided to ask for her. Seeing the cellar again was high on her list too. She was aching to examine some of the wine labels, never mind all those rooms she hadn't had time to explore before. Who knew what treasures they might hold – and clues.

Heavily accented English, she decided, would be most in character. Madame Merlin would do her best to speak the language of her host.

"*Ma fille...* my daugh-ter likes to go to *les caves -* ze cellars. *Elle s'interesse* in... in ze atmosphere, *n'est-ce-pas,* Patrice?"

"*Ah, oui,*" Nigel answered with a lift of his eyebrows that reminded her once more of his grandmother. "We will go then. But please watch your step. The stairs are very steep."

He ushered them to a door along the hall that led to the kitchen. Beyond it Laura saw stairs, which were indeed steep but not nearly as bad as the ones she had crawled up last night. She wished she had known about them before subjecting herself to the tunnel and the winding staircase, but at least she now knew there was another way to get from the cellar to the house. That could prove very useful tonight.

Nigel led them through the maze of the cellar, explaining the purpose of various rooms, if they had one, but mostly just letting them soak up the ancient and musty atmosphere. When they came to the room Laura and Catherine had entered from the big double doors, Laura noticed that the large chest of drawers had been moved back to its original place, covering the tunnel. She wondered if Nigel would mention that, but he didn't. Perhaps he was afraid some of the visitors would insist on exploring it.

The big freezer was still in use, she noted, if the long extension cord was any indication. An extra freezer would be handy, she supposed, when they had large groups of guests. She pulled it open a crack while the rest of the group was examining the old linen press, curious to see if anything was in it.

The lid fell back with a soft thump, and Laura felt the blood drain from her face. A hand was in the freezer, a human hand. She had seen it clearly sticking up past some large bags of ice. Barely visible beneath it was a body that almost certainly belonged to the missing cook.

Laura's stomach churned. To find her here, thrown carelessly into a cold freezer and surrounded by ice, was somehow far more terrible than finding her comfortably lain out in a bed and covered with a beautiful warm duvet. And the pale disembodied hand; it was sad, so horribly sad that anyone had been so neglected, so…so thrown away…

Laura stood perfectly still, her mind reeling with shock, and tried to recover her poise. She mustn't let anyone see how affected she was. Catherine especially mustn't see, mustn't look. Nigel, too - he didn't need this as well as the other burdens he must carry. The other tourists mustn't know, either.

She glanced at them and saw to her relief that they were still intent on the clothes press, all but the Scotsman, who was reading wine labels. Laura's gaze strayed back to the freezer. She had to look again, had to make certain she'd seen what she thought she'd seen. Easing the lid up, she peeked in. The hand was still there, and it was attached to a body that was faintly visible under all the ice.

Ignoring the sick feeling in her stomach and the faint ringing in her head, she straightened her shoulders and walked slowly toward the group. She was glad now that she had to be Madame Merlin. If she'd been Laura, she wasn't at all sure she would have been able to act normally.

She leaned over the linen press with feigned interest and then went on to the wines to peer at some labels. Catherine gave her a sharp glance that didn't look like Patrice, but she didn't speak, and Laura was relieved. By the time they reached the front hall again, she had recovered enough to thank Nigel in heavily accented English for a wonderful tour.

Walking into Murder

At that moment, Antonia came down the hall, and Laura was glad she had used English instead of French. Antonia would have picked up the lingering American in her French in seconds.

Antonia paused when she saw them, nodded briefly and moved on. Before she turned away, her eyes lingered on Laura's clothes, especially her fashionable purse. There was avarice in those cool eyes, Laura thought, and was vastly relieved. Her accoutrements had attracted Antonia, not her face. The Baroness had done a good job.

The small distraction helped to put the gruesome discovery out of her mind. So did Catherine's pleasure when she left to join Angelina and Mrs. Paulson. Laura was doubly grateful now to see the girl leave. Not only would it give Catherine a welcome break from being Patrice; it would give her a break from the strain of pretending she had nothing more than the general mystery on her mind.

She went back to her room and slumped onto a chair. The idea of rest seemed ludicrous now, but she could at least try to think. If there really was a body, she had to call in some kind of official help right away. But what if she was wrong again and there wasn't a body? Her mind had begun to work more clearly now, and she realized she could once again be jumping to unwarranted conclusions. The hand might not belong to a body at all, but to a mannequin, like the one Nigel had made of his grandmother. Now that she thought about it, the hand in the freezer had looked just like the fake grande dame's hands as she had grasped the back of the Victorian sofa, and she hadn't been able to see the body clearly enough through all those bags of ice to tell if it was real or not. Maybe for some reason Nigel put his models in the freezer. Perhaps it was part of the finishing process, to keep the wax from melting or to stiffen the body.

Laura shuddered. The only way to know with certainty was to examine the hand and whatever was attached to it more carefully. Before she called in the authorities, she had to be quite sure of her facts. She wished she could sneak down the cellar steps now and get the unpleasant task over with, but that could be disastrous. Someone would be bound to notice her. She would have to wait until tonight.

In the meantime, she decided to distract herself by using the computer at the local library. Thomas's dissertation on art forgeries in that horrible shed on the moor had been interrupted, and she needed to know more before she went on her search tonight. She was determined to find out more about Thomas, too, and this was the first chance she'd had to do it. Where was Thomas anyway? The man was like an elusive shadow!

To her surprise, the Scotsman who had been on the tour came into the library while she was struggling to find a useful site. He nodded politely and walked toward her. Laura nodded in response but then turned pointedly back to the computer. She didn't want one of the guests at Torrington Manor looking over her shoulder right now, with a large print headline announcing the latest art forgery techniques. What would he think?

To her horror, the Scotsman picked up a chair, placed it next to hers and sat down. He glanced with interest at the glaring headline.

"Ah! Art forgeries. Yes. Now where was I? I believe I had mentioned that the first major type is simply a good copy of a masterpiece which often fools even the experts. The second is the pastiche. A copyist uses typical scenes from paintings by a well-known artist to -"

"Thomas!" Laura hissed the name. Her first impulse was to slug him, but since she was in a library, she couldn't. Why hadn't she seen through his disguise before? He had obviously seen through hers, which was maddening. And how had he managed to look so old and uninteresting?

Thomas continued relentlessly, seeming to enjoy her discomfiture. "The typical scenes used by the copyist give the impression that this painting is also genuine. The third type is an original fake, which means a copyist imitates the style and subject matter of a well-known painter. Some painters are remarkably good at it. To sum up, any of these three types can and do fool professionals if they are well done, and they often are."

Laura gaped at him, speechless. She still couldn't find Thomas under all that bristly hair. Had the Baroness done him too? What a macabre sense of humor the woman had! And what talent.

"Of course, copies of masterpieces can be sold legitimately too," Thomas added with a grin that for a second made him Thomas again. "It's a good business for artists. Many collectors can't afford originals but will pay well for fakes they can pass off as originals to their friends."

Laura held up a hand of protest. "Enough," she said faintly. "I get the point. Forgeries are everywhere and not as hard to make as I'd thought." She sighed. "I will never look at a Rembrandt or a Vermeer with the same eyes again. Or for that matter, any of the paintings people gape at so reverently in museums."

"I could tell you all about what to look for to see the difference," Thomas promised, "but right now, the librarian looks annoyed."

Laura glanced at the desk. The librarian was indeed flashing fierce looks at them over her thick half glasses.

"How did you know who I was so easily?" she whispered. "I must be a lousy actress."

"If it makes you feel better, I don't think I would have known except for Catherine. She played her part extremely well, but I have an advantage. I saw her in a similar type of uniform not too long ago. Her mother's idea; it was a boarding school and Catherine left within a month. I couldn't blame her. The place was called a finishing school. Mostly they taught deportment and how to say the right things to the right people."

"Sounds ghastly," Laura agreed. "I gather, then, that the Baroness didn't tell you who we were."

"The Baroness seldom tells anybody anything, at least not directly."

"True," Laura agreed. "Is the Baroness responsible for your new and hairy appearance? And why are you disguising yourself?"

"I did most of it myself," Thomas answered breezily. "I've always wanted a beard, so every once in a while I don on one, just for the experience." He eyed her attire. "Do you occasionally crave stiff-looking designer suits?"

'No," Laura answered tersely. "I dislike them intensely. But why *are* you in disguise? I don't believe the beard bit. And ginger hair falling over your eyes and half your face is a bit much."

"You're in disguise, too," Thomas pointed out. "I imagine we have more or less the same reasons. What are yours?"

"I like donning new personas occasionally to remind me how pleasant my own actually is," Laura replied sarcastically. If he wasn't going to tell her what he was up to, she wasn't going to explain, either.

"Please could you continue your discussion elsewhere?"

Laura jumped. The librarian had come up behind them so quietly she'd never heard a thing. "Yes, of course, so sorry," she whispered. "I've got to go anyway," she hissed to Thomas. "I need to search the Baroness's supplies for an equally conservative outfit for dinner tonight."

'Not the sort of thing you generally bring along, I gather," Thomas remarked as they went outside. "Thank heaven," he added. "How about that green dress you had on before? I found it fetching."

"Thanks." Laura was pleased. He had actually noticed what she was wearing. Then she glanced at him suspiciously. Was he teasing her again?

"I gather you and Catherine have had some more unusual experiences since I last saw you," Thomas continued. "I must say that you demonstrate a great deal of ingenuity in extracting yourselves from difficult situations, but you seem to have an equal talent for getting into them. If I remember correctly, you did say you would keep my daughter out of trouble while I was away."

"I tried," Laura said, abashed. "All I did was get into the car Adrian had sent for us to take us to

Torrington Manor. That didn't seem dangerous until Roger pulled out his gun."

Thomas suddenly grasped her hands. "Laura, I really need you to understand that this is a job for professionals, not amateurs, however talented or brave they may be. Please, please, don't do anything rash."

"I never do things that are rash," Laura pointed out. "All I've done so far is go on a walking trip, and through no fault of my own I found a body and then I got chased with a knife and locked in a cottage, and then…"

She stopped abruptly. She wasn't about to mention the body in the freezer until she'd had a chance to make sure it really was a body.

"And then?" Thomas prompted. "What else have you found?"

"Nothing in particular," Laura hedged, and blushed. She always blushed when she lied. Maybe he wouldn't see through the makeup.

His suspicious eyes told her that he had. "You're a terrible liar," he commented, but to Laura's relief, he let the subject drop.

As soon as they returned to the manor, she went in search of a dinner outfit among the racks of clothes in the workroom. Her own clothes were much too comfortable for Madame Merlin to consider them appropriate. Funky, Donald had called them, which wasn't precisely true. Birkenstocks were not her style, nor were all those layers of shapeless cotton. The correct word, Laura decided, was individualistic. Her clothes seldom looked like anyone else's and she liked it that way.

Walking into Murder

In the end, she took the Baroness's advice and wore a black linen suit that looked impossibly conservative. Clip-on gold earrings that pinched her ears, black pumps that pinched her toes and a black clutch purse that did its best to pinch her fingers every time she opened or closed it completed the ensemble. Laura found herself wondering what Thomas would think.

A pang of guilt assailed her. Maybe she should have told him about the body in the freezer. He had seemed genuinely upset by his colleague's death, and he would want to know if the poor woman was lying in the freezer. But if she did tell him, he would try to stop her from looking in the freezer again - and from searching the outbuildings and the box room in the attic, all of which she was still determined to do.

2.

Laura took a last look in the mirror, hoping that Madame Merlin's image would inspire confidence. Then she marched downstairs for the requisite pre-dinner sherry.

Adrian and Thomas, alias the Scotsman, were both there and came to stand beside her. Adrian gave her one of his probing looks and asked in stilted French if she was all right. Had the Baroness alerted him to her disguise? Either she had, or those eyes were unusually perceptive tonight. They were also very worried, and she hoped he hadn't come to protect her.

"Ca va bien," she told him but his eyes only probed deeper. The man really did look as if he were trying to read her mind. It was most disconcerting.

Thomas managed to look mischievous despite the beard, making her wonder what he was up to. Like

216

Adrian, he sent her a searching look, but his purpose, she was sure, was to outwit her rather than protect her.

Dinner was announced and they filed into the dining room. The guests looked stiff and self-conscious, and Laura found herself hoping that Lord Torrington would serve a good wine to loosen them up. Otherwise this was going to be a very long dinner.

To her dismay, the Baroness directed her to a seat beside Thomas and directly across from Adrian. Now she wouldn't be able to escape those gimlet eyes or Thomas's effortless ability to disconcert her.

The torment began immediately. "*Je comprehend que vous aimez les cellars, Madame Merlin,*" Thomas asked in indifferent French spoken with what was probably supposed to be a Scots accent. Perhaps sensing the accent was off, he continued in English with a pronounced Scots burr. "I too am fond of cellars. So many treasures and secrets, are there not?"

"*Ma fille...my daugh-ter, aime les caves –ze cellars,*" Laura replied firmly, and pretended not to understand the rest of his query. Had he been watching when she looked into the freezer and noticed her shock? Probably he had, she realized sourly. Thomas was hard to fool.

"So the tour takes you to the cellars, does it?" Adrian remarked stiffly. "I am surprised. Rather musty down there, I should think."

Laura smiled at him as if he had said something brilliant. "*C'est vrai, Monsieur,*" she agreed. "*Tres moosty, ees it not?*"

Thomas tried another tack. "*Le box room aussi,*" he ventured. "*Il y a quelque chose tres interessante dans les attiques.*"

The Baroness regarded him quizzically. Thomas must know he couldn't fool her, Laura thought, so who *was* he trying to fool by playing the Scotsman? Adrian perhaps?

Thomas's next words, in Scots again, confirmed it. "I am very grateful, Baroness Smythington, for your introduction to Dr. Banbury. I found his gallery exciting, truly one of the most interesting collections I have come across recently."

The Baroness inclined her head graciously, and Thomas turned to Adrian. "I must thank you, too, Banbury, for permitting the tour."

"My pleasure," Adrian replied brusquely, but Laura was sure he hadn't enjoyed showing his collection to the Scotsman. Why had the Baroness helped Thomas to see the gallery? What was in there that Thomas wanted so badly to see?

Laura added a second visit to Adrian's gallery to her list of things to do. First thing in the morning, she decided. Vets were always up early.

"*Je suis tres interessante en les pientures des eighteenth century*," Thomas explained for Laura's benefit. She nodded politely.

Since his comment had elicited no response, he returned to his previous question. "*Les box room est tres interessante, n'est-ce-pas?*"

Laura nodded again and Adrian smiled at her protectively. No doubt he thought the garrulous Scotsman was irritating her – which he was. With a pointed glance at Thomas, Adrian answered the question instead. Laura was glad to see that for once Thomas looked discomfited.

"Yes, those old box rooms contain a host of treasures," Adrian told the Scotsman. "I remember spotting quite a valuable painting among the contents of an old house that were being auctioned off. Apparently it had languished in the box room for all those years. No one else seemed to realize its value, so I was able to procure it for an unusually low sum. Quite a scoop, if I do say so myself."

The German couple looked impressed and began questioning him in halting English about auctions. Adrian seemed to know a great deal about them, as did the Englishwoman, so the conversation became general

Laura took a deep breath, glad to have a break. Being Madame Merlin in public was exhausting, even without Thomas needling her and Adrian watching her obsessively. Twelve pairs of eyes were on her all the time. The Baroness's eyes were hardest of all to please. Occasionally, she uttered one of her discreet coughs, which Laura realized were to remind her to get back to her role.

Her reprieve didn't last long. "*Qu'est-ce-que vous faites après le diner?*" Thomas teased in a low voice, smiling seductively and edging closer. "*Je vous suivez, Madame! Tous le temps je vous suivez!*" He wagged a finger at her and shook his head flirtatiously, making his beard wobble.

Laura glared at him as she thought Madame Merlin would glare if she received an indecent proposal. He was saying that he would follow her wherever she went tonight, which really was indecent.

"*Arretez!*" she snapped under her breath, and pushed his hand away. He had actually had the temerity to place it suggestively on her thigh!

Walking into Murder

Fortunately, the Englishwoman began to pester Thomas with questions about Scotland, which as far as Laura could tell he answered very vaguely. She seized the opportunity to take a large gulp of her wine – not appropriate for a Frenchwoman, she knew, but an essential source of sustenance at the moment. By way of compensation she raised her glass to Lord Torrington and complimented him on the vintage. As before, he appreciated the gesture, since it provided an opportunity to drain his glass and refill it.

Dessert arrived, a blancmange that to Laura looked like a wobbly mass of protoplasm similar to those she sometimes saw washed up on beaches. She ate a bite to be polite and rearranged the rest on her plate.

The Baroness finally rose to her feet, signaling that dinner was over. Relieved, Laura trailed after the others to the library, where she tried to consume enough coffee to keep her awake for her search but not so much that it sent her scurrying for bathrooms.

The other guests went to their rooms soon after coffee was served, and Lord Torrington and the Baroness excused themselves to attend to various duties. To Laura's surprise, Thomas also left, without even teasing her again. She was instantly suspicious. Was he laying some kind of trap for her, maybe disguising himself anew and hiding somewhere so he could follow her when she left her room?

He had also left her alone with Adrian, who immediately confronted her. "I don't know why I allowed Charlotte to turn you into Madame Merlin," he said irritably, "but I hope you will go straight up to you room and lock the door. I don't trust that Scotsman.

There is something wrong about him. I can sense these things, you know."

Laura tried not to smile. "I'll be sure to do that," she promised, and ushered him firmly toward the door. Finally he left, still assuring her that she could call any time, day or night. Exhausted, she plopped onto a chair in a manner most unbecoming to Madame Merlin and then jumped up again. Time, finally, to get ready for her search.

She heard the murmur of voices through the half open door of Lord Torrington's study. He and the Baroness must still be in there. Laura decided to stop and congratulate them on the magnificent dinner. It seemed the right thing for a French tourist visiting their country to do. Her polite impulse came to a halt when she came closer to the study and the words took on meaning.

Lord Torrington was speaking. "Don't like the look of that French woman," he drawled irritably. "Too bloody inquisitive by half, with that long pointy nose of hers. Wanted to poke it into everything. Even wanted to go down to the cellar. Why must we have these people anyway?"

"We must have them for a while longer." The reply came in a voice Laura didn't recognize. "It's the best way right now. You know that as well as I do, darling. And the rest will be sorted out soon. We're almost ready." The voice was very soft, obviously female. It certainly wasn't the Baroness, but it didn't sound much like Antonia either. Was it possible that Lord Torrington had another woman in his life?

Lord Torrington uttered a contemptuous snort that seemed to imply the woman's argument was useless, and she continued her plea.

"Trust me, darling," she said, in a low, thrilling voice. "Just trust me for a little longer. I am quite sure my plan is working. Soon it will all be over." Rustling movements followed this appeal, and Laura was certain the woman had embraced Lord Torrington. She frowned. The woman had to be Antonia, in a loving mood for a change.

After a prolonged silence, more rustling sounds told her that the couple had finished the embrace, if there had been one, and would soon emerge. Pulling off her shoes, Laura ran up the stairs and hid behind the door of her room. She wanted badly to discover the identity of the unknown female.

She didn't have to wait long. Footsteps sounded on the stairs, and she peered out from behind the door. The hall lights were dim, but she had no trouble recognizing the two people. Her eyes widened in shock. Coming slowly up the stairs, hand in hand, were Lord Torrington and the Baroness.

CHAPTER SEVENTEEN

Laura lay on the bed, her mind – and her stomach - whirling. She was beyond shock now, or even disbelief. She felt as if she were caught in a maze, or a house of horrors with an endless series of twists and turns that had to be negotiated, and every choice led to a dead end where an unexpected and unwelcome sight awaited.

Lord Torrington and the Baroness holding hands was certainly an unwelcome sight, almost an unthinkable one. Did they really have a romantic relationship, or had she misunderstood the joined hands, the rustling sounds, the prolonged silence?

She must have, Laura decided. The idea of the Baroness indulging in an illicit and possibly incestuous liaison was simply unacceptable. Still, it did happen, as Shakespeare had known. Thinking of Shakespeare made her think of the Baroness again, but in another way. They were somehow connected; Laura was certain of it, but she still couldn't remember how.

Besides, she corrected herself, the relationship wouldn't be incestuous unless the Baroness was Lord Torrington's mother or sister. Maybe she was neither of those things. Maybe she was the mother of his first wife. In that case, though, she was involved in a relationship with her dead or divorced daughter's former husband, and that seemed almost as bad. It was also completely out of character for the grande dame, Laura decided stubbornly.

Too restless to stay still, Laura stopped trying to work it out and got up again. She had been afraid she would be too exhausted to stay awake until the house was quiet enough for her to begin her explorations, but that was no longer a problem. How could anyone sleep after a day like this one?

The only thing to do was to get on with her search. If someone was still awake, she could hide - even better, listen to their conversations. She looked at her watch, saw that it was almost midnight, and decided to get ready. The black suit was too tight for running or climbing, both of which she might have to do, and the outfit she had worn for the tour wasn't much better. But what else was there? The clothes she had come in had been taken away for washing. The only garment she had left was the one the Baroness had given them last night, the one that looked like a hospital gown. That would have to do.

Grimacing, Laura put on the gown, slung her dark jacket over it for warmth as well as a pair of grubby black tights and the spare hiking socks she always kept in her pack. Her clothes, or lack of them, would be an additional reason to make certain no one saw her. She would head for the cellar and tackle the most unpleasant task first, she decided, then search the outbuildings and the attic if she still had time.

She peered into the hall, but neither heard nor saw anyone, so she crept cautiously down the back stairs, heading for the cellar entrance. Its door creaked when she opened it; she held her breath, waiting, but no reaction came. She peeked into the kitchen just in case, but it was empty. The outer door, however, was ajar, and Laura hesitated. Someone must be out there, perhaps letting the dogs out for the night. They would give her away quickly if they spotted her.

Walking into Murder

A shadowy figure near the barn and the prancing figures of the dogs told her she was right. Lord Torrington, she realized with surprise. He must have left the Baroness shortly after she had seen them. There certainly hadn't been time for a romantic interlude. Maybe she had misread the situation after all. Then she remembered how young the Baroness had looked the evening she and Catherine and Angelina had emerged from the workshop closet, and wondered anew. Maybe Antonia was only playing the role of Lady Torrington but wasn't really involved with the lord of the house. The Baroness had too much spirit to put up with a new young wife or mistress, if she did have a prior claim. But why, then, had Antonia come?

"Come on, you idiots." Lord Torrington's voice was loud and genial. "Just for a while; then you can come out again. Biscuits if you come quickly."

Jasper and Lucy understood what *biscuit* meant and loped after him eagerly. Laura breathed a sigh of relief. He was putting them in their run, not letting them out. She wasn't afraid of the dogs anymore, but her search of the outbuildings would be easier without them. Maybe she should take advantage of the fact that they were locked up and search outside first, instead of starting with the cellar. Probably she was procrastinating because she really didn't want to look in the freezer again, but it did make sense.

Grabbing a few hunks of bread in case the dogs were let out again before she had finished, she slithered out the door into the shadows. As soon as the clang of their gate told her they were safely confined, she sprinted for the trees.

Walking into Murder

Whistling cheerfully, Lord Torrington strode toward the kitchen door, went into the house and slammed it behind him. Laura heard the sound of a key turning. Why hadn't she thought of this possibility before? Now she would be forced to go in again through the cellar. She shivered. Perhaps it was just as well. She would have to go right past the freezer and further procrastination would be impossible.

She crept cautiously toward the barn. A low light shone over the door, but the interior was in shadow. She stared in, eyes straining. Nothing moved and she heard no sounds, so she dared to turn on her flashlight. Hay littered the dirt floor and she could still see tracks where something heavy had been dragged across it. Thomas, perhaps? She followed the trail. It ended in a large clear space, as if someone had lain there. She turned her flashlight on it and was immediately rewarded. A stout stick, almost a club, had been thrown carelessly aside beside the cleared space. Was that the stick Morris or Stewart had used to knock Thomas out before rolling him in the carpet?

Laura knelt to examine it more closely and discovered a sticky-looking substance that could be blood on one end. She touched it delicately with a finger. Definitely sticky. Did that mean it was fresh blood? Or just reddish mud? How long did blood stay sticky anyway?

Laura shook her head. She had questions in abundance but no answers. Maybe the loft would provide more clues. She struggled up the steep ladder, trying to hold the flashlight in her teeth. It fell out half-way up and dropped to the ground. Irritated, she went down again to retrieve it. This time, she put it in her

226

pocket and climbed up with only the faint light from the doorway to guide her. Cobwebs stuck to her face and hair as she progressed. At the top she fell across a bale of hay and bumped her head on a large object. Fumbling for the light, she shone it around. Her eyes widened in astonishment. A pair of gold-framed paintings was propped against the large chest in front of her, paintings that looked exactly like the ones Thomas had examined so carefully in the study. They had the same dark background, the same slouched, almost caricature-like figures and touches of bright color.

Of course, Lord Torrington could have decided to sell them, hoping they had value, as Thomas had implied. There was no crime in that. She would look in his study later, Laura decided. If the two paintings were still there, one or the other of the sets had to be copies.

The photo of the three paintings she had found on the moor came to mind. They weren't the same as these; she was almost sure of that, so there must be another group of three. Remembering her forgery lesson from Thomas, she ticked them off: one was the original, one a copy to sell as an original to a shady or just a gullible buyer, the third might go to a buyer who could tell all his friends it was an original. A very profitable business, Laura decided. But who did the copies? And who got the profits?

Other paintings were scattered around the loft. Laura examined each in turn but quickly realized she didn't have enough light to see them clearly, nor did she have the knowledge and expertise to come to any conclusions about them. All she could do was try to remember each one in the hopes that if she saw another like it, she would know they were the same.

She sighed, discouraged. Every time she found clues, she only became more puzzled and more aware of her ignorance.

One of the dogs yapped, reminding her that time was short. Hastily she climbed back down the ladder and left the barn. Lights from a cottage-like building beyond the stable that she hadn't noticed before caught her attention. Maybe Stewart stayed in the place; he didn't seem to sleep in the house. She hoped Roger didn't stay there as well. She had no desire to confront him again.

A murmur of voices came from one of the open windows of the building. Laura crept closer, wondering if she dared to peer in.

"A bit more of the brown on the dress, I think," Antonia's voice said. She sounded tense, as if she were waiting for something to happen.

"I wish you'd stop looking over my shoulder like that," came the irritable reply. "You make me nervous and then I get the lines wrong and the color muddles."

"I'm only trying to help," Antonia snapped. "All I want is for you to finish the thing so we can get out of here."

Laura dared to peek in. Stewart stood in front of an easel, paintbrush poised over an unfinished painting of a woman in an old-fashioned bonnet. A completed painting was propped on another easel beside him. Even to Laura's inexperienced eyes, it was obvious that the finished painting was of museum quality. Even more remarkable, Stewart was making an identical and similarly lovely copy of it. The expression on the woman's face was the same, the colors perfect; the whole feel of the painting was right.

Walking into Murder

Laura stared, captivated. Maybe an expert could see differences, but she certainly couldn't, except for the fact that the copy was incomplete. Now she knew why there had been paint under Stewart's fingernails when he'd taken them to the cottage. Stewart really was a painter, and if she was any judge at all, an excellent one, or an excellent copyist at least. Did Thomas know that?

"Go sit down!" Stewart said sharply to Antonia. She complied, her lips set in a tight line.

"How long do you think it will take to finish?" she asked from her seat. "I'm not prodding," she added in an effort at conciliation. "I just need to know so that I can plan."

Stewart put down his brush and turned toward her. "Frankly, I am much more concerned about Angelina than about finishing this," he said, gesturing to the painting. "Don't you think we have enough already? I don't like the thought of her up there with a pair of strangers."

"We have been over this before," Antonia replied grimly. "Angelina is much better off up there than around here. She is quite safe, and the American women will look after her. Why do you think I told Roger to take them up there, for heaven's sake? I knew they were the types who would take care of a child. Angelina will be thrilled to order them about and eat all that food we put in. She'll be perfectly happy there for days if need be, so do stop worrying about her. She is not in any danger."

Laura gritted her teeth. So Antonia was the one who had ordered Roger to take them to the cottage! What a devil the woman was! She was also clever, diabolically so – though not clever enough to know that Angelina was no longer in the cottage. Stewart didn't know Angelina had escaped, either. That was one small victory.

Why hadn't the Baroness told her? Obviously, because she didn't want Antonia to know. Did she suspect that Antonia was involved in Angelina's disappearance?

Antonia must not be underestimated, as the grande dame had said. She was right. No doubt Antonia was also the person who had instructed Morris and Stewart to knock Thomas out, wrap him in a rug so no one would see him, and take him to the shed for further questioning. Morris was provided as the icing on the cake, so to speak, with his persuasive knife.

Stewart turned back to the painting. "I still don't like it," he muttered. "The whole thing has gone too far, got too complicated. It's too much, having to do all these copies as well as the ones we've already got. Maybe if Morris hadn't come and tried to horn in…"

"Morris won't be a problem any longer," Antonia interrupted harshly, her voice sharp with anger. "I can promise you that. The bastard had the nerve to steal his own sister's child, hide her in that cottage and then try to get money from me to get her back! That was the last straw for me. He is out of my life. Out for good!"

"I'll be happy to see him go, no doubt about that," Stewart commented mildly as he put down one brush and applied tiny gentle strokes with another.

Antonia smiled maliciously. "It gives me great pleasure, I can tell you, to turn my erstwhile brother's little plot with Angelina around and use it for my own ends. And what *I* get out of it will be more than petty cash."

Stewart, however, paid no attention to this further diatribe. He was bent over his painting again, concentrating, as if all other considerations had left his mind. Laura watched him, impressed by his skill. Still, she suspected he was merely a pawn in the forgery operation, despite the fact that his astonishing talent supported it. He just wasn't the type to run a complex organization. She felt oddly sorry for him. It wasn't easy to make a living as an artist, even for a good one, and he had probably been forced to do copies instead. A legitimate market did exist for them, as Thomas had said, but the world of illegal art undoubtedly paid more. The temptation would be great.

Stewart turned toward her briefly and for the first time the light shone on his face. Understanding came in a flash. That was where she had first seen Angelina's unusually pointed chin – on Stewart. He must be her father. No wonder he was so concerned for her. That meant Lord Torrington wasn't her father. Did he know? He acted a lot like a father, but that could just be concern for a child in his keeping, however unwillingly.

Antonia sprang to her feet and began to pace, and Laura decided she had better leave. The paces were getting too close to the window. She backed away and crept silently into the trees again.

The cellar had to be next whether she liked it or not. She had a few answers now, but not enough. She still didn't know who had murdered the cook, who had put the masks on the victim's face, who had turned down the lights, who had drugged Lottie, who had cut the telephone wires…. The list ran on and on. She might as well get busy.

Walking into Murder

Headlights glowed on the track that led to the manor and Laura heard a vehicle speeding up the hill. She ducked into the first building she saw, the old tool shed she had explored the first morning after her arrival. How long ago it seemed!

She sniffed. The place smelled odd, like disinfectant. Feeling her way into a corner, she crouched there. She heard a car door close; feet crunched along the gravel drive, and a squeaking noise she couldn't identify made her jump. Total silence followed. Laura dared to turn on her flashlight again. She might as well look at that box of rat poison again and see if any had been used recently.

She trained her flashlight on the shelves, then on the room. The container looked exactly as it had before. Tools were stacked against the walls or hung on hooks in orderly rows. Whatever his other faults, Roger was neat. The tools were clean, too – except for one shovel, which had been tossed down carelessly in the middle of the room. Laura bent over to look at it, wondering why Roger had left it there. Maybe he had been interrupted, or someone else had used it.

It was definitely not clean. Laura knelt to examine the shovel more closely and saw that it had been used quite recently. The dirt on it was damp and stuck to her fingers. She frowned. It seemed to her to have the same consistency as the substance on the stick she'd found in the barn. Could it be blood? What did that mean?

A bundle of old burlap bags lay under the shovel. She had seen other bags like them neatly folded in a corner, so why were these here? Laura touched them gently. There was a lump under them, a large one. Probably an animal, she realized. Roger had either killed or found a dead animal and brought it here to be buried in the morning. That would explain the strong disinfectant smell. Perhaps Roger wanted to mask the scent of decay.

Curious to see what the animal was, Laura pulled back one of the bags. Her hand shot to her mouth in a desperate effort to hold back a scream. Morris! Morris was under the burlap bags.

His eyes were staring sightlessly and he was very, very dead.

CHAPTER EIGHTEEN

Laura pressed her hand against her mouth, this time to hold back an urge to vomit. What was Morris doing here dead? She'd thought he was in the hospital. More urgently, who had killed him? Roger? Or could Antonia have done it?

Laura gagged. She had to get out of here. The person who had killed Morris could still be nearby. Stumbling to her feet, she almost ran out of the shed.

She had to alert someone too. There was no doubt in her mind that Morris had been murdered. His head was smashed in at the back. Had Roger done it on Antonia's orders? Was that why she had told Stewart that Morris was out of her life for good?

Against her will, Laura visualized the scene. She saw Roger hitting Morris with the stick to knock him out, then dragging him here and hitting him again with the shovel, maybe because Morris tried to struggle. He couldn't struggle very hard, though, with his injuries. He didn't have his knife for protection, either. She had it; she still had that horrible knife...

Panic rose in Laura's chest. She had to get into the house, into a place where there was light and safety. But how? The door was locked. The cellar. She would have to go through the cellar doors. She staggered toward them.

To her surprise, the double doors were already open, and a faint light showed inside. Could that mean whoever had killed Morris was hiding down there?

Laura crept closer and stood perfectly still, listening. Gradually, her breathing steadied and her heart stopped pounding. Rationality began to return, too. The murderer wasn't likely to be lurking in the cellar. That would look too suspicious. He or she would either be long gone or trying to act as normal as possible. Besides, right now getting into the house was more important. Whether she could force herself to look in the freezer when she got there was another matter. She was beginning to think Thomas was right, that this wasn't a job for amateurs. What she ought to do was to go straight up to her room.

On the other hand, it would be very useful to find out who was in the cellar and why. She had to go that way in any case. She would just look around quickly and then go straight to her room.

Laura approached stealthily, ears and eyes alert. When she reached the top step, she stopped. Still nothing. With infinite caution, she placed her feet on one step, then the next, until she reached the bottom. Then she came to a halt again. Unbroken silence. She stepped inside the cellar and stood still for a long moment while her eyes adjusted to the dim light. Then she began to walk slowly toward the freezer.

Without warning, her arm was seized and twisted behind her back. A hand came over her mouth, and something cold and hard was pressed against her back. Just like the last time, Laura thought hysterically, except worse. That was a gun!

Terror gripped her. She felt faint, and a surge of nausea rose in her throat. She tried desperately to wriggle away, but the man held her still harder. Opening her mouth as far as possible, Laura bit down hard.

"Ouch! Cut it out!" a voice ordered - Thomas's voice. Laura's jaw went slack. Thank heaven. Though why she should be thankful, she didn't know. Maybe Thomas was a member of this gang after all – or the person who had killed Morris.

"If you'll promise to be quiet, I'll let you go," Thomas hissed. "If you don't…" An unnerving pressure against her ribs made his meaning clear.

Laura nodded fervently, and he released her. A wave of dizziness almost made her fall. Thomas reached out to prop her up. His beard had disappeared, she realized, and that ghastly wig. He looked a great deal better without them.

A look of disgust spread across his face when he saw who she was. "Oh, Lord, not you again!" he exclaimed. "I thought there was something familiar about the way you felt, especially with those cobwebs and bits of straw all over you. Every time I think I've finally nabbed one of the villains in this case, it turns out to be you. And that is the most improbable outfit I have ever come across. Black stockings and a hospital gown? Really, you are matchless!"

"That's not very flattering," Laura snapped. "And I wish you would stop pointing that gun at me if you don't think I'm one of the villains. I've had enough trauma for one night."

She brushed ineffectively at the offending straw and cobwebs. "I've always suspected *you* were one of them," she went on. "You're still the most likely candidate to mastermind an art scam. If you aren't, I think it is past time you told me what really is happening. And don't start prevaricating again."

Thomas regarded the gun in his hand with surprise. "Sorry. I was so disappointed I forgot I was still holding it." He tucked the gun into a holster at his belt. "As for

236

being the mastermind, I can only say there have been times when the thought has crossed my mind. As you imply, I am ideally placed."

He sighed dramatically. "However, I am basically a conservative type who upholds the side of law and order. I suppose I should pull out a badge to prove it, but unfortunately I don't have one. A business card perhaps?"

He reached into his shirt pocket but came up empty-handed. "I guess I didn't bring them," he said lightly. "A bad idea, you know, in case the villains get hold of me. I can't lie as well if they know who I am."

Laura felt like screaming. Couldn't the man ever be serious? Gritting her teeth, she tried again. "Are you telling the truth? And please for once can you be serious? I really need to know. It's important."

She reached up to swipe defiantly at her eyes, which against her will were filling with tears. Her hand came away streaked with makeup, and heaven only knew what she had deposited on her face. She felt herself swaying again.

Thomas reached out to steady her. He looked into her smudged face, frowning, and then pulled her against him.

"Laura, it's all right! Seriously, I really am an art detective, as Catherine describes it, and I am *not* a part of this organization. I am trying to find out who is for the Baroness, so we can put a stop to it. She discovered who I was when I came looking for Catherine, and she asked me to help her. That is the truth, I promise."

His voice was very somber and Laura believed him. Relief washed over her, and she felt tears start again.

She pulled away, unwilling to let him see. Thomas turned her toward him again and peered into her face.

"You really are upset, and not just by me," he said, startled. "You're white as a sheet under all that make-up. What is it, Laura?"

"Morris," she answered tonelessly. "I found him in the tool shed just now. Dead. His head was bashed in."

Thomas was appalled. "And then I come along and grab you. I wonder you're still on your feet at all. You must have nerves of steel."

"I don't," she admitted. "I thought I was going to throw up on you when you grabbed me – or faint. It's a good thing I didn't."

"No, you bit me instead." Thomas examined his hand, which still showed the indentations of her bite. "At least you didn't draw blood. I suppose I should be glad you didn't spew all over me instead, or faint dead away like one of those old-fashioned maidens in books."

Laura smirked at him, feeling better now that they were sparring again. "Just a little love bite, you can tell your friends, so you don't have to explain that a lady with pancake makeup and cobwebs all over her got the best of you by protecting herself with a good old-fashioned bite despite the fact that she was just about to faint."

Thomas grinned. "You don't give up no matter what, do you? Rather like one of those terriers that go after rats."

Laura glared at him. "That is distinctly unflattering. Can't you ever say anything nice about me?"

Thomas considered. "Well, I could say that I have never known anyone before who so regularly came across bodies." He frowned. "That reminds me. I must go have a look at Morris. It's best not to delay, lest someone else have an interest in him."

The remark reminded Laura of the cook. "I found another one too," she admitted, feeling almost sheepish. "Or I think I did."

Thomas gaped. "Another? Who?"

Footsteps on the stairs from the kitchen interrupted them. Laura froze in terror. It could be Roger. That had probably been him driving up in the van. Worse, Antonia and Stewart might have seen her creeping away and followed her. In her present costume, it wouldn't take the canny Antonia long to penetrate her disguise.

Thomas, however, seemed unconcerned by the approaching footsteps, which suggested that he knew who was coming. Laura wasn't sure whether that alarmed her or reassured her.

"We have an unexpected visitor," he said lightly as the newcomer approached. "I must say, Baroness, you've done a masterful job. I wouldn't have recognized her during the tour except for Catherine. I'd seen her in a get-up like that before."

Laura's muscles relaxed. Not Roger or Antonia. But what was the Baroness doing here at this time of night?

"What do you think we ought to do with her?" Thomas inquired mildly as the Baroness came up beside them. She looked tired and rather sad, but as unruffled as ever. Laura looked at her own disheveled clothes and wondered if she would ever be able to achieve that look of dignified order.

The Baroness considered the question. "Actually, I rather expected Laura would be unable to resist the temptation to look around the manor," she answered calmly.

"I should have expected that, too," Thomas agreed. "She is not the sort to leave stones unturned in her search for the truth."

"An excellent trait," the Baroness pronounced. "Do not be so flippant, Thomas."

They were certainly on good terms, Laura reflected, which seemed to confirm that they were on the same side. Still, she mustn't jump to conclusions about the Baroness. Like everyone else in this household, she was clearly not the person she pretended to be.

"I suppose we shall have to ask you to remain while we supervise the task for which we have come," the Baroness said soberly to Laura. "It will not be a pleasant task but it is a necessary one."

Thomas nodded. "Yes, I suppose you're right. My preference would be to send Laura back to her room with stern orders not to come out again, but I doubt very much she would heed that sensible advice."

Laura decided it was time to speak for herself. "No, I do not intend to return to my room," she said crisply, "and if there is a task to be performed, I suggest you get on with it before other members of the family interrupt you. Antonia and Stewart are in the small cottage behind the barn. He is copying a painting, a portrait of a woman in a bonnet. I also thought I heard Roger coming in the van a few moments ago.

Thomas and the Baroness regarded her with respect, and Laura was gratified. She decided to take a chance: "Does your unpleasant task have something to do with the body in the freezer?"

To her disappointment, Thomas looked unsurprised. "So that's your other body," was all he said.

The Baroness didn't look surprised either. "Ah," she said. "I wondered if you had looked during the tour. I trust you kept your discovery to yourself?"

Laura's heart sank. So there really was a body. She had wanted badly to find only a mannequin when she looked again.

"Yes," she answered sadly. "I made sure no one else noticed, and I haven't spoken of it to anyone. Neither Catherine nor Nigel should see such horrors, nor should any of the other guests," she added with a shudder.

"Thank you, my dear," the Baroness replied gravely.

"However, I need to know how the woman got there and who put her there," Laura's voice was firm.

"I did not put her there, nor did I kill her," the Baroness stated. "I am not certain who did but intend to find out. Thomas is helping us in that regard. Does that satisfy some of your concerns?"

Laura nodded. It was simply impossible not to believe the grande dame. She turned to Thomas, awaiting his explanation.

"I certainly didn't kill her, but I too intend to find out who did. I found her only a short time ago. I didn't actually see you look in the freezer during the tour, but I did notice that you had seen something that shocked you badly. Naturally, I came down here to look for myself as soon as I could. I called the authorities right away, and then I went upstairs to notify the Baroness.

"I imagine the person or persons who did kill her are becoming very nervous about leaving her in the freezer any longer," Thomas added. "I intend to put her into safe hands before they can dispose of her in their own way." Once more, his voice had that implacable note. And so it should, Laura thought fiercely. Someone had to defend the poor woman, even if she was dead.

The Baroness coughed gently. "I believe I owe you at least a partial explanation for the events you have witnessed since you arrived in Torrington Manor," she said unexpectedly. "I shall endeavor to be brief.

"When Lord Torrington and I first came to the manor, it was in very bad repair. So were many of the town's finest buildings. Traditionally, the owners of the manor helped to maintain them as well as the manor. The necessary repairs, however, were costly, and we sought a means of raising the funds. A friend informed us that many of the paintings in the manor were very old and could be valuable. That proved to be the case. We hired Stewart, who is a master copyist as well as a painter in his own right, to make copies of some of them to use in the manor, and provided him with the basic equipment needed for the task. We wished to maintain the integrity of its furnishings, in appearance if not in reality. We also wished to avoid drawing attention to our plans and so conducted the transactions very quietly."

Which, Laura thought, was a discreet way of saying they didn't want the villagers or the general public to know that some of the paintings at the manor were now fakes, thus reducing the manor's value as a tourist attraction. No wonder Lord Torrington wanted to avoid the police, especially the local ones.

"The originals were sold, and with the proceeds we were able to begin the necessary restorations," the Baroness continued. "Some have already been completed, in particular the church and much of the manor."

She paused, and Laura waited patiently. "It seemed an excellent plan," the Baroness went on almost wistfully. "We did not think many people would notice that some paintings were copies, and indeed that was the case until Thomas arrived. At the same time we were able to fulfill our traditional obligations to the village and the villagers. They are in a sense part of the family heritage, and we take the responsibility seriously. Unfortunately, others with more personal motives discovered that there was money to be made at Torrington Manor, and we have thus far been unable to dislodge them. Once Thomas understood what was happening, he agreed to assist us in this matter. We hope to resolve it soon."

"As I said, I came here to look for Catherine," Thomas put in, "but I was also aware that a number of old masterpieces were entering the market that had originated in this area. That is all I knew, so it was just luck that brought me to Torrington Manor – and the fact that I was aware that Catherine had been sleeping in the barn."

"An excellent piece of luck for us," the Baroness commented dryly. "We were rather at our wit's end."

"Not surprising," Thomas agreed. "It's a nasty business." He turned back to Laura. "As soon as I arrived, I realized that I had stumbled into the proverbial hornet's nest. One of the first things I found was a sophisticated laboratory in Stewart's cottage for preparing canvases and mixing the paints required for forgeries – far more sophisticated than the Baroness had provided. I called a colleague, who told me that paintings passed off as originals, but which some experts thought were forgeries, were also turning up on the market. They, too, seemed to come from this area, possibly the manor. They had sent one of their investigators here, posing as a cook." He gestured toward the freezer, and Laura shuddered.

Tires crunched on the gravel driveway. "Ah, that must be the police," Thomas said with satisfaction.

"If you have no objections, Thomas, I believe I shall go upstairs now," the Baroness said. "I find I am not quite prepared to watch after all."

Thomas nodded sympathetically. "No need for you to stay, Baroness. I just thought it important that you know."

"Thank you, Thomas." The Baroness turned to Laura. "I must make one more request before I leave, and that is that you to keep your knowledge of what you have seen and learned tonight to yourself."

"Of course," Laura agreed. "I will not speak of any of this to anyone." The Baroness inclined her heat in thanks, and went slowly up the stairs.

"You can leave too, Laura," Thomas said, concern evident in his voice. "In fact I wish you would. This isn't going to be pleasant to watch."

Laura shook her head. "I feel a kind of responsibility since I was the one who found her – twice. I can't bear to walk out now," she admitted.

"If you're sure," Thomas agreed, walked over to the freezer. "I suppose I should get it open for them. Not so many fingerprints that way." Slowly he lifted the lid.

Steeling herself, Laura followed. Thomas stared in, total disbelief in his face. "The body's gone!" he said. "It's gone!"

Laura peered into the freezer. He was right. There was no sign of the body at all.

CHAPTER NINETEEN

Laura sat up abruptly, awakened by a rustling at her door. A piece of paper slid under it and she blinked. Who was sending her messages through a door?

An explanation presented itself and she lay down again. Thomas had probably left it there to let her know what happened after she left the cellar. He and the two men with the stretcher had gone to the tool shed to collect Morris instead of the missing cook, so the men hadn't come in vain. She had elected not to join them.

Time enough in the morning to read it, Laura decided. If she looked at it tonight, she would be wide awake again for hours. Yawning, she nestled under the duvet again and tumbled back into sleep.

When she woke again, it was light outside and this time she knew she wouldn't be able to go back to sleep. Might as well get up and get going, she decided. Remembering the note, she went to the door but found nothing there. Had she dreamed the whole thing? She must have, since there clearly was no paper. Her brain really must be overworked.

She stood and stretched, wishing she could talk to Thomas and find out what had happened directly from him. It seemed cruel to wake him, though. Between Morris and looking for the missing body, he probably hadn't got to bed until a few hours ago.

That poor woman – she seemed fated to disappear over and over again. The strange thing was that Thomas had left the cellar for only a short time after he had found the body, to alert the Baroness. That someone had managed to steal it in that short time was positively spooky. The man who had done it must have been nearby all the time, waiting for his chance.

And it probably had been a man, Laura realized. Only a very strong person could have hauled the stiff body out of all that ice.

She wondered if she should knock on Thomas's door anyway, just to check on him. He accused her of getting into trouble, but he was worse. She compromised. Instead of knocking, she turned the knob gently and eased the door open a crack. To her relief, he was sleeping soundly. She left him to it and went to get dressed.

A glance at her watch told her it was just past six-thirty. An excellent time to pay Adrian a visit, she decided. She wouldn't be expected, and she could surely wangle her way into the gallery again. Mrs. Paulson might even feed her some breakfast. She could walk. It couldn't be more than about two miles to Adrian's house, and walking always cleared her head.

She looked at herself critically in the mirror. The alterations to her face were holding up surprisingly well. She did her best to fix them up and then donned her hiking clothes, which fortunately had been returned. Holding her muddy boots, she went quietly downstairs.

She went first to Lord Torrington's study, to see if the two paintings were still there. A glimpse from the doorway told her that they were in place. That meant either they or the ones in the loft were forgeries.

On impulse, Laura stopped in the dining room to look at the portrait over the sideboard. The woman seemed to stare back at her, tantalizingly like the Baroness and yet not her in some subtle way. What was the difference, besides youth?

Walking into Murder

The article about the society wedding she had found on the moor came into her mind. It must have been about the Baroness, since the bridegroom was a Baron, but she had no idea why the cook had thought the article important. What had it said exactly? *The tall and glamorous bride was lovely in her satin and organdy dress* was one sentence, but that didn't tell her much. Maybe the next had meaning. *A lacy veil covered the bride's face and she held a bunch of wild-flowers picked that morning from a meadow, making her resemble Ophelia, one of her favorite...*

Memory returned with a physical jolt that made Laura gasp. She reached for a dining room chair and sat down heavily. A barrage of images poured in, with all the emotional impact they had aroused more than two decades ago.

Charlotte Gramercy. The Baroness was Charlotte Gramercy, the magnificent young actress who had burst upon the London scene over twenty years ago and then disappeared as abruptly as she had come. She had intelligence, discipline, grace and above all talent, the critics had gushed, and she played Shakespeare and Ibsen better than any actress in living memory. As Ophelia, she had brought tears to even the most hardened eyes. She had truly been a legend in her own time.

Laura rose again, too dazed by the discovery to sit still. She had seen the revered actress only once, when she had gone to London during a student year abroad. Charlotte Gramercy had played Ophelia that night, and the memory of her performance had never left Laura. Ophelia and Lady MacBeth had been the actress's favorite roles. They were polar opposites – the woman so cruelly used by her lover, and the woman who used her husband without scruple to further her ambitions. Charlotte Gramercy had played both brilliantly.

What an honor, to know her in person! But what had happened to her, and why had she so suddenly left the theater? Why was she so anxious to conceal the fact that she had once been Charlotte Gramercy? And how on earth had she ended up here, mistress of Torrington Manor?

Noises on the floor above roused her. Someone else was up. Laura tiptoed down the hall and slid out the back door. Donning her boots, she made her way out to the road, carefully avoiding the outbuildings. After this, she would leave body-finding to people who were more inured to such gruesome discoveries.

It was a beautiful morning, and Laura almost forgot the manor and its problems as she listened to birds singing in the hedgerows and took in the scents of trees and flowers. She was surprised when she saw Adrian's house already coming into view. It really was an attractive place. The golden Cotswold stone gleamed in the early morning light, and the flower gardens all around it were full of color.

Adrian was standing, lost in thought, near the well-tended front garden. When he spotted her, he called out an enthusiastic greeting.

"Laura! What a marvelous surprise! I am delighted to see you, even as Mme Merlin, though I must say I like Laura better. Come on in and we'll make a cup of coffee, or tea if that's your preference."

He came up to her as if to embrace her, but seemed to think better of the impulse and took her arm instead.

"You are up early. Good. I like early risers. I can offer you some breakfast if you like, though we are on our own in that, I'm afraid. For some unaccountable reason Mrs. Paulson decided to stay at her sister's last night."

"Are Catherine and Angelina with her?" Laura was vaguely alarmed at the thought that they were alone in the house with Adrian. He was well-meaning, but probably not very adept at handling children.

"They are indeed," Adrian assured her. "I suspect their desire to stay with her involves puppies," he added with a twinkle.

She asked for tea and looked around curiously as Adrian prepared it. The kitchen wasn't at all modern, but it had all the necessary appliances and looked efficient and comfortable.

"I do hope the remainder of your night was peaceful," Adrian remarked as he filled the kettle. "I did not like leaving you with that Scotsman in the house."

"He seems to have left," Laura assured him. "He didn't even spend the night." It seemed an easy way to make the Scotsman disappear, along with his beard and wig.

"I am immensely relieved." Adrian presented the tea with a flourish. Laura thanked him and eyed the cup dubiously. The tea was weak and lukewarm. The coffee he poured for himself, however, looked hot and strong. Maybe she could pour the tea unobtrusively down the drain and have coffee instead.

"I can make some breakfast," she offered. "What do you usually have?"

"Adrian looked perplexed. "Whatever Mrs. Paulson puts out for me," he answered vaguely. "I guess I don't pay much attention. I'm not much of a cook, I fear, especially when it comes to breakfast."

"I can make some toast," Laura suggested.

"Toast sounds excellent," he replied. "Then I can show you around the house. All you saw was the gallery last time."

Laura was delighted by the idea, not because she had any great desire to see the house but because Adrian had so conveniently provided her with an opening to ask if she could see the gallery again.

"That would be nice," she agreed. "I would especially enjoy seeing your gallery again before I leave."

Adrian looked dismayed. "I do hope you aren't leaving soon. I had hoped we could pursue our acquaintance over the next few days."

"I'm not sure of my exact plans," Laura hedged, "but I should be back in London soon to get ready for a course I am teaching there."

Adrian beamed. "Excellent. Then we can surely look forward to more time together. I had not known you were staying on in this country, and I am very pleased that you are." He settled back in his chair. "Business brings me often to London," he went on. "Perhaps we could take in a show together, or go to a few galleries."

"That sounds very nice," Laura temporized, wondering if it had been wise to tell him she was remaining in England. Did Adrian view her as a friend or as an extension of his favorite lady?

When they had finished, Adrian stood up. "It's time for me to show you my house and then to see my little collection again. After all, you are in it, are you not?" he added playfully.

Laura smiled tepidly and took a last sip of her coffee, which she had covertly substituted for the insipid tea, and followed him out of the kitchen. He led her on a tour of the house, providing the history of each antique they passed. He owned quite a few: china, furniture, even some tapestries. Adrian's tastes were far richer than those of a simple country veterinarian, Laura reflected. Where *had* the money to pay for all these treasures come from?

"Now, the gallery," Adrian said at last, taking the key out of his pocket. The hushed note of reverence, the possessiveness, came into his voice again, and again, Laura felt that small shiver of apprehension.

Despite her uneasiness, the extraordinary glow of the room captured her as it had before. She stood in the middle of the room, gazing around her.

"Where did you find them all?" she asked. "That must have been a job in itself."

Adrian's answer was illuminating. "It wasn't that difficult, actually. Many of them came from the manor. That's how I got started. I had come into some money when my wife died, and when I saw the wealth of treasures languishing in the manor and heard that Charlotte, the Baroness I suppose I should say, and Lord Torrington wanted to sell some of them to raise funds for restorations, I couldn't resist the opportunity to embark on what had been a life-long dream."

He must have been the friend who had alerted them to the value of their paintings, Laura realized, and wondered why the Baroness hadn't said so.

"I was also lucky," Adrian went on. "The Torrington ancestors who had collected the paintings had tastes very similar to my own – and had the wits to hide their treasures during times of trouble, to keep them out of the hands of their enemies."

"Were they Royalists?" Laura asked, struggling to remember the history books she had read in preparation for the trip.

"Well done!" Adrian was impressed. "Yes, they were Royalists, and they were Catholics as well. They committed the double sin of wanting to see the monarchy restored and of sheltering fugitive priests, who were presumably hidden with the paintings."

"Priest holes," Laura murmured, thinking of the tunnel Angelina had showed them. "So then you bought some of the paintings?" she prompted.

Adrian nodded. "We had various pieces appraised, and I bought most of them once my late wife's estate had been settled." He smiled, remembering. "Actually, I was their first buyer. We had a wonderful time together. We did some bargaining, more for the pleasure of it than anything else, and arrived at a good deal all around."

"When did your wife die?" Laura asked sympathetically.

Adrian's face closed. "Three years ago," he relied shortly. Perhaps her death was a subject that was still hard for him to talk about, Laura thought. He seemed an unusually sensitive man.

"I am sorry," she offered. "That must have been hard."

Adrian shook his head. His lips compressed into a thin, disapproving line. "No, it wasn't in fact. We had little in common except a love of art, and even that had begun to change. She preferred a different style," he added with a touch of contempt.

Laura couldn't think how to answer. Adrian obviously had very firm views on artistic taste. She began to feel sorry for the dead wife, whose money had been used to pay for an art collection she might not have liked.

"She was a semi-invalid for a long time," Adrian went on. "Finally she took a little too much of whatever it was the doctors gave her. I could hardly blame her. It seemed the sensible thing to do. She was not very happy."

Laura could find no response to this honest but callous assessment, either. Perhaps veterinarians were so accustomed to putting animals out of their misery that it seemed normal for a suffering woman to choose the same path.

Adrian had moved away from her and was staring up at his favorite painting, the one of the lady with the big hat that he now called Laura.

"It seems so extraordinary that I should actually find you, the living embodiment of the woman I have always adored," he said, his voice awed. "I have always believed that we must consider seriously what such coincidences might mean. Life does not offer them often, does it, my dear?" Smiling, he grasped her fingers and pressed them to his lips.

It was a courtly gesture and well-intentioned, but Laura was still alarmed. Adrian sounded as if he were about to declare his love on the spot. She had better defuse the situation fast.

Pulling her fingers firmly away from him, she pointed to the painting. "She's much better looking than

I will ever be," she commented wryly, hoping that humor would have the desired effect. "All her hair is in place, her clothes aren't filthy, and she hasn't had her face rearranged by the Baroness."

Adrian was offended. "This is not a joke, Laura," he reproved her. "It is the woman inside who counts."

Laura sighed. Humor was clearly not the right approach. "No, I suppose it isn't funny," she answered. "I'm sorry, Adrian."

Adrian's face relaxed and he became his genial self again, though now his affability seemed forced. "I guess I do get carried away," he admitted. "I feel so strongly about paintings, and that makes me go overboard with you as well."

Laura nodded, but the statement didn't reassure her. It was definitely time to leave. "I should get back to the manor," she told him. "They will wonder where I am."

Adrian seemed not to have heard her, or if he had, he paid no attention. "We must look at some of the others," he said, and stopped in front of another portrait of a woman. Laura was relieved. At least it wasn't the one he thought was her this time.

"Can you believe," he said in the same wondering tone, "that I once thought she was the right woman for me?"

Reluctantly, Laura examined the painting. The woman was beautiful, but there was a secretive air about her that made further speculation difficult.

"She's very beautiful," she offered tentatively.

"Oh, she is beautiful." Adrian was contemptuous. "Certainly she is that, but can you see the coldness, the ambition?"

"Who is she?" Laura asked.

"She was a French aristocrat," Adrian replied. "I believe she went to the guillotine."

Laura shuddered. "Poor lady. That seems a cruel fate."

"I suppose it is," Adrian agreed. "Perhaps, though, she deserved it."

"No one deserved to die that way," Laura objected.

Adrian didn't answer. "Of course, it's Antonia, too," he remarked instead. "You can see that, I'm sure."

Laura sighed. This business of putting people into paintings was becoming tedious. "I suppose there is a resemblance," she replied doubtfully. The woman didn't look much like Antonia to her, except that they were both blond and had classic profiles.

Adrian shrugged. "There is no doubt about it," he asserted, dismissing her response. He shook his head ruefully. "I thought at first she was so perfect, but of course she was just her trying to wangle herself into my life so she could get her hands on my money. She was wrong, very wrong, not the right person for me at all."

She had been right. Adrian was the other man Maude hadn't wanted to talk about. Laura could understand her loyalty. Adrian might have strange views about his paintings, but he was basically a decent man.

Adrian returned to the first painting. "How do you know she wouldn't be wrong for you, too?" Laura asked mischievously. The moment the words were out of her mouth, she regretted them. Adrian didn't have a sense of humor about his paintings. Or her.

Adrian was shocked. "Laura," he said reprovingly. "I am surprised at you! Surely, you know that is impossible."

Laura sighed again. She certainly didn't know that, but she could see it was useless to argue the point. "It was only a joke," she said instead.

"This is not a joking matter," Adrian rebuked her sternly. "I have told you that once already. Please do not forget it again."

Laura's temper snapped. "Oh, for goodness sake, Adrian, stop talking to me as if I were the Victorian woman in that picture. I am not! I am Laura, who is quite a different person. I do appreciate your collection, and I am grateful to you for showing it to me, but now I really must get back to the manor."

Adrian stared at her. A strange expression came over his face, as if he had finally understood something, but he didn't speak.

"I must leave now," Laura repeated, edging away from him.

The expression vanished. "Of course," Adrian replied courteously. "I can't think what got into me, to rattle on like that way. I got carried away."

That was an understatement, Laura thought, but she was glad that he seemed to be himself again.

"Never mind," she reassured him. "These last days have upset everyone. There has been so much going on, and so much that is unsettled."

"I imagine it will all be settled soon," he replied calmly. "Things have a way of working themselves out."

Unsure what he meant by that, Laura headed for the door. The two paintings she had noticed on her first visit were beside it, and she glanced up at them. Even a quick scrutiny told her that they were the same as the paintings in Lord Torrington's study as well as the two in the loft.

Were they the reason Thomas had gone to such lengths to see the gallery?

The painting next to them caught her eye. Unless her memory was faulty, it was the same as the trio of paintings in the photograph she had found on the moor. One was here, where were the other two?

A painting on the other side of the door came into focus. It was a portrait in the same style as the one she had seen Stewart copying last night. Surely, it must be by the same painter. The woman wore the same type of clothes, almost the same bonnet. The whole look of the painting was remarkably similar. If one of an artist's paintings could be copied, others could too, and there was an empty space beside this one that could have held the original she had seen in Stewart's cottage…

Laura's heart seemed almost to stop as a terrible suspicion entered her mind. Was that how Adrian was financing his acquisitions now? Had he gone through his wife's money and turned to peddling fakes to satisfy his obsession? After all, no one knew about the originals hanging anonymously in his small gallery, and to sell Stewart's copies as originals would be easy. Was it Adrian who had provided the funds for the new and more sophisticated equipment Thomas had found, so Antonia and Stewart could make near perfect forgeries? Was Adrian the man behind the criminal operation?

A glimpse of Adrian's face told her that he knew what she was thinking. "I am so sorry," he said, but his voice held no hint of remorse. "It would be better if you had not understood."

Fear thudded into Laura. She backed away, afraid to take her eyes off him.

Adrian gave a deep sigh. "You are not what I thought you were," he added sadly. "I suppose no one is, are they?"

"No," Laura answered as she turned and sprinted for the door. Adrian took three fast steps and caught up with her.

"I fear I shall have to keep you here for a time," he told her, grasping her arm firmly. His eyes were cold now, cold and dangerous.

Wrenching herself out of his grasp, Laura ran - straight into a pair of waiting arms.

CHAPTER TWENTY

Thomas disentangled himself gently from Laura and sauntered into the gallery. "Good morning, Banbury," he said. His voice was debonair and unconcerned, and infinitely reassuring to Laura. "I am glad to find you at home. Hope you don't mind if I join you?"

He looked around the gallery with interest. "This is indeed a fine collection," he added admiringly. "I have seldom seen its equal. "This painting is particularly fine," he added, pointing to the one he and Laura had seen in the trio of photographs. "I believe I saw one very like it recently in a barn, of all places."

Laura felt dizzy with relief. She sat down in the nearest chair, then got up again and walked unsteadily back to Thomas. His eyes were fastened on Adrian and he didn't look at her, but she felt him touch her arm lightly.

"Perhaps you would like to make us all a cup of coffee? There are various matters we need to discuss."

"Yes, I can do that," Laura replied, but she didn't move. Thomas was trying to get her out of the room and therefore out of danger, but she wasn't going to disappear meekly and leave him to handle Adrian alone. In this latest incarnation as master criminal, the man was terrifying.

A large frying pan, she thought irrationally. She could grab one from the kitchen, come back, and hit Adrian over the head with it.

She looked at Adrian and changed her mind. He had slumped into a chair, and he looked numb, without strength, as if both body and mind had ceased to function. Pity flooded her. He must realize that he had lost.

"I wonder if you showed your collection to a friend of mine?" Thomas asked the unresponsive Adrian. "She was a great lover of art, though she often worked as a cook."

Adrian's head jerked up. "I didn't kill her. I have never killed anyone," he said, and there was a note of pride in his voice.

"Ah!" Thomas replied, studying the other man. "Not even your wife?"

Laura was startled, but Adrian only frowned irritably. "She was dying anyway," he snapped. Laura's moment of pity dissolved.

Thomas changed the subject. "How many did you let them copy?" he asked, his tone businesslike now.

"I have told them they cannot take any more," Adrian answered with finality. "Antonia is not a good woman," he added as if that explained his decision. Disapproval was thick in his voice.

"No, she is not," Thomas agreed. Laura noticed that he placed a finger very delicately against the corners of a few of the paintings. Did he suspect that some of these were fakes too?

"Well, Banbury," Thomas said finally, "shall we adjourn to the kitchen? I believe Laura will have finished the coffee by this time."

He shot Laura a reproachful glance. "Don't you ever do as you're told?" he muttered under his breath.

"Seldom," Laura replied, but she went ahead of him into the kitchen and rummaged in the cabinets for the coffee.

"Coming, Banbury?" Thomas called back as he followed her, but Adrian didn't move. His voice answered faintly from the gallery.

"Did you send her here?" he asked. "Was she a spy too?"

"No," Thomas called back, but his eyes were on Laura. "Laura came here of her own free will, presumably because she wanted to see you. Despite strict, and I had hoped persuasive instructions not to pay you a visit," he added sotto voice to Laura.

She turned, surprised. "Instructions?"

Thomas shook his head wearily. "The note under the door. Surely you took the trouble to read it?"

Laura was indignant. "But I didn't get it! I thought I saw something white being pushed under the door, but when I went to get it this morning it had disappeared, so I thought I had dreamed it."

Thomas stared at her. The annoyance in his face shifted to astonishment and then to dawning horror.

"I've had it all wrong," he said incredulously. "Of course! He couldn't really be the one, could he?"

Without waiting for an answer, he grabbed Laura's arm. "We have to get back to the manor now, pronto. Are you coming?"

"But what about Adrian?" Laura was baffled by the abrupt mood change, and his question. "What do you mean, he can't be the one?"

"That he can't be the one behind all this, as we'd thought," Thomas answered impatiently. "Come on! I'll explain as we go. If that is, you wish to come," he added stiffly.

"Of course I do!" Laura expostulated. "Do you think I want to be left behind with this... Well, I don't know what he is, but I would just as soon get out of here."

"Good," Thomas sounded relieved. "Let's go. I've got a car." He grabbed her hand, and they sprinted for the front door.

Tires squealed on the driveway just as they reached it. Thomas pushed Laura behind him and opened the door a crack. He closed it again fast.

"Too late," he whispered, and thrust Laura into a closet, leaving the door slightly ajar. She struggled to find footing among a welter of boots and space to breathe instead of being smothered by coats, then stood perfectly still, waiting. She heard Thomas run back the way they had come, heard the front door open. Peering out through the coats, she saw Antonia and Roger creeping down the hall. Both of them were holding guns.

They went past her toward the gallery, and Laura opened the door a bit wider, straining to hear. There was no need. Antonia had found Adrian still sitting in the gallery and didn't bother to lower her voice.

"We have a deal, you bastard," she said furiously, "and you are going to abide by it. How dare you tell Stewart he can't do any more? I have a buyer who is prepared to pay very well, and he is not the patient type."

Adrian didn't answer, seemed not even to hear her. That made Antonia even angrier. "What is the matter with you, Adrian?" she demanded. "I want answers, and I want them now."

Still, he made no response. "Cat got your tongue?" Antonia taunted.

Walking into Murder

Unable to resist the urge to watch as well as listen, Laura crept noiselessly down the hall and peeked around the study door. She was rewarded with a view of Antonia, hands on hips, furiously challenging the unresponsive Adrian. Incongruously, she was clad in a close-fitting silk dress that emphasized every curve in her slender but well-rounded body. Roger stood beside her, looking immensely pleased with his role as Antonia's sidekick. There was no sign of Thomas.

"He talked a good deal before whenever I came to see him before," Antonia told Roger in a taunting voice Adrian was also intended to hear. "In fact, he told me the whole story of his life and all about his late unlamented wife, every time we got into be-"

Roger's unpleasant snicker cut off the word and finally aroused Adrian from his stupor. "Be quiet!" he thundered. "I would like you to leave now," he added, with a dignity that to Laura sounded pathetic.

Antonia paid no attention to the command. Her fit of temper had passed without a trace, and she was intent now on the paintings. Her eyes were practiced as she scrutinized them, assessing, judging.

"We'll take those three," she said to Roger. "Be a dear, will you, and bring the replacements from the van?"

Obediently, Roger lifted the three paintings from the wall and carried two of them out of the room. Alarmed, Laura pressed hard against the study wall and watched him trudge down the hall and out the front door.

Adrian came to life. "What are you doing?" he asked frantically, rising from the chair to place a protective hand on the remaining painting. "That is mine and you cannot have it. I paid for all these paintings. They are mine."

Antonia laughed. "Don't worry, darling," she told him. "Roger has gone to get you another. It's in the van."

"But that one's a copy," Adrian protested.

Antonia shrugged her elegant shoulders. "Yes, darling, it is, but then, so are most of these." She gestured toward the other paintings with a sweeping arc of one silk–clad arm. "I switched them, you see, while you were at the surgery. This particular client wants the real thing and it isn't easy to fool him."

Adrian looked stunned. "But Mrs. Paulson... Mrs. Paulson wouldn't let you in," he stammered. "And you haven't a key. Only I have a key."

Antonia gave a mocking laugh. "Darling, I don't wait for people to give me keys! I just take them and get copies, and if I can't..." She gave a deep and theatrical sigh. "Well, that's one of the things Morris did well. He was helpful in certain ways, I admit. And no, I don't suppose Mrs. Paulson would let me in. She never did seem to like me, even when we were... shall I call it close? But she always goes to her sister's teashop at ten o'clock sharp, to help with the food and that sort of thing. Had you forgotten?"

Adrian looked at her in horror, then at his paintings. "Do sit down again, darling," Antonia urged him. "You look apoplectic."

Adrian moved slowly toward her, his face tight with fury, and she shrugged again. "I can't see why you're upset," she said coldly, leveling the gun at his chest. "You never noticed the difference before, did you darling, so what difference should it make to you now?"

Ignoring the gun, Adrian came closer. "I could not care less if you kill me," he informed her through gritted teeth. "I have one desire now and one only, and that is to place my hands around your throat and squeeze until all the life has drained from your worthless body."

Antonia took a step backward, but her voice held neither fear nor shock when she answered. "But darling, I wasn't going to shoot you," she taunted. "I was going to shoot her." For a moment Laura thought she had been seen, and she shrank back. Then she saw Antonia gesture toward the painting of the woman with the big hat, the one Adrian confused with her.

"I know that one's your favorite," Antonia went on remorselessly. "She wouldn't look nearly so well with a bullet in her face, would she? Or shall it be her eye?"

Laura's fists clenched convulsively, as if, like Adrian's, they wanted to wrap themselves around that pale throat. The woman was a devil. She had not known anyone could be so cruel.

"Let's see," Antonia went on in the same tightly controlled voice. "The right eye or the left?"

She had gone too far. Adrian sprang at her, unstoppable now. Several things happened all at once, and Laura was never able afterwards to put them in their proper order. She felt the coldness of a gun at her back, heard a gun explode, saw Thomas catapult into the room, Adrian crumple to the floor, and fell heavily to the floor herself as Roger sprang at Adrian, or perhaps Thomas, and heard another sharp report from a gun.

For a moment she thought she had been shot. There was a terrible pain in her chest. Then she realized that Roger had slammed her against the doorknob in his hurry to get at Thomas and Adrian.

265

Walking into Murder

Dragging herself upright, Laura stared into the gallery. Adrian was still on the floor, with blood seeping from his head. The others were standing, Thomas on the far side of the room, Antonia and Roger facing him. Both of them were pointing their guns at his chest. Their backs were toward her.

Laura grabbed the only potential weapon in sight, a heavy plaster bust, and crept into the gallery. Maybe she could hit one of them on the head and even the odds a bit.

Roger foiled her. "The nosy walker lady's behind you," he informed Antonia in a laconic bad-guy voice that was clearly meant to impress.

Laura frowned. How did he know who she was through her disguise? Probably her hiking clothes, she realized. From behind, they would give her away.

Antonia stiffened. "I thought she was still at the cottage. How did she get here?" Her voice sharpened. "Where's Angelina?"

"At the manor, I guess," Roger answered. "I heard her there. Can't keep that kid quiet for a minute. I saw this lady there, too, sneaking through the bushes like she always does. Must have escaped somehow."

Antonia flushed with fury. "Why didn't you tell me, you fool!"

Roger looked surprised at her anger. "You didn't ask," he pointed out, "and anyway I thought you already knew."

Antonia gave him a long look and sighed audibly. For once, Laura sympathized with her. Roger might be obedient, but he wasn't very bright.

Antonia recovered quickly. "Keep him covered," she told Roger crisply, and turned to point her own gun at Laura.

"Well, this is a surprise," she said sarcastically. "You don't give up, do you? You could have stayed safe and sound in the cottage where I so thoughtfully put you, but no, you had to get out so you could play detective again. I gather you had some help from the Baroness, or was it Nigel?"

Laura didn't answer, but Antonia seemed not to notice. "I thought I had him out of the way, too," she went on with a disdainful glance at Thomas. "Heaven knows I did my best to convince him that Torrington Manor was not a healthy place to be."

She uttered another theatrical sigh. "And then, in spite of all my efforts, both of you had to come back so you could get yourselves killed. I suppose we will have to oblige you, but remember that it's your fault, not mine."

The gleam of satisfaction in her eyes infuriated Laura, and she decided to ignore both the gun and Antonia. Still holding the bust, she went to Adrian and knelt beside him. He wasn't dead, only unconscious, she discovered with relief. A deep gash on the back of his head told her that he'd been hit hard, no doubt by the butt of a gun. His pulse and breathing were ragged, though, and there was blood seeping out underneath him, which made her suspect he'd been shot, too. She dared not move him to find out.

She rose and walked slowly over to Thomas. "I might have known," he muttered morosely as she approached. "Simply can't stay away from the action."

Laura flinched. He looked terrible. His face was ghostly, and one arm hung limply by his side. "Were you shot?" she asked fearfully, putting the bust down beside him.

"Just a bump," he assured her bravely, and quickly spoiled the effect of this manly dismissal. "Actually, it hurts like hell," he complained as Laura examined the arm gently, looking for blood or some other sign of injury.

"There's no blood," she pointed out.

"No," he said grimly. "Dislocated shoulders do not bleed, but if you would prefer some blood, I imagine that can be arranged."

"I am sure it can," Antonia agreed unpleasantly.

Laura ignored both of them. "I took a first aid course once, and learned how to put them back in place," she volunteered, hoping she remembered the technique and had sufficient strength.

Thomas looked at her appraisingly. "How many times have you done it? And how long ago was that course?"

"I haven't actually had to do it on someone whose shoulder was out," Laura admitted. "I guess the course was about ten years ago."

Thomas turned a greenish color. "Thank you, but I think I'll wait for the doctor. I have had it done once or twice and it isn't pleasant even in experienced hands."

"If you two have finished discussing your health," Antonia interrupted irritably, "you might want to remember that two guns are pointing at you and unless you start paying attention, your life span might be rather too short to worry about things like shoulders and first aid."

Just as she finished this cold-blooded little speech, a sound distracted all of them. Laura looked up and saw the painting of the woman with the big hat sliding in slow motion toward the floor. It landed at a rakish angle on its side, so that the woman was on her back. Maybe she had tired of standing after so many hundreds of years, Laura thought with more than a touch of hysteria, and had decided to try lying down for a change.

The bullet had hit the wall just above the painting, she observed more rationally, not an eye. Antonia wasn't a very good shot.

Her head whipped back to Antonia, and she almost cursed aloud. Both Antonia and Roger had been caught off guard for a few seconds, and she had missed a heaven-sent opportunity to leap at them and maybe grab one of the guns. Now it was too late. Antonia was covering both of them while Roger pulled a length of rope out of a bundle he had brought in with him.

"Tie them to the chairs," Antonia ordered coldly. "I want them out of commission until we've finished. Then put them back to back and tie their hands together, too." The thought seemed to please her and she smiled.

"Him first," she added. Roger nodded and pushed Thomas into one of the chairs Adrian had thoughtfully placed in the room for viewing purposes. None too gently, he grabbed one of Thomas's wrists, then the other and twisted them behind him. Thomas promptly fainted and fell forward onto the floor.

"Stop that!" Laura screamed. "He's got a dislocated shoulder!"

Roger shrugged and looked at Antonia. She too gave a shrug, an infinitesimal one that made the gesture seem positively evil.

"Prop him up on the chair and tie him anyway," she instructed the endlessly accommodating Roger. "Then get on with her."

Roger complied. Looking pleased with his assignment, he tied Thomas to one chair, her to another and then tied their hands together with vicious jerks. Rubbing his hands together in satisfaction, he went back to Antonia to await further orders.

Thomas looked as if he had fainted again, and Laura pressed his hands gently. A brief returning pressure told her that he was still conscious. That was a start. He wasn't going to be able to give her much help, though, which meant she had to get them out of this predicament on her own. She should have taken a knife from the kitchen, she thought glumly. If that was in her pocket now...

An image of Morris's knife came into her mind. It was still in an outside pocket of her pack, she remembered, and her pack was only a few feet away. If Antonia and Roger left the room, she could try to get to it - if Thomas had the strength to walk the few steps with her. They would have to drag the chairs, too.

Antonia's voice interrupted. "We have only an hour, so we shall have to work fast," she told Roger in a businesslike tone. "Are you sure they're securely tied?"

Roger looked hurt. "Of course," he replied, his voice sulky.

Antonia slid her arm into his. "Don't be cross with me, Roger," she pouted. Her full lips parted in a sultry smile. "You know how I depend on you. You're the only one I can trust, you really are. Everyone else..."

She let the sentence dangle, but Roger got the point. He glowed with pride, and Laura felt a little sick. What did he expect from Antonia, and why did he obey her so slavishly? Did she reward him in the usual way, or was she canny enough to dangle promises in front of him like carrots so he would keep waiting on her, asking for nothing but praise, until he was no longer useful?

"We are going to have to work together, you and I," Antonia went on, contriving somehow to sound as if she and Roger were alone in a bedroom. "If you take the heaviest paintings and I take the others, we can be out of here quite quickly. That's why I wanted to make sure they were tied."

"How do you know which ones are the originals?" Thomas asked innocently, and Laura jumped. She had thought him barely conscious.

Antonia shrugged her slender shoulders. "I keep track."

"So do quite a few other people," Thomas observed with a maddening drawl. "There's been a lot of interest in those paintings."

Antonia whirled on him. "What do you mean?" she demanded.

Thomas began to shrug in imitation of her gesture, grimaced and thought better of it. "The Baroness, for one, Lord Torrington for another."

"Oh, them." Antonia was dismissive. "They don't know what's going on. Charlotte just thinks she does and Bark hasn't a clue. Hasn't much of a clue about anything else, either. Never did have."

"I gather you've known him for some time," Thomas remarked.

Antonia looked at him sharply. "That is none of your business," she snapped.

"Perhaps you're right," Thomas answered lazily. "It's just that I've been in France recently and come across some documents - interesting ones, I must say, and quite unexpected. Still, I've had them checked out..." He left the sentence unfinished, watching Antonia's face carefully.

Her reaction was fast and furious. "Shut up!" she told him. "You talk too much. You know too much, too."

"Want me to shut him up?" Roger asked eagerly.

Antonia considered. "Not just yet," she told him. "I rather enjoy watching his face. But believe me, you will get your chance to shut him up - permanently."

Thomas persisted. "You haven't answered my question. How do you know which ones are originals?"

"It's not hard," Antonia said indifferently. "Stewart's good, one of the best, but I can still tell."

"I suppose you can," Thomas conceded. "It's just that I've been keeping an eye on the manor recently, and I've seen the Baroness and Lord Torrington replacing the paintings you've brought from here with their copies. Clever, I thought. The originals from here are replaced by Stewart's fakes, and the fakes by the originals all over again. Hard to tell what's what now."

So that was why Nigel had been helping Lord Torrington yesterday! Laura was astonished. The family must have known all along what Antonia and Roger were up to, and were replacing the originals they had stolen from Adrian with their own copies. That meant Antonia could be sending out fakes she thought were real to her discriminating buyer. But what did they hope to gain from that?

Antonia had the same thought. "I can't see what they would want to do that for," she replied, but she sounded worried now.

"Maybe," Thomas drawled, "they want you to get caught."

Antonia stiffened. "Charlotte and Bark know better than to do that," she snapped. Her eyes were intent on his face.

"Perhaps you are right," Thomas said. "But maybe they are no longer concerned about it. They could have information of their own."

Antonia stared at him, grasping a meaning in his words that Laura couldn't. "I see," she said finally, and gave him a look so hostile that Laura cringed.

"At any rate," Thomas went on blandly, "are you still sure you know which paintings are the originals?"

Antonia turned to examine the paintings still hanging on the wall. For a moment she looked uncertain; then an odd expression came over her face. It was part acquisitive, part triumphant, part gloating, and part just nauseating. Laura looked away in distaste.

Roger was staring at the paintings, too. "What about the ones in the van? Are they the ones we want or not?" he asked, confused. "Shall I bring them in here?"

Antonia laughed. It was a chilling sound. "Oh, I think we'll just keep them *all* for ourselves now that we're not sure which is which," she cooed, giving his arm another lingering pat. "Adrian had his chance and lost it, so we needn't bother with him anymore. Besides, we might as well sell them all and get twice the money. After all, no one seems able to tell the difference anyway. Don't you agree?"

273

Roger glowed again, and she favored him with a brief peck on the cheek. Thomas glowered.

Adrian groaned suddenly, surprising all of them. Antonia glanced down at him. "I do wish he would wake up," she said, and there was genuine disappointment in her voice. "You shouldn't have hit him so hard, Roger. I would have enjoyed watching his face as his precious art collection disappeared. He crossed me, and he should pay with more than just a bump on the head. Now it's too late."

She stared down at Adrian for another moment; then her face became businesslike again. "No more talk," she said crisply. "We have work to do and it's getting late."

Roger went into action, struggling manfully with the heaviest painting. Antonia confined herself to the smallest one, and they went out the door.

"Quick," Laura whispered. "There's a knife in my pack. Can you stand up? I can grab it if you come with me."

"I'll try," Thomas stood, swaying slightly. Together they shuffled crab-wise to the pack, their chairs dragging noisily behind them. Feeling like a contortionist, Laura bent backward as far as she could and felt for the knife. Her stiff fingers finally found it. Trembling with the effort, she bent her knees as far as she could so she could get some leverage to pull it out.

"Got it," she breathed, and they shuffled back again.

They had just managed to sit down again when Antonia and Roger returned. Laura hoped no one would look behind her and see the knife in her hand. She hoped she wouldn't drop it either. Her fingers felt numb.

Antonia regarded her suspiciously, but she said nothing and picked up another small painting. Roger took two this time; together, they went out again.

Laura sawed as carefully as she could at the rope between their hands. Thomas winced and she knew she must have cut him. If only she could see what she was doing!

"Sorry, it's an awkward angle," she apologized, struggling to maneuver the knife into a more effective grip. The strain on her arms and shoulders was already intolerable. How Thomas was enduring it she couldn't imagine.

Twice more Roger and Antonia went out. Laura sawed through a few strands each time, until finally the rope that tied them together came apart.

"Hold our hands together with the frayed pieces inside, so they can't tell," Thomas whispered as they heard Antonia and Roger returning. Laura obeyed as best she could, and they held their hands close together. The touch was comforting, and Laura was very glad not to be here by herself.

The feeling didn't last. Only three paintings were left, the one that had fallen, and two others on the wall. She and Thomas didn't have much of a life span unless they could get free soon, Laura thought gloomily.

Thomas seemed to share her thought. The next time they were left alone, he jerked hard against the ropes that bound him to the chair, at considerable cost to his injured shoulder, while she sawed diligently. Finally, the last rope snapped. Thomas grabbed the knife and freed her. Handing her the knife, he shook out his numb fingers. Laura did the same; then, hearing the returning footsteps, she tucked her hands and the ends of the rope back into Thomas's grasp.

"We've done it!" she whispered exultantly. One knife and three free hands against two guns wasn't much, but at least it was a start.

She looked down in horror. The knife! She had put it on her lap when she shook out her fingers. Dislodged by her movements, it was sliding slowly off her knees. It dropped to the floor with a thud just as Roger and Antonia came through the door.

CHAPTER TWENTY ONE

Thomas jerked spasmodically, as if he were having an uncontrollable fit. One leg thrust out in one direction, one in the other. The first foot landed squarely on the knife. With a dramatic groan, he pulled the leg slowly back into place, the knife beneath it.

"He's in terrible pain," Laura babbled as Antonia and Roger entered. "I think he's going into convulsions." Antonia regarded Thomas with curiosity, a gleam of prurient pleasure in her face. Then her mood changed.

"Oh, for goodness sake!" she snapped irritably. "So much drama for one small shoulder that won't know the difference soon anyway."

Relief flooded through Laura. Antonia hadn't seen anything but Thomas's dramatic performance. Her off-hand comment, however, cast a shadow over their reprieve. They still had two guns to contend with.

"Take those last two off the wall, there's a dear," Antonia cooed to Roger in another complete change of tone. "I'll take one of them and you take the other, along with the hat lady. She will bring quite a bit, so treat her carefully." Roger obeyed and trotted out of the room after Antonia.

"This is the first and I hope only time in my life I will be glad someone is a sadist," Laura muttered as she grabbed the knife. "Antonia enjoyed your convulsions so much she didn't even see the knife."

"As bad as her brother," Thomas commented. "Where can we hide it?"

"In here." Laura slipped the knife delicately into the wide pocket of her walking skirt. How convenient! In pants the knife might show. In her full skirt, it wouldn't.

Roger eyed them nervously when he came back. "What do we do with them now?" he asked anxiously. Laura felt a spurt of hope. Maybe Roger liked the idea of shooting them better than the reality. He might even be waking up to the possibility that Antonia intended to leave the dirty work – and the murder charges – to him, while she escaped with the goods. A reluctant assassin might be even more help than the knife.

"I know I can safely leave that to you, Roger darling," Antonia purred, providing him with another of her seductive glances. "What would I ever do without you?"

Roger shuffled his feet. "I'm not all that sure…" he began.

Antonia patted his arm. "If you should feel the least bit squeamish, and I doubt a man as brave as you ever would, remember that it's not our fault if they end up dead. They insisted on getting in the way, so really, they asked for it."

"How did you kill Marie? And Morris?" Thomas asked so suddenly that Laura jumped. Who was Marie?

Antonia's head whipped around. She looked frightened. "I had nothing to do with Marie. I have no idea how she got there," she said emphatically. "I didn't kill Morris either. I don't know who did but I swear it wasn't me."

"I guess she'll blame both murders on you," Thomas said blandly to Roger.

"I didn't even know Morris was dead," Roger protested. "No one told me that. I swear I didn't know, so I couldn't have killed him."

Laura frowned. It was hard not to believe them. But if neither of them had killed Morris, who had?

"And Marie?" Thomas pressed.

"Marie did it to herself," Roger answered self-righteously. "Fell down the stairs. You'll see when you look at her. No bullets, nothing. She just fell down those stairs. Dangerous stairs."

"Which stairs?" Laura asked, understanding now. Marie was the missing cook, the other detective. "The stairs to the cellar, or the ones..."

"Yes, that's them," Roger interrupted, "You believe me, don't you? I mean they're terrible steep, those stairs. I was nowhere near Marie then. Morris was behind her, not me, but he said he didn't push her or anything like that. She just tripped, I guess."

"Or got tapped," Thomas suggested. "There's a bruise on the back of her head."

"That was from before," Roger protested, "when she was poking around earlier. I only gave her a little tap, just to make sure she did what she was told. She was only out for a minute."

"Who put her in the green room, and who put the mask on her face?" Laura asked, determined to take full advantage of this unexpected flow of information.

"That wasn't me either," Roger said defensively. "It was Morris. He's the one. Switched the mask later, too. I wouldn't play a trick like that, but Morris got a kick out of it. All I did was help him carry her up there and fix up the lights a bit so no one would see it was a mask."

"I guess you helped carry her down to the freezer and then helped take her out again, too," Thomas remarked casually.

Roger stared. "I put her down there, but I don't know who took her out. Why would they do that? She was all right in there. Preserved her."

Laura shuddered. "I suppose you gave Thomas just a little tap, too," she inserted. "Twice, if I remember correctly."

Roger bristled. "I only do what I'm told. I didn't really hurt him, only knocked him out for a bit. Morris was supposed to finish him off that second time, once he'd talked, not me."

Laura frowned, wondering why Antonia was letting Roger speak so freely. The answer came quickly. So far Roger was only incriminating himself.

"I suppose you were told to drug Lottie as well," Thomas said to Roger, but Laura noticed that his eyes were on Antonia now.

"I didn't do that either," Roger muttered, with a guilty glance at Antonia. "It wasn't me," he repeated. "That was her id -"

"Shut up!" Antonia interrupted furiously. "Can't you see they're just trying to get you to talk so you incriminate yourself? I don't want you to talk anymore. No more, do you understand?"

"Now that your name is under discussion, his wagging tongue must be stopped," Thomas observed sardonically, confirming Laura's thought. "But you did drug Lottie. And me, so you could search my room. We found the sleeping pills ground up as face powder on your dressing table. Horrible things. Made me fuzzy for days."

Antonia stiffened. "That's ridiculous. Why would I drug Lottie?"

"So that when she reappeared from the dead, so to speak, the others would think there hadn't been a body after all. That way, no one would know that Marie had been murdered. Very clever, actually."

"Until you thought Lottie really was dead," Laura observed. "That must have been a shock. If she had died of a drug overdose, you would be charged with murder."

"But she didn't and I wasn't," Antonia taunted, and Laura felt her spurt of hope evaporate. A woman who could flawlessly execute an art heist as complicated as this one, down to the smallest detail like cut telephone wires, wasn't likely to let a reluctant Roger bungle the job of silencing them.

Antonia's words confirmed her fears. "Enough," she snapped. "Everything you've said is pure speculation, and I shall make sure you don't last long enough to tell anyone about your pretty little theories anyway."

Her expression changed as she turned to Roger. "Well," she said softly, letting her long-lashed eyes linger lovingly on his face, "we've got all the paintings, haven't we, darling. I'll wait in the van while you finish up here."

Smiling lazily at Roger, she lifted her arms and stretched voluptuously, so that her breasts were clearly outlined against the thin silk of her shirt. Roger goggled at her and began visibly to sweat.

She blew him a kiss and walked slowly toward the door. "They're all yours, Roger dear," she called back in her sweetest tone. "I'll be waiting for you. And then..." She let the sentence dangle and smiled seductively.

Roger swallowed hard and licked his lips. "Wait!" he exclaimed urgently. "Maybe it would be better if you did it," he added tentatively. "I mean…"

"Darling! Are you getting cold feet?" Antonia stopped beside the door, a trace of impatience on her face. "What you have to do, Roger dearest, is to think of us basking on a beach somewhere warm, or perhaps - "

She stopped abruptly as a car door slammed. The unexpected sound was jarring. A voice piped up, a very familiar voice.

"Can I pour out the milk for him? Mama never let me have a puppy, but now I've already got Muffin, and she can't give him back, can she?"

Angelina's childlike question was so incongruous in the midst of Antonia's sadistic plotting that all of them froze.

"Oh my God," Thomas muttered. "I told Mrs. Paulson she could come back any time after eleven. I was sure I'd have Adrian in handcuffs and out of here by that time."

"Maybe they won't come in here," Laura said hopefully, but at just that moment, she heard the clipped sound of a dog's toenails trotting along the uncarpeted hall to the gallery. Other feet followed, Angelina's feet.

"You better bring the puppy back in here," Mrs. Paulson warned from the kitchen. "The doctor won't want him peeing on the rugs."

Angelina giggled from the study. "He already has." The puppy burst into the gallery, wagging its tail frantically, and went to sniff at Adrian's prone form.

"What's Uncle Adrian doing on the floor?" Angelina asked from the door. "Is he hurt?" She ran after the puppy and knelt down beside Adrian.

"Angelina, I want you to go back to Mrs. Paulson," Antonia said. Her voice had a strangled sound. Laura saw that she had hidden the gun behind her.

"Right now, Angelina!" she ordered, but there was no authority in the command. There never was when she spoke to Angelina. It was as if she had no idea how to deal with someone she couldn't manipulate, even when that person was her own child.

Stewart's child, too, Laura remembered suddenly. Where *was* Stewart?

"If you're a good girl and go back to Mrs. Paulson with the puppy right away, you can keep him," Antonia offered, resorting to bribery. Angelina didn't cooperate. Instead, she got up and went to her mother.

"Why are you holding a gun?" she asked. "Roger has one too. Can I see it, Roger?" She reached out a hand.

"Don't give it to her," Antonia snapped. "I... I mean, we are playing a game," she told Angelina with an oddly pleading glance at Roger. "We're almost finished. You take the puppy back to the kitchen now, and I'll come in a few minutes and explain."

Angelina regarded her solemnly; then she turned to Laura. "Will you come with me? I'll go if she can come with me," she told her mother.

"Laura has to stay for just a few more minutes." Antonia said weakly.

Angelina went to stand beside Laura, close enough to touch her. "I don't like it here, with Uncle Adrian on the floor and Mama has a gun," she said tremulously, pressing her pudgy body against Laura. "It's all wrong. I want you to come with me." Blinking hard, she bit her lip and looked down at the floor.

"Let's ask your mother if I can come with you," Laura said gently. She wished she could reach out to reassure Angelina, but she dared not reveal the fact that her hands were free, not just yet.

"Can she come with me now?" Angelina didn't look at her mother but kept her eyes firmly on the floor.

Antonia stood perfectly still. A series of expressions crossed her face: shock, disbelief and then capitulation. She seemed to shake herself, and when she spoke her voice was perfectly controlled. "Roger and I will go back to the manor now," she announced. "We will finish our game another time."

She turned to her daughter. "I'll see you there later, Angelina. As soon as I have gone, Laura can come with you." She walked slowly to the door and lingered there for a moment, to look back at her daughter, at the room, as if memorizing the scene of a failure so she wouldn't repeat it.

"Bye, Mama," Angelina said nonchalantly. Stooping, she picked up the puppy. "I'm going to give Muffin his milk now," she told Laura. "You have to come with me, though, okay?"

"I'll be right behind you," Laura promised. She rose and shook out her arms ostentatiously, both of them, and decided she would never again enjoy anything so much as the look of incredulity on Antonia's face.

"Maybe you should come too, Thomas," she added silkily. Taking his cue, he stood up, his limp arm hanging free by his side. At the same time, Laura drew out the knife and let it dangle tantalizingly from her fingers.

Antonia gave a small yelp of dismay and her face turned white. Laura smiled at her. "It was knocked out

284

of Morris's hand when the horse kicked him up on the moor. I picked it up because I thought it might be useful."

Antonia shot her a glance filled with loathing and walked stiffly away.

"See you later," Laura called to her retreating back. "Though in rather different circumstances, considering what we know," she added with a theatrical sigh that rivaled Antonia's own. "Still, I understand that some of the jails in this country are quite comfortable."

Antonia turned again, and now her face was dark with rage. Laura thought she was going to bring out the gun and shoot her, despite Angelina's presence. With a visible effort, Antonia controlled herself. Without speaking, she walked slowly out the door, her demeanor once more imperturbable.

Laura started after her. Antonia and Roger would vanish as fast as they could with their precious cargo of paintings. They had to be stopped.

Thomas had the same thought. Grabbing the knife from her hand, he picked up the plaster bust she had left on the floor and charged out of the room. She ran after him, ignoring Angelina's furious protests. To her relief, Mrs. Paulson appeared behind the child and guided her gently into the kitchen.

Thomas gave a flying leap toward the car just as its engine turned over, and slashed the nearest tire. A loud hissing noise followed; he slashed the next one, rolling to avoid being run over as Roger gunned the engine. Then he flung the bust at the window on the driver's side. Laura heard glass shatter as the van roared away, its rear end sagging almost to the ground. It wouldn't get far, she thought with satisfaction.

The bust was in pieces at her feet, and for the first time she saw who it was, or had been. Adrian, she realized, or what was left of him. His sightless eyes stared up at her. She hoped that wasn't symbolic.

The sound of a loud crash startled her. The van! It had come to rest against a tree where the road turned sharply. She turned to tell Thomas but he was already running back to the house.

Mrs. Paulson met him half-way and pressed a small instrument into his hand. "The doctor has one of these newfangled contraptions," she said disapprovingly. "Don't like them myself, but I suppose they come in handy.

"I've called that number you gave me already," Mrs. Paulson went on calmly. "The line's a bit crackly but I told the police to come right away."

She turned to Laura. "Wasn't hard to see that something was wrong around here," she said, shaking her head. "Once I saw that van and had a peek inside, I knew, anyway. The doctor's been acting ever so strange these last weeks, always staring at those paintings, and his poor wife, dead so sudden you know, and I couldn't help but wonder. That's why I spoke to Mr. Thomas here. Heard he was a detective and all that.

"I called Dr. MacDonald, too," she added complacently to Thomas. "He's the doctor. I'll have a look at Dr. Banbury now, poor soul, if that's all right with you."

"Thanks, Mrs. Paulson. You're a gem." Thomas punched in some numbers.

Laura shivered and moved closer to his warmth. "I'm glad that's over," she said fervently.

Thomas sent her a quizzical look. "Not all over, I fear," he said, and began to issue crisp instructions into the phone.

Laura straightened. He was right. There were still missing pieces to this puzzle. The answers, she knew, could only be found at Torrington Manor.

CHAPTER TWENTY TWO

Laura crept quietly up the three flights of stairs to the attic. The box room, she was sure, would provide answers to some of her remaining questions. The others, she hoped, would come from Antonia and Roger. They had emerged almost unscathed from the crash, and the police had been there to greet them. Thomas insisted, however, that everyone at the manor be told that they had been killed.

"Do not divulge the fact that they are alive unless there are no other options," he had warned her. Laura wasn't sure why he was so insistent, but she had no intention of giving the secret away. So far Antonia had sat stony-faced, saying nothing, but being in police custody had shifted Roger's loquacity into high gear. He was spouting like a faucet. Interestingly, he swore that the van had crashed because someone had tampered with the brakes, not because of flat tires or lack of skill on his part.

The crowded box room almost defeated Laura before she began to look. Old trunks, cardboard boxes, packing cases of all sizes were piled in every available space. Laura decided to start at the back and move forward on the theory that what she was looking for would be well hidden. She was right. At the very back of the room at the bottom of a pile of heavy boxes she finally discovered what she sought. A glossy photograph of the young woman in the painting above the sideboard stared up at her when she pried the box open. Below it were more photos and best of all, London theater programs, and the reviews that had followed the performances.

Laura sat down and dug into the piles of papers. Slowly, bits of the story began to emerge – Charlotte Gramercy's successes, her marriage at the height of her career to a young European Baron who had been the catch of the season, the trips to Monte Carlo and other glamorous places, but there was nothing, at least so far, to tell Laura why it had all ended. It seemed a fairy story, one that must have gone bad, but why?

Another photograph fell from the box, instantly recognizable as a much younger Lord Torrington playing Julius Caesar. According to the reviews, he had been a fine actor. He certainly had the voice, Laura thought, and found she could easily imagine him in that commanding role.

A clipping about two English actors making a living in France was attached. One was called Charles Morrison, the other Barkeley Smythington. That must be Lord Torrington! No wonder he was so good at playing his present role. She peered at the accompanying photographs. Oddly, the one called Charles Morrison looked more like Lord Torrington than the other, though it was hard to be certain since both men were in costume and stage make-up. Perhaps the writer of the article had mixed the two men up.

A slight noise behind her made her look up sharply. She rose to her feet and saw Mrs. Murphy, the new cook, standing in the doorway.

"Hello," Laura said, unable to think of anything else to say. Mrs. Murphy didn't answer. She only looked at Laura coldly, and then sighed.

"I suppose it takes all types, doesn't it?" she asked rhetorically. "Well, she warned me - the Baroness that is - but she said it was all right. I'm not just going to take her word for it, though. I'm here to make sure." Planting her hands on her hips, she sent Laura a threatening glare that made her blood run cold.

"Perhaps you had better explain what you mean," Laura said faintly.

"What I mean is that if you give her away, I'll...I'll..." Mrs. Murphy's voice failed and to Laura's astonishment, tears came into her eyes.

"Mrs. Murphy," Laura said gently, "I have no intention of doing anything that would hurt the Baroness, if that is what you mean. I think she is one of the finest people I have ever met."

Mrs. Murphy wiped her eyes with her apron. "That she is, and it is good of you to say so, Miss. Not everyone understands. But I still can't just..."

"Can't just take it on faith that I can be trusted?" Laura ventured, and Mrs. Murphy nodded.

"You know her well, then," Laura went on, wondering how that was possible even as she realized it must be so.

Mrs. Murphy's face changed, and a dreamy look came into her fierce eyes. "I was her dresser, you see, all those years. Every piece of clothing she wore I fixed for her, got her into them and out of them and my, sometimes we had to move so fast I hardly got her buttoned. Been with her ever since, but for the last few years, when I had to go tend my sister. Dying of cancer, but now I wish I hadn't gone. Still, I came back as soon as I could. I pretended to answer that ad in the paper, but the Baroness and I had it all fixed up ahead. *Just don't tell Antonia who you really are,* she told me."

Mrs. Murphy paused, smiling at the memory. "You should have seen the look on Lord Torrington's face when he saw me. He didn't give me away, though. Great actor, he was, still is, if you ask me. Antonia never guessed. But I should never have left to start with. Look what happened! That dreadful woman, and all her terrible schemes, and I wasn't here to help my poor lady the way I should..."

"But why didn't the Baroness just stop her?" Laura interrupted. "Why did she let Antonia come here in the first place?"

Mrs. Murphy sent her another threatening look. "I'm not telling you that but if you find out - and you probably will because you'll snoop around until you do - I want a promise, a promise on your mother's grave that you won't talk," she said fiercely.

An unexpected voice came from the door. "Murphy Darling, don't take on so. It's all right." The Baroness entered the room and put her arms around Mrs. Murphy's tense shoulders. "I'm sure we can trust Laura not to say anything. After all, she's been a great help already, hasn't she?"

Mrs. Murphy glowered at Laura. "She better not talk," she muttered, and sat down on a packing case in front of the Baroness. She reminded Laura of one of those fierce little terriers who plant themselves in front of a beloved mistress, ready to leap at the throat of anyone foolish enough to come too close.

The Baroness sat down beside her and gestured for Laura to find a seat too. "As you have already discovered," she began without preamble, "I was once an actress. I was aware from the beginning that you were puzzled by my familiarity and that you would try to ascertain its source. You are a woman who seeks answers."

The ghost of a smile touched her lips before she went on. "I decided, therefore, to let you discover the facts for yourself and then to tell you my story in the hope that you will keep my secrets - our secrets, I should say, for they involve others as well. Under the circumstances, it seemed the only sensible course of action."

Laura nodded dumbly, too mesmerized by her presence to speak. Even sitting on a cardboard box, the Baroness was commanding, awe-inspiring. It seemed impossible to Laura that she hadn't recognized her sooner – until she recalled that Charlotte Gramercy was one of the finest actresses the London stage had ever known and could probably fool anyone at any time, if she chose.

"I only saw you once," she said softly, "as Ophelia. It was a performance I have never forgotten."

The Baroness nodded graciously, accepting the compliment. She looked down at the floor of the cluttered box room, thinking, remembering, and when she resumed her story, she spoke not as herself but as an observer, as if distancing herself from memories that were still too raw to confront directly. Her voice changed too; it was still grave and memorable, but now it was beautiful as well, deep and warm, vibrant with passion and intensity. Laura sat motionless, enthralled.

"Many years ago," the Baroness began softly, "a young woman called Charlotte came to London, looking for work as an actress. The classics were her goal, especially Shakespeare, the great bard whose understanding of human nature has never been surpassed and from whom she learned all she needed to know of people and their ways.

"Unlike so many others she succeeded in the theatre. What they saw in her she has never fully understood, but simply accepted as a gift. The praise flowed, the flowers and the champagne, the offers of marriage, of more and better roles, of movie contracts and plays written just for her, but she was seldom tempted. She wanted Shakespeare still, and later Ibsen, a few other classicists. She seemed to know even then that if she diverged from the path she had set herself, disaster would follow. And so it did."

Laura's stomach clenched. She was about to hear, finally, the rest of the story she had sought, but now she wasn't sure she wanted it. She knew already that the telling, and the listening, would be painful.

The Baroness made no effort to spare herself, or Laura. On and on her voice went, mesmerizing in its intensity, describing Charlotte, the roles she had played, the cities that had welcomed her, the people who had lavished gifts and attention and praise upon her. At first her story was inspiring, a tale of hard-earned praise and success, but gradually Charlotte's faults, the arrogance she began to develop, the expectation of adulation, were laid out too, as if for renewed examination.

Murphy remained always at her side, barring the door with fierce protectiveness to unwanted admirers, reluctantly admitting others when Charlotte insisted. "A redheaded terror from Yorkshire," the Baroness said, her voice taking on a Yorkshire lilt, and Laura saw

Murphy's thin lips curve in a proud smile that was
quickly tucked away.

Above the words, seeming to float in her own clear
atmosphere, as objective as she was painful or amused
or joyous in turn, was the Baroness of today, a woman
so schooled by life that she had no need anymore to act.
She had only to understand, to assess, and then to watch
as others played the roles she assigned them, never
suspecting they were being manipulated by her unseen
hands, hands that knew, as her mentor Shakespeare had
known, all there was to know of human folly and
greatness.

Laura sighed without knowing that the small burst
of air had been expelled. She understood now what had
mystified her most of all: that the Baroness was the
unseen puppeteer she had sensed when she sat captive in
the kitchen of the cottage. Power dwelt in those skillful
hands – too much power perhaps?

A niggling doubt crept into Laura's mind. Had they
been wrong in believing that Antonia was the brains
behind the art forgeries? Maybe the Baroness had
manipulated them into suspecting her. And now the
Baroness believed that Antonia was dead.

"Charlotte's most persistent admirer was Baron
Zorolaskowitz," the Baroness went on. "We called him
Zorro to tease him, but he was not amused. That should
have warned Charlotte, and perhaps it did, but she did
not want the knowledge."

For a moment her voice faltered. Then it went on
steadily to tell how Charlotte was finally won over by
the handsome young Baron, by his charm and
sophistication, his desire for her, his fervent promises of
eternal adoration. *Why not some personal happiness?*

Charlotte had asked herself. *Others have it, why should I not?*

So she had yielded to his entreaties, had married him and then been forced to watch as his attention flagged and his adoration faded into petulance. Weary of her fame, her constant absences, the very absences he had assured her would only enhance the passion of their reunions, and jealous of the demands made by her career and the attention paid to her by others, he drifted slowly into dissipation and drink, gambling away first his money and then hers.

Laura felt tears prick her eyes for the young woman who had known all along in some deep part of herself that this would happen but for whom the enactment must still have been so intensely painful. It wasn't an unusual story, she supposed, but in the grande dame's exquisite telling it had all the elements of tragedy. But then, Shakespeare's plays told ordinary tales, too – a jealous husband who killed his wife, lovers separated, men and women of overreaching ambition or fatal attraction to the wrong person. The words, the manner of delivery gave them epic proportions, and a profound understanding of the human mind and heart, with all their tragic flaws.

Did the Baroness, too, have a tragic flaw – the flaw of overweening pride – hubris, the Greeks had called it – so that she believed she was justified in deciding other peoples' fates? Who should live and who should die...

Unexpectedly, the Baroness smiled, and Laura felt suddenly comforted. Her persistent feeling of unease began to dissipate as the next part of the story unfolded. How could a woman like the grande dame be a criminal?

"But there was Lucy," the Baroness was saying, "my darling Lucy. She was my younger sister, far more beautiful than I and as kind and playful as I was hard and watchful, as irreverent as I was over-serious. For Charlotte had become those things, though at the time she did not know it. She went to France to rest and to think what to do, and Lucy came there to console her. In doing so she helped Charlotte to recover, so she could act again, and that truly was a joy, for now she knew better how to keep the arrogance at bay. No one could be arrogant with Lucy watching.

"Lucy met her husband there, a Frenchman as kind as she was herself and even more gentle. Too gentle perhaps," she added with a touch of asperity that might have made Laura laugh had she not been so enthralled.

"We were happy together, Murphy and Charlotte and Lucy and her husband, and then Nigel came along…" The Baroness's voice faltered and a look of inexpressible sorrow crept slowly across her face. Laura waited, tense with horror for the disaster she knew must come. It was in the form of a car accident. Lucy's husband was driving; Lucy was beside him, Charlotte and Nigel were in the back. When they were finally extricated from the wreckage, only the baby, Nigel, was unscathed. Lucy and her husband were dead, and Charlotte had multiple fractures and burns across much of her body. Her young husband did not come to her nor did anyone else, only the faithful Murphy. Nigel went into her care, and so did Charlotte, once she came out of the hospital.

"There was one other," the Baroness continued softly, speaking as herself again now that the tragedy was over. "His name was Charles then, although you know him as Lord Torrington."

Laura stiffened. Charles, not Barkeley. How could that be? A frisson of fear crept up her spine. Maybe the article she had found on the moor wasn't wrong, if the man named Charles Morrison was now Lord Torrington. What had happened to Barkeley Smythington? With that name, surely he was the rightful heir. Where was he now?

"Charles was an actor, too," the Baroness went on imperturbably. "He was some years younger than I, but he had always been my friend. Not just an admirer, a friend in the truest sense of the word. He was English, but he was working in Paris that year, and he was always there, to help us all, to force me to move my limbs when I thought I could not or make me laugh when I was certain that was impossible, to wheel Nigel about in his pram and help him learn to walk, to joke with Murphy and jolly her into creating the delectable French dishes he loved but hadn't the patience to make for himself."

"Prodded me terrible, he did," Murphy remarked unexpectedly.

The Baroness smiled at her fondly. "Murphy was the one who kept food on the table and a roof over our heads for quite some time. And Charles. When his acting job came to an end, he stayed on, working at whatever he could get to help us make ends meet. One of his jobs was at an art gallery, where he learned what art was worth and what the rich would pay for old masterpieces, a lesson that proved valuable later. So did Murphy's cooking and dressmaking skills. She did better than any of us in those early days, as a seamstress and cook.

"Eventually, I was able to help. I could no longer act nor did I wish to, with my stiff body and stiffer face, which had suffered injuries that affected the mobility on one side. I learned a great deal about facial structure in those days, and became intrigued with the many ways in which the human face and body could be altered and character changed. I began to work for museums, actors, sculptors, artists, anyone who needed to be transformed or to have a life-like facsimile created. And so our lives took form, and Nigel grew. He did not have parents, but he had more care and attention lavished on him than most children, since at least one of us was always there - too much attention perhaps, but it did not seem to spoil him unduly."

Another piece of the puzzle fell neatly into place in Laura's mind. The Baroness was Nigel's aunt, and "Gram" was short for Gramercy. Nigel must have made up the name when he was small and now Angelina used it too.

"Charles met a young man called Stewart at the gallery," the Baroness continued, "a painter with an uncanny ability to copy masterpieces. He also met a very beautiful young woman named Antonia."

She sighed, a long sigh of regret. "Charles had asked me many times to marry him, but always I refused. I was older, maimed, too proud, perhaps; it is hard to say. I was also aware that to obtain a divorce in my husband's Catholic family would have been very difficult. It was a decision I came to regret many times. So did Charles, for in the end, he gave up on me and married Antonia instead. We were unhappy that year. Very unhappy indeed."

Mrs. Murphy nodded in agreement. "Not our best." Her bony face assumed a dolorous look.

"The marriage did not last," the Baroness went on in her usual measured tones. "Antonia tired of Charles as soon as she realized he was not going to be a great star. She disappeared, and he did not hear from her again for many years. Stewart went away soon after she had left. We had no way then of understanding how significant those dual departures would one day become.

"Charles came back to me, and I…" the Baroness drew a deep breath. "I saw what I should have seen long before, that Charles and I would be happy together. And so we have been for many years. More than happy, in fact. We were quite delirious for a time, though eventually we settled down. A little," she added thoughtfully, and smiled.

Laura remembered the passionate voice she had overheard in the study and the embrace that had followed. It seemed right now, almost inevitable. But was it true? Had all of this really happened or was it just a story the Baroness had concocted to seduce her into silence?

"But how did Charles Morrison become Lord Torrington instead of Barkeley Smythington?" she blurted out.

She was immediately aware of a subtle change in the atmosphere of the room. Murphy's eyes seemed to shoot sparks at her. The grande dame's face changed, too, became oddly secretive. She kept her eyes on Laura, but it was to Murphy she spoke. "Murphy, dear, would you be kind enough to get us some tea? My voice, you know. It gets so dry. We could have a little tea party up here, Laura and I."

Mrs. Murphy got to her feet. "I shan't be long," she promised the Baroness. She sent Laura another threatening look and then went out, closing the door hard behind her.

"Murphy is protective of me," the Baroness observed with the touch of humor that was so characteristic of her. "I see that you understand the implications of what I am saying," she went on gravely. "There is more to come."

Laura wondered numbly what it was. Drugged tea perhaps? Probably she ought to get up and leave, but she couldn't. She knew now why a mouse being tormented by a ruthless cat didn't dart away. It couldn't. It was too mesmerized by those batting paws, the glowing intensity in the cat's eyes. Like the mouse, she couldn't leave until the game was over. She had to hear the rest.

"We had another special friend in those years," the Baroness said, and Laura knew at once that she was coming to the heart of her story. "His name was Barkeley Smythington. He and Charles had grown up together in a village near Torrington Manor, and often played in the manor grounds. Barkeley had even been taken inside, for the manor belonged to distant relatives. He did not know them personally, but he cared deeply about the manor and the town and spoke often of them, with great nostalgia. He wished he could see them again, but he was dying of AIDS, and was too ill to travel.

"Shortly before his death, the letter came. The old Baron at Torrington Manor had died and there was no direct heir. Barkeley, to his astonishment, was next in line as the new Baron. He wanted desperately to go, and became frantic with grief because he could not assume the responsibility. The manor property would fall into ruin, he told us, would be divided into ugly estate homes or worse. There seemed to be only one solution."

Laura didn't need to be told what it was. Charles Morrison had taken Barkeley Smythington's place, and that meant the present Lord Torrington was an impostor. That was the secret that could not, must not get out. The world Lord Torrington and the Baroness had built would come crashing down if it did.

And everyone who knew the secret was dead, all but Antonia, and the Baroness didn't know that.

Laura shrank back against her box. Now, she too knew the story. Why had the Baroness told her? Did she really trust her not to talk? Or was the Baroness offering this virtuoso performance as a kind of last gift?

Inexplicably, the grande dame's lips twitched with amusement. "Barkeley came up with a novel solution," she said, humor clear in her eyes. "He looked at Charles and saw the new Baron. 'You are perfect,' he told him over and over again. 'You *are* a country squire, a lover of horses and all things British,' and it was true. Charles had always wanted fine horses. He was the very epitome of an English country gentleman. And so, on his deathbed, with great drama, for Barkeley was an actor too and a very dramatic one, he extracted a promise from us both that we would try at least. Charles was to assume his identity, use his papers, *be* him, and go to London to talk to the trustees. I was to come later, with Nigel and Murphy."

The Baroness looked down at her hands, and Laura was sure she was trying not to laugh. "It was so outrageous, you see," she explained, "like something

301

Lucy would have done for a lark. I had the feeling the whole time that she was laughing, urging us on. Even more important, we had promised, and for Charles to become the new Baron was the greatest gift we could offer our old friend. We *wanted* to do it, too, wanted to rescue the manor. Perhaps most of all, we wanted badly to go home. England was our home and Murphy's, and none of us had been back for so long."

The Baroness spread out her hands as if to say: "What else could we do?"

Laura laughed, relieved at the explanation. Why not uphold a friend's dying wish and take on Torrington Manor, which so desperately needed to be kept intact?

"Charles went to London as Barkeley and succeeded in establishing himself as the new Baron. He had the time of his life, to use a rather vulgar phrase," the Baroness told her, smiling at the memory. "The trustees were delighted with him. They were elderly, eager to be rid of the responsibility of the manor, and I doubt they looked carefully at the documents. It all seemed too easy, as if it were meant to be, *fated*, as Lucy would have put it. There were no problems at all, about me or Nigel. The trustees were very pleased to have the next heir in place. I simply came as a relative, and no one bothered to ask any more questions. After all, I was already a Baroness, and that seemed enough.

"I also had money. My husband had died the year before, and I inherited what was left of the family fortune, mostly from a trust he could not touch. Some money was left from the old Baron at the manor as well, not a lot after death duties and years of profligate spending, but with my funds it was enough to begin the restorations.

"I also took great care to hide my former identity. I was well known, and if anyone became interested in how Charlotte Gramercy came to Torrington Manor they would no doubt have stumbled upon Charles's past, too. So I presented myself simply as the Baroness, though I gave out Smythington when a surname was required. To be still safer, I took to making myself look older so no one would put us together but would think I was Nigel's grandmother instead. I became the grande dame of the manor, as I am aware you and Catherine have dubbed me, and Charles became the quintessential English country gentleman. It is a role he dearly loves to play - and loves even more to overplay," the Baroness added with a wry twist of her lips.

Laura sighed. It all sounded so delightful - and so very believable. Surely, it must be the truth?

"Eventually, my money began to run out and we decided to sell some paintings, as you have heard. Charles located Stewart and hired him to make copies, and then... then the nightmare began."

The Baroness closed her eyes and a spasm of pain crossed her face. "Perhaps you can guess the rest. Antonia had been living with Stewart, though we had not known it, had in fact been selling copies for him for years, using Roger as her enforcer, if that is the right term. She knew the business well, though we did not realize how well until these last few days. Scenting money, she followed Stewart here, bringing their daughter, Angelina, and later Roger, first as a butler, then as gardener when it became clear even to her that his surly manner made people suspicious. There was nothing we could do to make her leave. She also knew who we were, you see, knew we were as fake as the paintings Stewart was providing for our walls, and she made it clear that she would publicize that fact if we thwarted her. All we could do was try to sabotage her plans, as you have no doubt learned from Thomas."

She looked up at Laura, desperate now to be understood. "We did not mind exposure for ourselves," she cried passionately. "It was the town, the manor itself; the many people who would suffer from what seemed such a benevolent deceit. They are the ones we worry about. We have come to care deeply for them, for the townspeople, the buildings, the manor itself. But most of all, we worry about Nigel. We tried to keep Antonia's purpose from him, tried to protect him, but it became impossible after a time. Nigel knows who he is - we have never hidden that from him - but we are the only parents he has ever known, and the manor is his home, even more than it is ours. If you could have seen his face when we first came here... He was only ten then, and had been happy in France, but here... here, he has flourished. Every object, every piece of furniture in the manor is his friend, every inch of the grounds he knows intimately. To wrench Nigel from this place would be to...to..."

Laura looked up as the door burst open. Lord Torrington stood there, holding the tea tray and smiling affably. His large bulk seemed to fill the doorway.

For the first time since she had known her, Laura saw the grande dame's face collapse with an emotion so strong she had no power to control it. Fear. The Baroness was terrified.

Abruptly, menace pervaded the room.

CHAPTER TWENTY THREE

Lord Torrington set the tray down on an old table near the door. He was still smiling affably. Laura relaxed a little. Maybe she was letting her imagination run away with her. She glanced at the Baroness and changed her mind. The grande dame hid her terror well, but it was still there under her guarded look. Laura's tension deepened.

"Thought I'd save Murphy the climb," Lord Torrington announced genially. "She's looking a bit peaked, so I gave her a cup of tea and sent her off to have a rest. Ought to get off her feet once a day, I told her. None of us as young as we once were."

"That was thoughtful of you, Charles," the Baroness replied. Lord Torrington looked startled at her use of the name *Charles*.

"It's quite all right," the Baroness assured him. "Laura already knows a great deal. She has no intention of using that knowledge." She stared at him intensely as she spoke, as if willing him to agree.

"Just as you say, my dear," Lord Torrington replied, and began to pour the tea into first one cup, then the other two.

The Baroness watched and so did Laura. She could see no sleight of hand to suggest that he was pouring powder into the cup intended for her. Did that mean it was already there? Or was she imagining things again?

No, she wasn't. Milk and sugar – with ground-up sleeping pills added in this case - were already in the cups as the ritual of English tea making required. They went in first and the tea was poured over them.

Walking into Murder

A chill settled over Laura despite the heat of the attic room. Did he really mean to kill her?

With a gallant gesture Lord Torrington handed a cup to the Baroness. Then he crossed the room to hand one to Laura. His back was to the tea tray.

"Thank you, Charles," the Baroness said politely. Her hand flashed out as she spoke. With a deft movement she put her cup noiselessly back on the tray and took the one Lord Torrington had poured for himself.

Laura's eyes widened. Was that a warning not to drink her tea? The Baroness looked straight at her and Laura knew that it was. Was the Baroness on her side after all?

She picked up her tea, pretended to take a sip, and then contrived to pour some of it into a box of old clothes while Lord Torrington returned to the tray. The Baroness saw her do it, and looked relieved.

Laura watched Lord Torrington surreptitiously as he sipped his tea. He looked younger now, and very alert. Why hadn't she noticed the intelligence in those sleepy blue eyes before? Probably he was far more capable than he pretended to be. He knew the value of fine art, too. The Baroness had just told her that. Maybe he had been working with Antonia and Stewart all along, only none of them had guessed. If so, he was vulnerable to exposure on two counts: his involvement in the forgeries and the all important secret of his true identity. Both were excellent motives for murder.

Lord Torrington interrupted her thoughts. "Well, all settled now, problems over," he said cheerfully. "Must say, Laura, you've been a great help. And Thomas. Good to have the foxes out of the henhouse finally, so to speak. Had to get rid of them of course, but hard to know how."

"Thank you, Lord Torrington," Laura said faintly. Her mouth was so dry she could hardly get out the words. She coughed harshly. "Thirsty," she explained, pretending to take a gulp of tea.

Lord Torrington looked pleased. Smiling, he turned to the Baroness and patted her arm. As he did, Laura quickly dumped out more of her tea.

"No need to worry any more, m' dear," he told the Baroness gruffly. "All over now. Antonia's gone, Roger too. "Good thing, too," he added. "Didn't know one end of a shovel from another." Laura flinched, remembering the bloodied shovel and Morris's battered head.

Her eyes widened in shock. Could Lord Torrington have done that to him? Antonia and Roger still insisted they hadn't killed Morris.

"Stewart too," Lord Torrington grumbled. "Fine painter but a terrible groom. Not good for the horses. Got to find one who knows his stuff. Have a superb pair of trotters in mind, doncherno. May need help with them."

"I am indeed relieved to think that we might be able to lead normal lives for a time," the Baroness said with a trace of her old acerbic humor. "These last days have been most trying."

"There, there, m' dear," Lord Torrington comforted, patting her hand again. "All simmered down now. Got to get you a rest." Tucking a finger under her chin, he kissed her on the lips. Laura upended her cup into the clothes.

"Maybe a little trip together, eh?" Lord Torrington continued. "Haven't been away for a long time now.

Due for a holiday, I'd say. Greece, maybe, or the Mediterranean."

He acted as if he knew she was aware of his real relationship with the Baroness, Laura realized. How long had he been outside the door listening as the grande dame told their story? The tea had felt quite cool when she had held the cup to her lips, so he must have been lurking there for quite a while. What else had he heard?

The Baroness noticed, too, and for a second the terror was back in her face. She controlled it quickly, and turned to look straight at Laura. Her gaze was so intense that Laura was unable to look away. And then she realized that there was a message in those brilliant eyes. *Take advantage of the opportunity I have offered you,* the Baroness was telling her. *It is time to get on with the play. You must be the actress now. If you can do that, you might save your life.*

It was a chilling message.

Laura took a deep breath, trying to control her racing heart and the thudding in her veins. Never in her life had she been so terrified. All that lay between her and death was this flimsy chance.

She must try anyway. Yawning ostentatiously, she slumped against the pile of musty clothes. "Sleepy," she muttered apologetically. "So sleepy suddenly…"

She yawned again, a real yawn this time that stretched her mouth so wide it hurt, and sank further into the soft clothes. As she did so, she pulled a lacy bit of blouse over her face in a way that she hoped looked inadvertent. She intended to watch as well as listen, and she didn't want Lord Torrington to see her alert eyes.

One limb at a time, she willed her muscles to go limp, the way she'd been taught years ago in a yoga class. How strange that those half-forgotten lessons might save her life now. Perhaps there was more to yoga that she had thought.

After a suitable interval while sleep presumably overtook Laura, the Baroness took her cue. "You know all this must stop, Charles. It is getting out of hand," she rebuked.

Lord Torrington looked offended. "Of course it will stop, my dear. Very soon, I promise you. I thought you understood that. But I must do what is necessary to protect us. People who know about us cannot be permitted to speak. We have no choice."

Laura realized that his voice, even his diction, had changed completely now that he thought she was asleep. He was no longer a typical country gentleman who mumbled in short "barks", but a sophisticated man with a clipped upper-class accent and a mellifluous voice that would have enhanced any Shakespearean role.

"Antonia could never keep her thoughts to herself under pressure and Roger was a weakling," he went on. "I dared not take a chance. It is not difficult to arrange accidents when you know how, but I was damned lucky that this one worked as well as it did. One can never be quite sure until afterward, which is a nuisance."

How cold-blooded he sounded! Laura tried not to shudder. So Lord Torrington had engineered the van's crash, probably by tinkering with the brakes as Roger said. She peeked at the Baroness and saw that she was startled. Maybe she hadn't thought of that possibility.

The grande dame's surprise showed for only an instant. "And the others?" she prompted.

"Damned cook was trying to blackmail us," Lord Torrington burst out, reverting to his bark-like speech in his agitation. "Can't have that! Had to be stopped. Would have stopped it myself but Morris gave her a good push first. He liked that sort of thing. It did the trick, too. Great help, that, since I didn't have to. Morris was a menace with that knife of his, but he had his uses. Still, he had to go in the end."

He glanced at Laura, now supine on the floor, before he continued. "We had to get rid of him. You know how volatile he was." His tone was persuasive and entirely reasonable. "Morris knew too damned much about everything, and he could wriggle information out of Antonia like a snake charmer. He would have blackmailed us as well if I had given him the chance. Stewart is hopeless at that sort of thing and so was Roger, under all that bluster, and Antonia didn't even want to hear about it. So I had to. No choice."

He shook his head sadly, appealing to her. "I don't like it, you know, but it simply had to be done. Morris was a devil," he added. The venom in his voice made Laura cringe.

"And once it starts it's hard to stop," the Baroness murmured, so softly Laura barely made out the words. "I should have realized that for you it would be like an addiction." For an instant, her face was desolate.

"Nonsense," Lord Torrington repeated, reverting again to his country speech. "That's the lot, I should think. No need for any more after today, and that will be over soon. So cheer up, darling girl. After this, everything will go back to normal.

"Except better, much better." His tone was unabashedly cheerful, and he rubbed his hands together in anticipation. "Plenty of money, an excellent stable, valuable art collection. Paintings hardly hurt at all. In the back, tied in. Antonia was always good about that.

"All ours again, too," he added triumphantly. "Adrian left them to you in his will, m' dear, did you know that? Solicitor told me in confidence. Poor man – shot in the chest as well as hit on the head, so he didn't last long."

He smiled affectionately at the Baroness. "No more nosy guests either," he added with a snort of disdain. "Still, I rather liked the American woman over there. Thomas too; he was a great help to start with. Showed up Antonia at least. Too bad they have to go."

The Baroness didn't respond directly. "The tea is very bitter," she remarked instead, taking another sip. "I feel quite sleepy." Suiting action to words, she closed her eyes. Perhaps she couldn't bear to look at him any more, Laura thought with sympathy.

Lord Torrington looked uncomfortable. "Never could fool you, could I? Sorry about that, my dear. But I couldn't let your tender feelings get in the way now. There is too much at stake to take any chances."

He indicated her cup. "I only put a small amount in yours. You'll soon be right as rain again."

Alarm shot thorough Laura. That meant Lord Torrington wasn't getting a very strong dose of whatever it was. She had hoped he would soon be incapacitated or at least weakened.

The Baroness didn't answer. Laura saw that her eyes were still closed and her face devoid of expression.

Lord Torrington stood up. "Time to finish up. Won't take long," he assured the unresponsive Baroness.

Crossing the room, he hauled Laura to her feet and grabbed her roughly under the shoulders. Still feigning unconsciousness, she let him pull her out the door to the stairs. Clumsily, she let one foot slide after the other as he half-lifted, half-dragged her down one step at a time, grunting with the effort. Maybe she could wear him out, Laura thought desperately. Unobtrusively, she allowed her feet to tangle in the banister, then wished she hadn't when one of them got stuck and he yanked it out with a savage jerk.

Where was everyone anyway? Surely someone had heard their noisy progress down the stairs. And then she remembered. No one else was here. Thomas was probably still with the police, Nigel and Catherine were in the woods looking for suitable sculpting stones and Mrs. Murphy was no doubt sleeping off her own cup of drugged tea. Even Angelina was away, so another unexpected rescue from that quarter wasn't going to materialize.

Laura decided the circumstances were dire enough to mention that Antonia was alive. If she wanted to live, she had no other option. "Talked to Antonia," she mumbled, trying to make her voice sound drugged. "Didn't die... talking... police..."

Lord Torrington stiffened. "How do you know that?" he demanded.

Laura frowned, as if unable to think clearly. "Thomas... Thomas said..."

"Thomas told you? Damnation!" Lord Torrington grabbed her arm so tightly that Laura cried out. "Down!" he ordered, and dragged her toward the last flight of stairs. Laura let him propel her awkwardly down, certain that if she didn't he would simply push her instead. She thought she heard quiet footsteps behind them. The Baroness?

Walking into Murder

The front door was already open and Lord Torrington pushed her through. Thomas's car was parked just in front of it. The motor was purring and Thomas was lying motionless on the back seat. Laura's heart sank. He must have come back, and Lord Torrington had found him. What had he done to him? How was she to get out of whatever it was he planned to do next with Thomas unconscious or even dead?

She tried again. "No point," she muttered. "They know…police waiting… over there…" Vaguely she pointed into the trees, wishing that her bluff was true.

Lord Torrington peered into the woods. There was no sign of movement, not even an unusual shape. He yanked her upright. "A bluff," he said furiously. "Always knew you were too smart for your own good."

Viciously he shoved her into the front seat. Laura's head cracked hard against the steering wheel, and for a moment she thought she was going to faint. Then the car started moving and she jerked herself upright.

She froze, horrified. The car was pointing straight down the hill toward the big tree at the bottom, the one that Lord Torrington feared had fallen over and brought down the telephone wires.

The car gathered speed as it careened down the hill. Grabbing the wheel, Laura yanked with all her strength. It was useless. The steering was broken. She pumped on the brakes instead. Maybe if she brought the car to a screeching halt it would swerve. The brakes didn't work either. She tried the handbrake, but that had been disabled too. Desperate, she flung the door wide open. Maybe she could jump out, open the back door and haul Thomas out somehow. Could she do it in time? Do it at all?

Walking into Murder

The car suddenly twisted sideways. Laura tensed. Why had it done that? She looked at the door. It was bent backward and down, as if it had become stuck on some large and unyielding object that had wrenched it away from the car. It was dragging against the ground, making a ghastly scraping sound.

She watched wide-eyed, caught between horror and wonder as the car twisted again and headed drunkenly for a field filled with grazing sheep and cows. It slowed, bumped heavily over the earth, splashing mud all over her as it ground through the puddles, then came to a gentle stop against a bale of hay.

The sheep scattered, bleating indignantly, but the cows barely moved. If they were startled by the sight of a car leaning against the haystack, they didn't show it. Lowering their heads, they resumed their contented munching.

Laura sat perfectly still, frozen in place. Shouting aroused her and she stumbled out of the car, still stiff with shock. Who was shouting?

Lord Torrington. Screaming obscenities, he ran headlong into the house and came back with his shotgun.

Holding it straight in front of him, he lumbered down the hill towards the field. His face was purple with rage. "Not going to get away with this," he shouted. "Not after all this... get you yet..."

The Baroness came up behind him and clutched his arm. "No Charles, no more. You can't do that. They're here, watching. Thomas called them."

Lord Torrington seemed not to hear. Brushing her hands away, he kept running. A rock tripped him and he fell. He got up again, swearing mightily, but Laura saw that his legs were unsteady. The Baroness stooped, picked up the rock and chased after him again.

Why was she just standing here? Wrenching the back door open, Laura shook Thomas. Let him just be drugged, not dead...

Moaning, he rubbed his eyes. He tried to sit up and fell back again. "What's happened?"

"Lord Torrington, shotgun, after us," Laura panted in staccato fashion as she struggled to haul him out of the car and onto his feet. "Get behind those bales of hay. They'll protect us."

Thomas looked at her as if she'd lost her mind. Then her meaning dawned on him. He grabbed at his chest and Laura was afraid he was having a heart attack. Instead, he pulled out a whistle hanging around his neck and blew three long blasts.

The sound pierced through Lord Torrington's unintelligible curses and brought him to a startled stop. He peered around as if trying to get his bearings. Then his eyes focused on Laura and Thomas. Raising his shotgun triumphantly to his shoulder, he pointed it at them.

Thomas moved – not toward the concealing bale of hay but up the hill toward Lord Torrington.

"Thomas! You can't get to him in time," Laura screamed.

He didn't need to. The Baroness got there first. An expression of anguish so terrible Laura knew she would never forget the sight crossed her aristocratic face before she raised her arm and hit Lord Torrington over the head with the rock. The gesture seemed to Laura less an intent to harm than a benediction.

For a few seconds Lord Torrington's face registered only profound astonishment. He tried to speak, but then his legs gave way and he toppled heavily to the ground. The Baroness stared at her hand in horror. Then she fell to her knees beside Lord Torrington and wept as if her whole world had fallen with him. And perhaps it had, Laura thought with a rush of pity. Like the fallen heroes her mentor Shakespeare described, the grande dame did have a tragic flaw, but it wasn't pride. Instead, her flaw was to cleave too hard and too long to the man she loved.

Impulsively, she knelt beside the Baroness and stroked her heaving shoulders, oblivious to cars screeching to a halt or the people surging down the hill. The Baroness was oblivious too, aware of nothing but the sobs that wracked her body.

The field was crowded with people now. Had Thomas's whistle brought them? She couldn't seem to think; all she could think of was the woman beneath her caressing fingers, the woman she had so admired whose life had been torn apart.

Someone tapped her on the shoulder. A policeman. He pointed toward the house. Laura stood and stretched out a hand to the grande dame to help her up.

The Baroness finally became aware of the people around her, and her sobs ceased. Clasping Laura's hand, she rose proudly to her feet. Her face showed signs of her distress, but her body was straight as a ramrod. Head high, she nodded graciously to the crowd and walked slowly back to the manor.

CHAPTER TWENTY FOUR

Laura and Thomas sat at a table in a quiet corner of Maude's bakery. From time to time Angelina appeared, clutching one of the puppies in her grubby fists. She looked superbly happy. Surprisingly, so did the puppy.

When Angelina disappeared into the back again, Laura asked the question that had been haunting her all day. "What will happen to the Baroness? Will she be charged as an accessory?"

"I doubt it," Thomas answered. "They would have to prove she knew about Lord Torrington's role in the art forgeries and in the murders. He'd been sending Antonia paintings for Stewart to copy all along, even from France, and pocketing his share of the proceeds. I don't think the Baroness knew. As for the murders, from what you said, she hadn't known, only suspected."

Laura sighed. "Or she didn't want to face the fact that the man she loved was a killer," she answered. "In the meantime, two people died. If she'd been willing to face the truth earlier, they might be alive. Knowing that seems to me punishment enough for a lifetime."

Thomas nodded and then clutched his head to stop the pounding. He sported an array of bruises in various unattractive shades, depending on their provenance. The new ones were a livid blue-purple-red; the old ones were lurid yellow and an odd shade of brownish maroon.

"I don't know why you're still upright," Laura remarked. "Probably you shouldn't be. Or why Lord Torrington didn't just kill you instead of knocking you out."

"Cars hitting trees are useful because they muddle the evidence about how a person died," Thomas said wryly. "Hard to tell what caused what, once someone has hit his or her head on the steering wheel or the roof."

"How did he manage to sneak up on you anyway?" Laura asked. 'You're always accusing Catherine and me of getting ourselves into trouble, but you're much worse. I think you need us to look after you."

Thomas grinned. "Sounds like an excellent arrangement to me, and I suggest we start immediately. As for how Lord Torrington snuck up on me, he didn't. I walked right into him. I'd heard him leave, or thought I did, so I went to his study to look for evidence about the forgery operation. He was behind the door with his shotgun and conked me as I came in."

"Not very smart," Laura observed. "You definitely need a minder."

"No, and yes," Thomas agreed. "My brain seems not to be functioning in optimal condition, and I do need someone to look after me." He pressed her hand and gave her a ridiculously exaggerated meaningful look.

Laura blushed, not because she was embarrassed but because she didn't know how to respond. Her future with Thomas, if any, was a subject she couldn't figure out how to deal with. Murders were easier.

"Whatever happened to Stewart?" she asked hastily, by way of changing the subject. "And have you found the cook's body, or figured out who took it out of the freezer?"

"Stewart vanished, leaving nothing but a note asking the Baroness to look after Angelina. And we found the body in the woods not far from the cellar. We suspect Lord Torrington hauled it out there in the few moments when I left to tell the Baroness. He and Antonia probably planned to get rid of it permanently. No body, no case. I imagine Lord Torrington meant to do the same with Morris but you found him first."

Laura shuddered. "He would have removed us the same way, if the Baroness hadn't helped me. It was a last resort for her, though. Until then, she thought she could control the situation by having Antonia caught for peddling fakes, and for all I know she took the missing silver herself, hoping that Morris would be arrested for stealing it. Nonviolent solutions that removed them from the scene – clever ones at that."

"They might have worked, too, if Charles hadn't decided to take matters into his own hands," Thomas put in. "His solution was simpler and much more ruthless. He just got rid of people who threatened his well-being."

Laura frowned. "Why in heavens name didn't we suspect him before? That mistake was almost lethal for both of us."

"Don't forget he's a consummate actor," Thomas reminded her. "I'm not sure I would ever have suspected him if Antonia and Roger hadn't insisted that they didn't kill Morris, or take the body. That's why I set up the trap by saying they were dead. You and I were the only ones left who threatened the killer, so he or she had an open field to finish things off."

Laura rolled her eyes. "Gee, thanks for setting me up so nicely."

Thomas had the grace to look abashed. "I almost got us killed instead," he admitted.

"You did indeed," Laura agreed. "But Lord Torrington had me fooled, too, at least until I saw that the Baroness was afraid of him."

"The Baroness is also a consummate actor," Thomas reminded her. "She can take on any identity or spin any tale that serves her purpose."

Laura nodded. "She certainly can. And in her own way, she's equally ruthless - not on behalf of herself but for others. She's a tigress when the people she cares about are threatened.

"I'd be one too, in similar circumstances," she admitted candidly.

"I imagine you would be," Thomas observed. "Maybe one day I'll get to see the tigress in action on my behalf." There was a wistful note in his voice and Laura had the odd feeling he meant what he said.

Who was Thomas anyway, and how many times had she asked herself that question? Was he the conservative husband and father Catherine described or the complex, ever-changing half-scoundrel she had come to know?

Finding out was more fun than knowing, Laura decided. Besides, if she could jump feet first into a murder and emerge more or less unscathed except for an aching ankle and a feeling that she'd been put through some kind of mangle machine from being dragged down three flights of stairs, she ought to be able to jump with equal vigor into a new relationship.

She smiled at Thomas. "Maybe you will one day," she answered coyly.

Thomas smiled back; then he leaned over and kissed her lightly on the lips. Another, deeper kiss was imminent when Catherine burst though the door.

"If you two have something going on, I want to be in on it from the very beginning," she announced, hands on hips. "It's my life too."

"Would you like that?" Thomas's voice was carefully neutral.

Catherine's eyes lit up. "You bet! It'll be exciting! I mean murders all the time, between Laura walking into them and Dad coming along to solve them, and me helping. And then I'll pass on the plots to Nigel so he can put them in his plays. He's doing one now called: *The strange events at Torrington Manor.* It'll be seething with affairs and passions and intrigues about who's the rightful heir to the title and the manor, just like Shakespeare's plays," she enthused, revealing a knowledge of literature Laura hadn't expected.

Thomas looked momentarily speechless. No doubt that wasn't the answer he had expected. Laura hid a smile. Like her father, Catherine responded in unpredictable ways. A taste of his own medicine would do him good.

"I imagine Nigel will make a fine playwright along with all his other talents," Thomas said, recovering his wits. "Still, all of this must be pretty hard on him. The man he thought of as his father stands accused of murder, never mind helping to run an art forgery ring. Is he all right?"

Catherine shrugged. "To tell you the truth, he wasn't all that close to Lord Torrington. He was kind of afraid of him. He knows he wasn't his father, too. The Baroness told him who his real father was a long time ago.

"Which is why he'll never have to leave the manor," she added cheerfully.

Laura was puzzled. "I thought Lucy's husband was his father – the one who got killed in the car crash, and I don't see what that has to do with Torrington Manor."

"Who's Lucy?" Catherine asked.

"The grande dame's sister. She was killed too," Laura explained.

"Well, I don't know anything about that," Catherine replied. "What I do know is that Nigel's father was the real Barkeley Smythington, which means Nigel is the rightful heir even if Lord Torrington is a fraud and a murderer."

Laura laughed. The Baroness was indeed creative – brilliant, really. She could change her story to meet any circumstances, and make everyone believe it. Would they ever know the truth about Torrington Manor and how Nigel and the Baroness had come there? Probably not, she decided, and maybe that was just as well.

"Well, I for one like Barkeley Smythington as father best," she declared, "since it means that Nigel and the grande dame can stay at the manor. They belong there.

"Now, however, I am going to forget all about it and let them get on with their lives while I get on with my own - which means getting on with my walk. I've got almost fifty miles to go, I calculated last night."

Thomas looked dismayed. "Fifty miles? I can't do that in my present battered condition."

"You don't have to," Laura pointed out.

Thomas leered. "For you, my darling, I would walk a thousand miles."

Catherine regarded him quizzically. "He's not like that usually," she informed Laura. "He must really be smitten."

She jumped up as a motor buzzed outside the door. "That's Nigel. He has a motor scooter. That's one good thing Lord Torrington did before he got caught. He said

Nigel needed a way to get around so the Baroness didn't always have to take in his broken glasses. People thought she was going blind because she spent so much time at the eye doctor's getting them fixed for him." With a wave, she ran out the door.

Laura grinned. "I had heard that rumor too, from Maude, the first time I came here, and I'm glad to find out it's not true."

Thomas didn't seem to hear her, and Laura regarded him anxiously. He really had been battered these last few days. Maybe he should see a doctor.

Thomas cleared his throat. "How soon do you have to leave?"

Laura looked at him in surprise. He sounded like a nervous adolescent. Maybe he felt as insecure about forging new relationships as she did. It was a new and interesting thought.

She leaned closer and smiled seductively. "I don't have to leave, not right at this moment. Why don't we fix ourselves up as best we can and treat ourselves to a really nice dinner tonight? If there's one to be had in this part of the world other than Torrington Manor," she added hastily.

Thomas's face lit up with pleasure. "I thought you would never ask!" His debonair self was once more in place, but Laura had seen his relief. "I know just the place," he added. "Quite romantic, actually. I think you'll enjoy it. They even have tablecloths and candles."

"Excellent!" That multi-colored silk tunic worn over deep russet pants with a fake gem-studded belt would be just right, Laura mused, glad now that she had tucked it into her suitcase. It was definitely outré but she had the feeling that Thomas might actually like it.

He was about as different from Donald as any man could be, she reflected later, as they settled into a corner table and ordered a bottle of wine. That was a big point in his favor. She wondered if, like Catherine, he even knew his Shakespeare.

"I feel as if I've been Beatrice to your Benedick during this last week," she commented, referring to the heroine and hero in one of Shakespeare's plays whose favorite pastime was exchanging verbal barbs.

"The situations we've found ourselves in have hardly been *Much Ado About Nothing*," Thomas countered.

Laura was delighted. "More tragedy than comedy," she agreed. "For tonight, however, we definitely need comic relief. Who shall we be?"

"Kate, in *Taming of the Shrew* might suit you," Thomas suggested. "Or perhaps Rosalind, that stalwart defender of justice," he amended when Laura glared at him. "What's the name of that play?"

"Just *As You Like It*," Laura quipped. "You ask the questions and I answer them."

Thomas laughed. "Keep in mind," he teased, "that every one of Shakespeare's feisty heroines succumbs in the end to a determined suitor."

"*All's Well That Ends Well*," Laura replied with a grin, and held up her wine glass in a toast.

THE END

Walking into Murder

A note from Joan Dahr Lambert:

I hope you enjoyed <u>Walking into Murder</u>. The next book in the Laura Morland Mystery Series, <u>Babes in the Baths</u>, will be online very soon, so be sure to watch for it. Here's a brief look at the action:

This time, Laura walks (or more accurately slithers down a slick wall and swims through noxious, rat-infested water) into a kidnapping when she rescues a baby hidden in the depths of the famous Roman Baths. All over England babies are being stolen, the papers say. More puzzling, the thefts seem related to Laura's current research: the treatment of women and girls in areas of religious upheaval.

Intrigued, Laura investigates, a move that triggers an alarming chain of near-fatal accidents, among them entombment in a pitch-black cellar, a wobbly escape on a stolen bicycle for which she is arrested, and a night being stalked by a sadist in a safari park while free-roaming lions roar and wolves howl.

The mystery deepens when a member of Laura's bus tour is murdered in an ancient cottage in Stourhead Gardens, a well-known tourist attraction. Laura's irrepressible curiosity and intrepid spirit shift into high gear, and she sets out to find the killer, ably assisted by an elderly umbrella-wielding aristocrat, her talented, metal-studded grandson, and an ungainly six-foot-tall woman improbably named Violet. But are these friends really on Laura's side? Violet might actually be a man, and like everyone else on the tour the titled aristocrat has a dangerous hidden agenda that has nothing to do with sight-seeing.

Walking into Murder

Laura must summon all her imaginative powers and more courage than she thought she possessed to solve the mystery of <u>Babes in the Baths.</u> But even she cannot be sure of the identity of the exceedingly clever villain until the very end. A meeting is called, a trap set, the lure baited. Not until the tension in the room becomes almost unbearable does a witness step forward. Then, with a dramatic and utterly unexpected accusation, the killer is exposed.

<u>Babes in the Baths</u> takes place in some of England's most atmospheric and historic tourist sites: the ancient towns of Bath, Glastonbury and Wells, the glorious, mist-saturated gardens of Stourhead, and Longleat House, owned by a six and a half foot tall Baron of impeccable lineage who turned his estate into a Safari Park, to the dismay of his more conventional peers.